FOREVER FAMILY: Newfound sisters
Bliss, Tiffany and Katie learn more about family
and love than they *ever* expected!

Luke felt a sense of belonging, of finally having a place in the world he could call home.

For the first time in a long time, he experienced a need to be connected, to be a part of something bigger than just himself. It was an odd sensation, really, one he'd hoped he would avoid for the rest of his life. And he suspected it had more than a little to do with Katie Kinkaid. That mite of a woman had found a way to bore herself under his skin, and he found himself thinking about her far too much.

He envisioned her dark red hair, spread around a face that was flushed with desire, imagined kissing the freckles on the bridge of her nose, saw vividly within his mind's eye her swift intake of breath and seductively parted lips as he began making slow, sensuous love to her.

If Luke didn't know better, he'd think he was in love....

Dear Reader,

Special Edition welcomes you to a brand-new year of romance! As always, we are committed to providing you with captivating love stories that will take your breath away.

This January, Lisa Jackson wraps up her engrossing FOREVER FAMILY miniseries with *A Family Kind of Wedding*. THAT SPECIAL WOMAN! Katie Kinkaid has her hands full being an ace reporter—and a full-time mom. But when a sexy, mysterious Texas rancher crosses her path, her life changes forever!

In these next three stories, love conquers all. First, a twist of fate brings an adorably insecure heroine face-to-face with the reclusive millionaire of her dreams in bestselling author Susan Mallery's emotional love story, *The Millionaire Bachelor*. Next, Ginna Gray continues her popular series, THE BLAINES AND THE McCALLS OF CROCKETT, TEXAS, with *Meant for Each Other*. In this poignant story, Dr. Mike McCall heroically saves a life and wins the heart of an alluring colleague in the process. And onetime teenage sweethearts march down the wedding aisle in *I Take This Man—Again!* by Carole Halston.

Also this month, acclaimed historical author Leigh Greenwood debuts in Special Edition with *Just What the Doctor Ordered*— a heartwarming tale about a brooding doctor finding his heart in a remote mountain community. Finally, in *Prenuptial Agreement* by Doris Rangel, a rugged rancher marries for his son's sake, but he's about to fall in love for real....

I hope you enjoy January's selections. We wish you all the best for a happy new year!

Sincerely,
Karen Taylor Richman
Senior Editor

Please address questions and book requests to:
Silhouette Reader Service
U.S.: 3010 Walden Ave., P.O. Box 1325, Buffalo, NY 14269
Canadian: P.O. Box 609, Fort Erie, Ont. L2A 5X3

LISA JACKSON

A FAMILY KIND OF WEDDING

Published by Silhouette Books
America's Publisher of Contemporary Romance

SILHOUETTE BOOKS

ISBN 0-373-24219-0

A FAMILY KIND OF WEDDING

Copyright © 1999 by Susan Crose

Printed in U.S.A.

Books by Lisa Jackson

Silhouette Special Edition

A Twist of Fate #118
The Shadow of Time #180
Tears of Pride #194
Pirate's Gold #215
A Dangerous Precedent #233
Innocent by Association #244
Midnight Sun #264
Devil's Gambit #282
Zachary's Law #296
Yesterday's Lies #315
One Man's Love #358
Renegade Son #376
Snowbound #394
Summer Rain #419
Hurricane Force #467
In Honor's Shadow #495
Aftermath #525
Tender Trap #569
With No Regrets #611
Double Exposure #636
Mystery Man #653
Obsession #691
Sail Away #720
Million Dollar Baby #743
*He's a Bad Boy #787
*He's Just a Cowboy #799
*He's the Rich Boy #811
A Husband To Remember #835
*He's My Soldier Boy #866
†A Is for Always #914
†B Is for Baby #920
†C Is for Cowboy #926
†D Is for Dani's Baby #985
New Year's Daddy #1004
‡A Family Kind of Guy #1191
‡A Family Kind of Gal #1207
‡A Family Kind of Wedding #1219

Silhouette Intimate Moments

Dark Side of the Moon #39
Gypsy Wind #79
Mystic #158

Silhouette Romance

His Bride To Be #717

Silhouette Books

Silhouette Christmas Stories 1993
"The Man from Pine Mountain"

Fortune's Children
The Millionaire and the Cowgirl

*Mavericks
†Love Letters
‡Forever Family

LISA JACKSON

has been writing romances for over ten years. With over forty Silhouette novels to her credit, she divides her time between writing on the computer, researching her next novel, keeping in touch with her college-age sons and playing tennis. Many of the fictitious small towns in her books resemble Molalla, Oregon, a small logging community, where she and her sister, Silhouette author Natalie Bishop, grew up.

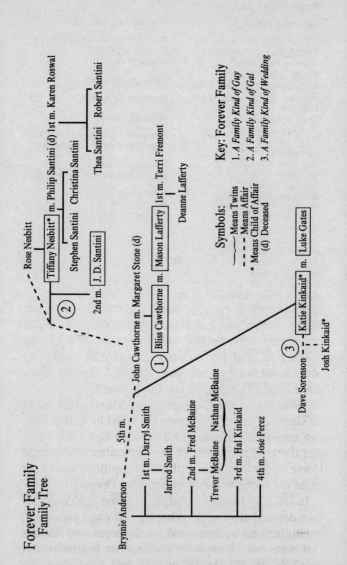

Forever Family
Family Tree

Key: Forever Family
1. *A Family Kind of Guy*
2. *A Family Kind of Gal*
3. *A Family Kind of Wedding*

Symbols:
— Means Twins
- - - Means Affair
* Means Child of Affair
(d) Deceased

Rose Nesbitt

Tiffany Nesbitt* m. Philip Santini (d) 1st m. Karen Roswal

Stephen Santini   Christina Santini

2nd m. J. D. Santini

Thea Santini   Robert Santini

John Cawthorne m. Margaret Stone (d)

① Bliss Cawthorne m. Mason Lafferty 1st m. Terri Fremont

Deanne Lafferty

②

Brynnie Anderson — — — 5th m.

1st m. Darryl Smith

Jarrod Smith

2nd m. Fred McBaine

Trevor McBaine   Nathan McBaine

3rd m. Hal Kinkaid

4th m. José Perez

Katie Kinkaid* m. Luke Gates

Dave Sorenson - - - Katie Kinkaid*

③

Josh Kinkaid*

Chapter One

"I'm countin' on you, boy. Now that Dave's gone, all his mother and me got left is the thought that he might have left himself a son or daughter. Don't know if it's true, you know, but he mentioned something about it the last time we spoke to him." The old man's voice cracked. "You let me know, hear?"

"Will do," Luke Gates promised, cursing himself as he slammed the phone down. How had he gotten himself roped into this mess? Sweat ran down his back, and the sweltering heat of the September day seemed worse in the confines of this tiny top-floor apartment of an old carriage house in Southern Oregon.

In Luke's estimation, Ralph Sorenson should do his own damned dirty work. What the hell was Luke doing, getting caught up in an old man's hopes and dreams that were bound to cause nothing but heartache and pain? So the old man thought he had a grandson. So he hoped that Luke would find the kid. So he was going to pay him to do it. Big deal.

But it was. When it came to money, Luke had been born with a weakness, a hunger for it. Having grown up dirt-poor, tossed around from one aunt to another, constantly reminded that he was "another mouth to feed" and that he must "earn his own keep" had only fostered his drive and need to chase after the almighty greenback.

But this job might be too much.

Ralph was pushing. Too hard. But then, the old man was desperate.

Luke's stomach curdled as he thought of the heavy-bodied man who had helped turn him from a hellion into a decent-enough businessman. Luke had never known his own father, and Ralph was the closest thing he now had to family. He supposed, under the circumstances, the reverse was true, as well.

But still, the thought of dragging forgotten skeletons out of closets and digging up innocent people's lives didn't appeal to him.

Not so innocent, he reminded himself.

Ralph Sorenson deserved to know his own flesh and blood. Who cared if it fouled up some woman's life? And besides, there was a pile of money involved.

Telling himself it didn't matter what he thought, Luke yanked on his favorite pair of boots and headed outside. Pausing on the upper landing of the staircase, he felt the impact of the late afternoon. The air was as dry as a west Texas wind and the September sun merciless. Just the way he liked it.

Sliding his key ring from his pocket, he hurried down the flight of stairs and strode across the patchy dry lawn to a spot of concrete by the garage where his pickup leaked a little oil. He'd lived here for a couple of weeks and planned to stay until he could make the old ranch house livable. It would take a little doing, even by his spartan standards.

A crow cawed angrily from an eave of the main house, a massive Victorian complete with gables, shutters and gingerbread trim. The turn-of-the-century home had been divided up some years back and now had several apartment units ensconced within its century-old walls.

He heard the sound of tires on gravel. A convertible, belching blue exhaust, the engine knocking out of synch, careened into the drive. The driver, a red-haired woman he'd caught glimpses of before, stepped on the brakes. She was out of the car before it stopped rolling.

"Hi!" She waved.

What was her name? Katie Something-or-other, he thought—a relative, maybe a sister, of Tiffany Santini, the widow who was his landlady.

Katie strode toward him with an air of confidence he found refreshing. A mite of a thing with fiery red hair, a sprinkling of freckles over a pert little nose and a pixie-ish jaw, she didn't dally. Sunglasses covered her eyes. "You're Luke Gates, aren't you? I've seen you around here and I always wanted to introduce myself." She flashed him a smile that wouldn't quit, the kind of thousand-watt grin that beautiful women used to get what they wanted. Her hand was already outstretched as she marched up to him. "I'm Katie Kinkaid, Tiffany's sister—well, half sister really." Her teeth were a set of pearls that were straight enough except for a small, sexy overlap in the front two and her face was flushed, as if she'd been running. He could do nothing but accept the small hand that was jabbed his way.

"Glad to meet you," he drawled, though he wasn't really sure. Katie struck him as the kind of woman who could steamroll right over a man even though she was only a couple of inches over five feet.

"Me, too." She shook his hand crisply, then let it drop. "Don't suppose you've seen my son around here, have ya? He's ten going on sixteen, got reddish-brown hair and is about yea tall." She gestured with the flat of one hand to the height of her opposite shoulder. "He's usually moving about a billion miles a minute and he's been spending a lot of time hanging out here with Stephen in the last day or two."

Luke knew the kid she meant. A gangly kid always on the go. "I think I've seen him," Luke allowed with a flick of his gaze toward the back porch. "But not today."

"Hmm." She shoved her bangs from her eyes and the scent of some flowery perfume teased at his nostrils. "Tiffany said something about taking the kids out to the farm—you know, the old Zalinski place that Santini Brothers Enterprises bought for their latest vineyard and winery. They probably just haven't gotten back yet." She slid her sunglasses off her nose and chewed on one bow as she squinted down the length of the driveway. "I guess I'll just have to wait." Pausing for a second, she turned her attention back to Luke. "So, I've been meaning to ask ever since I first saw you, what brings you to Bittersweet?"

"Business."

She was a pushy little thing. She gave him the once-over, a swift glance up and down his body, and her expression said it all. In faded jeans, a T-shirt and his scruffy boots, he didn't look like the typical three-piece-suit-and-tie businessman. But then this was Bittersweet, Oregon, not New York City or LA.

"What kind of business?"

He had to get the word out sooner or later. Though he was going to do a little bit of detective work for Ralph, that was only part of his reason for hanging around. The ranch was his real purpose and now that the sale of the property was a done deal, he saw no reason to keep it to himself anymore. "I bought a spread a few miles outside of town and I'm hoping to convert it into a working dude ranch."

Her eyebrows arched up as she slid her shades onto the bridge of her nose again. "You mean for tourists to come down here and round up wild horses, and brand cattle, and, well, do all that macho outdoorsy cowboy thing—kind of like the movie *City Slickers?*"

He couldn't help but smile. "Not that elaborate, but, yeah, that's the general idea." There was a whole lot more to it than that, but he didn't see any reason to fill her in—or anyone else, for that matter—with the details. Not just yet. Until he was sure of them himself. Besides, she had a way of distracting him. In white shorts and a sleeveless denim blouse, she showed off a tanned, compact body with more curves than a logging road in the Cascade Mountains. The V of her blouse's neckline gave him a quick glimpse of cleavage between breasts that were more than ample to fit into a man's palm.

He caught himself at the thought and shifted his gaze back to the truck. Katie Kinkaid's all-American-girl-next-door good looks were heightened by a bit of raw sensuality that gripped him hard and caused a ridiculous tightening in his groin.

Obviously it had been way too long since he'd been with a woman.

He even noticed the dimple that creased her cheek when she smiled. She was sexy and earthy, yet exuded an innocence and charm that, if he let it, might get under his skin.

"When do you plan to open the doors?" she asked, and he cleared his throat for fear his voice would betray him.

"By early next summer. Soon as the winter snowpack melts." He wasn't used to being grilled, wasn't sure he liked it.

"Where is your ranch, exactly?"

"Outside of town about three miles or so." He decided to end the conversation before she dug too deep. She was a nosy one, this Katie Kinkaid. If he let her, she'd talk to him all afternoon. "I gotta run."

"Wait a minute. I'm a reporter with the *Rogue River Review*—that's our local paper—and I'd like to do a story about the ranch when you open."

So that was it. He should have known.

When he hesitated, she barreled right on. "You could think of it as free advertising." She angled her face upward for a better look at him and he thought he noticed a hint of defiance in the tilt of that impish chin.

"Thanks. I'll let you know."

"Here—let me give you my card." Whipping open a small purse, she scrounged around for a second, extracted her wallet and edged a clean white business card out of a slit behind a picture of her son obviously taken a few years back. "Here. Just give me a call, or I'll contact you." She looked up at him expectantly as he flipped the card over and over between his fingers.

"I don't have anything like this yet," he admitted. "The deal just went through, but I'll call you later."

"Or I'll call you," she repeated quickly, as if she thought he was giving her the brush-off. Apparently she was used to being in charge.

"Fine. Nice meetin' ya." He slid her card into the back pocket of his jeans and walked to his truck. A black cat that had been sunning himself on the hood, perked up his head; then, as Luke opened the driver's door, the animal shot to his feet and hopped lithely to the ground.

"Oh, come here, Charcoal," Katie said, bending down and picking up the slinking feline. "That's a boy."

As Luke rammed the truck into gear, cranking on the steering wheel, he caught a glimpse of Katie in the rearview mirror. One hip thrust out as she cradled the cat against her chest, dark glasses hiding her eyes, lips tinged a soft peach color, she exuded a natural sensuality that caught a man off guard and squeezed tightly. Too tightly.

His gut feeling about her was simple: Katie Kinkaid was a woman to avoid.

Katie was still petting the cat, staring down the driveway and asking herself a dozen questions about the enigmatic cowboy who had taken up residence in Tiffany's carriage house when J. D. Santini's Jeep roared into the drive. J.D., Tiffany's brother-in-law and soon-to-be husband, was behind the wheel.

Katie stepped aside as the rig rolled to a stop.

"I'm sorry we're late," Tiffany apologized. Her face was flushed, her gold eyes bright as she climbed out of the Cherokee. "We went to the farm and the kids swam in the lake and... Well, we just lost track of time.''

J.D. stretched out of the rig. His grin was wide, a slash of perfect white teeth against a dark complexion.

"Don't let her kid you," he said, winking at Katie. "Stephen, Josh and Christina amused themselves and this one—" he slung his arm familiarly over Tiffany's shoulders "—couldn't keep her hands off me.''

Tiffany burst out laughing and nudged him in the ribs with her elbow. "Dream on, Santini," she teased, but she wasn't able to hide the sparkle in her gaze. She was, without a doubt, totally and gloriously in love.

Katie didn't feel the least little bit of envy. She believed in love—for other people. It just wasn't in her cards. "I haven't been here long and besides, I got to meet your new tenant.''

"Luke? Hmm." Tiffany frowned slightly. "He keeps to himself most of the time.''

The boys climbed out of the back of the Jeep and Christina, Tiffany's three-year-old daughter, hopped to the ground. The minute her sandals hit dry grass she ran, black curls bouncing at her shoulders, plump little arms stretched upward to J.D., the man who was her uncle and was about to become her stepfather. "Piggyback ride!''

"Sure, dumpling." J.D. lifted her to his shoulders. Christina giggled and clung to J.D.'s head and for the first time in a long while, Katie felt a touch of sadness that her son hadn't yet met his father. In time. All in good time, she told herself.

"Hey, Mom, what're you doin' here?" At ten, Josh had teeth that were still too big for his face, freckles that stood out and huge, deep coffee-brown eyes.

"Picking you up.''

"Already?"

"You've got soccer practice."

"Not until five."

"He can stay—" Tiffany started to offer but caught the quick shake of Katie's head.

"Another time."

"Okay, but at least come into the house for a quick glass of iced tea or lemonade. There's something I need to talk about."

"It sounds mysterious," Katie said.

"Everything sounds mysterious to you. Believe me, this isn't anything you'll want to write in the paper."

"You never know," she teased. After having grown up in a houseful of older half brothers Katie was overjoyed to discover she had not one, but two half sisters. For most of her life she hadn't known that Tiffany was her sister; it was only after her husband died that Tiffany had decided to move to Bittersweet where her grandmother, Octavia Nesbitt, had spent most of her life.

The boys took off for the house at a dead run and by the time Katie, Tiffany and J.D. had crossed the shaded backyard and climbed the few steps to the back porch, the wail of an electric guitar screamed through the open window of Stephen's room. "My son, the rock star," Tiffany said with a laugh.

"I wanna see!" Christina wriggled unsteadily on J.D.'s shoulders until he helped her down to the floor. She scurried ahead of them through the open door of the house and clambered up the stairs. The airy kitchen smelled of dried herbs and wildflowers that were bunched and hung from the exposed beams overhead. Artwork, schedules and old report cards decorated the refrigerator while a rack of copper pans was suspended over a center cooking island.

"I'll bet the boys arc gonna love her wanting to get in on the action." Tiffany opened the refrigerator and hauled out a pitcher of iced tea.

"If they're like my brothers," Katie said, "they'll lock the door and tell her that because she's a girl she's not allowed inside. It's a plot by all older brothers to mess up their younger sisters' self-esteem."

"Didn't seem to take in your case," J.D. observed as Tiffany poured them each a glass.

"Careful, Santini, you're outnumbered here," Tiffany warned him as she sliced a lemon and dropped wedges into the drinks. She handed Katie her glass and waved her into a chair at the table. Leaning thoughtfully against the counter she asked, "So, are you ready for the wedding this weekend?"

"Can't wait." Katie took a long sip of tea. "How about you?" She pressed the cool glass to her forehead as Tiffany settled into a chair.

"I'll be okay, I guess. I'm thrilled for Bliss and Mason, but..." She let her voice trail off as she took a swallow of cold tea.

"Don't tell me," Katie guessed. "You're still having trouble dealing with dear old Dad."

Small lines of concern appeared between Tiffany's eyebrows. "Let's just call him John."

"Okay, so the fact that John Cawthorne is going to be there is bothering you."

"Not only that he's there, but that he's giving the bride away." Tiffany sighed and, resting her chin on her open palm, stared through the window. "It...it brings it all out in the open again."

Katie knew what her half sister was talking about.

The situation had been painful for everyone involved. John Cawthorne had sired one daughter out of wedlock and hadn't bothered to marry the girl—Tiffany's mother. According to Tiffany, there was no love lost between Rose Nesbitt and John Cawthorne. But he hadn't finished fathering daughters. He'd married a woman named Margaret from San Francisco and she'd borne him a second daughter—the legitimate one— Bliss.

Not one to ever be satisfied, John had started living a dual life—part of the year in Seattle with Margaret and Bliss, the other down here in Bittersweet where he met and fell in love with Brynnie Anderson, who, in between several husbands, carried on an affair with Cawthorne. As luck would have it, Brynnie, who already had three sons, got pregnant with John's third daughter. However, Katie had always assumed her father was Hal Kinkaid, her mother's third husband, whose name she was given. No doubt about it, the family situation was one tangled mess of relationships and emotions. "So, what're you going to do when you and J.D. get married?" Katie asked.

"I want to go before a justice of the peace."

"No way." J.D. set his glass on the table and skewered his bride-to-be with determined eyes. "This is my first and last marriage and I want it done right."

"I know, I know. Then…then I suppose that Stephen will give me away."

"Fine." J.D. seemed satisfied. "Now that I've exerted my testosterone-filled rights, I think I'd better make a quick exit." He walked to Tiffany and brushed a kiss across her ebony crown. "Besides, I've got some paperwork to finish, then I've got to call Dad. I'll be down in a couple of hours." He hoisted his glass in

Katie's direction. "Ms. Kinkaid," he said with a lift of one corner of his mouth. "It's been a pleasure. As always."

"You, too, J.D."

Carrying his glass, he walked briskly out of the room and Tiffany's gaze followed longingly after him.

"Boy, have you got it bad," Katie observed.

"That obvious, huh?"

"You could hang a flashing neon sign that reads 'I Love J.D. Santini' around your neck and it would be more subtle."

"Oh, well, I guess I should be more discreet."

"Not at all! Love's great." Katie believed it with all her heart; it just didn't seem to work for her. "Which brings us back to Bliss's wedding this weekend. How're you gonna handle the John situation?"

"I don't know," Tiffany admitted. Rubbing one temple, she leaned back in her chair. "What do you want me to do? Make up with the man? Let bygones be bygones and pretend that he didn't ignore me for over thirty years?" She shook her head and swirled her glass. Ice cubes and slices of lemon danced in the amber liquid. "I'm sorry. I didn't mean to sound bitter, and in all fairness, John…he's been good to the kids and to me lately, ever since his damned heart attack. But I can't just erase the past."

"No one's asking you to."

"Just to sweep it under the carpet for a while?"

"No way, but maybe… Well, if you want to, just give him a chance. That's what I've decided to do."

"You don't have a mother who uses his picture for a dartboard." Tiffany's lips pulled into a tight little knot.

"Nope. My mom married him. Imagine that." Katie

let out a low, disbelieving whistle. The conversation had turned too heavy. Way too heavy. "So what about you and J.D.? When're you going to tie the knot?"

"Later in the fall, we think, though… Well, I don't think I'm ready for all the fuss of a big wedding."

"But you have to!"

"I've been married before."

"So were Brynnie and John."

"I know. My point exactly." Tiffany studied her glass and frowned. "We'll see. I think we should give it a couple of months."

"Why wait?" Katie knew she was impetuous to a fault but when two people were so obviously in love with each other it seemed silly to put off the inevitable. Though she tried to ignore it, she was a romantic at heart.

"Actually," Tiffany admitted, "there's something I was going to discuss with you, something that has to do with me getting married."

"What?" Katie asked, unable to contain her enthusiasm.

"Well, J.D.'s dad has finally convinced him that he and I and the kids should move out to the new farm that Santini Brothers is converting into a vineyard and winery."

"The old Zalinski place." Katie had already heard the news.

"Right. Even though J.D. argued with him and told him there was no way he was going to be involved with the company business again, Carlo can be *very* persuasive when he wants to be, so… as the old saying goes, he made J.D. an offer he couldn't refuse. Not only did Carlo give me the deed to this house free and clear, but he is offering us the farmhouse if we'll agree to live on the grounds. J.D. will still practice law for other people but he'll be a consultant of sorts for Santini Brothers.'' Glancing around the kitchen, Tiffany added, ''It's probably time I started fresh anyway. I moved here when Philip died and both of the kids hated it. Stephen openly rebelled and Christina suffered from nightmares. All that seems to have gone away, but J.D. and I and the kids need a new start. A place of our own.''

''Sounds great. Too good to be true.''

''Almost. But the problem is I'll need someone to run this place—you know, manage the apartments and live on the premises. I thought it would be perfect for you and Josh. You could stay here rent free, collect a salary and still work for the *Review.*''

''You're kidding!'' Kate's head snapped up.

''Dead serious. You could sell your place or rent it out,'' Tiffany said, before draining her glass.

Katie didn't know what to say. She gazed at the kitchen filled with all of Tiffany's things—her baskets and shiny pots and hanging bundles of dried herbs. ''I...I don't know. I'd have to think about it. Talk it over with Josh.''

''Do. You've seen the place, of course, but let me give you the grand tour, show you what you'd be in for. Let's start at the top.'' They climbed two flights of stairs to a studio apartment set under the eaves. J.D. sat at a small table with his laptop computer glowing in front of him.

''Missed me?'' he asked, as Tiffany approached him.

''Terribly,'' she replied dryly. ''I just couldn't stand it.''

His smile stretched wide and he leaned back in his chair to stare at his fiancée. The silent message he sent her fairly sizzled and Tiffany's cheeks burned red. "Well…uh, this is the smallest unit." She pointed out the tiny kitchen and bath, then, with a sidelong look at her husband-to-be, led Katie down to the second floor. "He's incorrigible," she muttered.

"Along with a whole list of other things," Katie teased. When Tiffany eyed her skeptically, she added, "All good. All very good."

They toured the second story with its three bedrooms and bath. The rooms were compact, with high ceilings and tall windows. The master bedroom, Katie noticed, had a view of the carriage house where Luke Gates had taken up residence. She thought of the rangy Texan— a sexy, rawboned cowboy with a slow-growing smile and a quiet manner. But beneath his easygoing exterior she sensed there was a deeper person, a man who had more than his share of secrets. Or maybe her reporter instincts were working overtime. Everyone accused her of searching out mysteries, stories and scoops where there were none. Nonetheless, she stared through the glass at the carriage house and said, "Tell me about Luke Gates."

"Not much to tell," Tiffany admitted. "But he's the perfect tenant. Quiet. Clean. Keeps to himself. Pays on time."

"He's from Texas, right?" Katie asked, spying the bridesmaid's dress for Bliss's wedding hanging from a hook on the back of Tiffany's closet door. Draped in plastic, it was a blue gown identical to the one Katie was to wear.

"Somewhere around El Paso, I think, although it seems to me he mentioned something about spending some time working at a ranch near Dallas. But I really can't remember. As I said, he doesn't say much.'' She slid an interested glance in Katie's direction. ''Why?''

''Just curious.'' The truth of the matter was that Luke was the most interesting man to show up in Bittersweet in years. Not that it mattered.

Tiffany raised one dark brow. ''Good-looking, isn't he?''

Katie lifted a shoulder. ''Only if you like the cock-sure, I-don't-give-a-damn cowboy type.''

Tiffany laughed. ''Don't we all?'' she said in a whisper, as if she expected J.D. to hear her.

Katie didn't answer, only grinned as they left Tiffany's room, walked down the short, carpeted hallway and stopped at a six-paneled door with a large Keep Out sign swinging from the knob.

''Yeah, right.'' With a wink at Katie, Tiffany gave the door a sharp rap with her knuckles, then twisted the knob and walked into what could only be described as a ''healthy mess''—just the kind Katie's own boy loved. Cards, marbles, shoes and clothing were strewn over the floor, a bookcase was crammed with video games, books, baseball cards, tennis racquets and empty soda cans. Posters of rock stars and baseball greats decorated the walls, and the bed was a disaster, the edges of the mattress visible beneath rumpled sheets and a cover that was draped half on the floor. In the middle of it all, Josh and Stephen were thumbing through a sports magazine while Christina rummaged through the closet. In Katie's estimation this was a ten-year-old boy's idea of heaven. ''We have a deal,'' Tiffany explained. ''Every Saturday morning—which is coming up in a few days, Stephen—he cleans this up, changes his sheets and puts everything away to my satisfaction. Then he can go out with his friends and I don't bug him until the next Saturday.''

"Awesome," Josh said, showing off his preteen vocabulary as if he knew the meaning of straightening up.

"If you guys need any snacks, I bought some chips and cookies this morning."

"Cool," Josh said and the boys, with Christina hurrying after them, scrambled out of the room.

"I quit fighting this mess because I had bigger problems with Stephen," Tiffany admitted and Katie remembered the boy's run-in with the police. Stephen had been questioned about Isaac Wells's disappearance because he'd been hired by the reclusive farmer to do odd jobs and had, at one time, stolen the keys to Isaac's classic car collection.

"How's Stephen doing?"

"Better." Tiffany sighed. "I hate to admit it, but J.D. has been a big help. Everyone told me that a boy needs a positive role model, a man to look up to, but I didn't want to believe it. After Philip died I wasn't going to ever get married again." She picked up a couple of empty cans and brought them with her. "Then J.D. came along—well, actually kind of pushed his way into my life. I had to let him because he was Philip's brother and the kids were his niece and nephew, but I never expected... Oh, listen to me. I'm rambling. Come on, let me show you Christina's room."

They walked through a half-open door to a charming room filled with a canopied bed, stuffed animals and a box of toys. A lacy dust ruffle matched the curtains that framed a view of the side yard. Katie's heartstrings tugged a bit. She'd always wanted a little girl, a sister for Josh, but, of course it wasn't going to happen. Hav-

ing a daughter was part of a pipe dream—one she'd
given up long ago. Now, she had to concentrate on her
son and her career. Period.

In the next twenty minutes, Tiffany showed her
through the living quarters on the first floor of the
house, then pointed out two apartments in the base-
ment, and an upper and lower unit in the old carriage
house.

The boys were shooting baskets near the garage and
Christina was chasing Charcoal across the lawn by the
time the tour was over.

"So, what do you think?" Tiffany asked as Katie
slung the strap of her purse over her shoulder.

"It's definitely a possibility." The truth of the matter
was that she wanted to say yes right then and there.
"I'll think about it," Katie promised, but she'd already
half made up her mind. She could rent out her house
and save money, spend more time with Josh and concentrate on her career without constantly worrying
about making the mortgage payment. She might even
be able to trade in her car for a slightly newer model.

"Right now all the units are occupied except for the
third floor that J.D.'s using as his office. I'll start advertising the space as soon as we move. Uh-oh. Chris-
sie! Watch out!" Tiffany raced across the backyard.
Her daughter had tripped and tumbled over an exposed
root. For a se ond there was no noise as Christina's
tiny face screwed up and turned a deep shade of purple.
The scream was next, a pained wail loud enough to
cause the boys to give up their game.

Tiffany scooped Christina up off the ground. "It's
okay," she said, brushing bark dust from the little girl's
tangled black curls.

Tears streamed down Christina's cheeks and she

cried, "Mommy, Mommy, Mommy!" over and over again.

"I think it's time for us to leave," Katie said. "Josh! Let's go."

"Oh, Mom, can't I stay a little longer?"

Christina was sobbing and gulping air now.

"Nope. It's time."

"But—"

"Hop in the car, bud. Now!" Josh cast her a I-can't-believe-you're-so-unfair look, but she ignored it and turned back to Tiffany who was brushing aside Christina's tears with a finger. "Thanks for the offer. I'll talk to Josh and give you a call."

"Good."

The back door of the house burst open, then slammed against the side of the house. J.D. hurtled down the steps. His face was a mask of concern and his eyes focused hard on Christina. "What happened?" he demanded, sprinting across the backyard with long, athletic strides. At the sight of J.D., the child brightened visibly.

"A minor catastrophe." Tiffany was holding her daughter close and Christina, who had been quieting down, started crying hysterically again.

"Is that right? Looks pretty major to me. Come here, dumpling," he said, prying Christina from her mother's arms. "Let's make sure you're gonna live."

Christina's tears stopped and she offered J.D. an impish smile that made Katie think her injuries weren't quite as painful as she'd let on. But then, she was only three.

"I'll see you later," Katie said as Josh climbed into the passenger seat. She waved to the small family as she climbed behind the steering wheel. She tried to start her car. The ignition ground and she pumped the gas before the convertible coughed twice, then sputtered. She swore under her breath and said a quick little prayer. Again she twisted the ignition. With a sound like the crack of a rifle, a spurt of blue smoke shot out of the tailpipe and the engine caught. "Good girl." Katie patted the dash. At least the darned thing was running. She only hoped that the temperamental car wouldn't die as she backed out of the drive.

"Can we stop and get a hamburger?" Josh asked. He adjusted his seat belt and leaned his seat into a half-reclining position.

"I suppose. I was planning pasta salad for dinner but—" she glanced his way and saw the expression of distaste on his oversize features "—I guess a bacon cheeseburger and a basket of curly fries sounds better."

"And a milk shake."

"Chocolate."

"Good deal, Mom." Josh gave her a thumbs-up. "I *hate* pasta salad."

"I know," she said and swallowed a smile as she reached over to rumple his stick-straight hair. Right now, staring out the bug-spattered window, he reminded her of his father; a man she hadn't seen in eleven years, a man who probably still didn't know he had a child. Her hands started to sweat against the wheel. For years she'd told herself that Dave didn't need to know he had a son, that he'd run out on her and left her pregnant without a backward glance, that he didn't deserve Josh's attention.

Lately, however, seeing all the mistrust and damage that had occurred because of her own father's lies, she doubted the wisdom of a hasty, emotional decision made when she was a scared, pregnant teenager.

Wouldn't it be better for Josh to know his dad? To understand where he'd come from?

Wouldn't she, as a teenager growing up, have given her right arm for the truth? She owed that much to her son.

Chapter Two

"I hate to say it, Katie, but what you need is a man." Jarrod Smith, Katie Kinkaid's oldest half brother, slammed down the hood of her old convertible and swiped at a mosquito that had hovered near his head. The minute she'd arrived home after dropping Josh at soccer practice, she'd called her brother to check under the hood. But she hadn't wanted or needed his advice on the sad state of her love life.

"I think what I need might be a new car." Katie frowned at her ancient two-door—a gem in its day— and wondered how she could possibly afford the payments on a newer model. Her gaze traveled from the single-car garage to her little bungalow, the place she and her son had called home for nearly a decade. Two windowpanes were cracked, the dryer was temperamental and the carpet should have been replaced years before. No, she couldn't swing buying a new car right now.

"This—" Jarrod thumped a greasy finger on the faded finish of her convertible "—is the least of your worries." Wiping the oil from his hands onto a soiled rag, he shook his head. Sweat dampened his brown hair and slid down the side of his face. "You've got Josh and—"

"And I don't need a lecture. Least of all from you," she said, irritated that the subject of her being a single parent was a matter for discussion. Just because their mother had married for the fifth time this summer and her two half sisters were planning to "do the aisle-walk thing," as the media now called it, didn't mean that she needed to hook up with a man. Independent to a fault, she supposed people thought her, but she couldn't imagine being tied down to one man. Not that she didn't have a fantasy now and again. Raising a boy alone was no picnic, but she wasn't sure a husband and stepfather would help the situation. In fact, she was certain it would do more damage than good. "No one ever *needs* a man, Jarrod," she said, leveling a gaze at him that she hoped would burn into his hard-edged heart. "Least of all, me."

"I'm just telling you that it wouldn't hurt." He glanced around the backyard where a rusted basketball hoop hung at an odd angle from the garage and the dandelions battled it out with the crabgrass for control of the lawn. Weeds choked the flower beds and the patio furniture needed to be treated for a severe case of rust. Yep, the whole place needed a makeover—and badly. Even her old hound dog, Blue, who was lying in the shade of the porch, one silvering ear cocked though his eyes were closed, could probably use a flea

bath, a teeth cleaning and a "buff and puff" from El-
sie, the local dog groomer.

It didn't make Jarrod's suggestion any more palat-
able. She was a woman with a mission, imagined herself launched into a career in high-profile journalism.
It was coming her way, and soon. She might already
have been sent her one-way ticket to fame and fortune—if the anonymous letter she'd received in this
morning's post was to be believed.

"A man, Katie," her brother repeated.

"You're like a broken record or CD, these days."
Planting both fists firmly on her hips, she asked, "So
what do you suggest? That I take in a roommate so
that I don't con my lazy, no-good self-serving half
brothers into doing odd jobs like fixing the dryer or the
dishwasher or the car for me?"

A crooked smile tugged at the corner of Jarrod's
mouth. "Now, that's an idea." He swiped the beads of
perspiration from his forehead and left a grease stain
on his brow.

"Or should I just take out an ad in the personals,
hmm? 'Wanted: Handyman and part-time father. Must
do light housework. References required.'"

"Maybe you should just get married," he said, and
Katie bristled at the thought.

She wasn't interested in marriage with anyone.
Wasn't even dating. For a second her thoughts skipped
to Luke Gates, then, horrified, she cleared her throat as
well as her mind. "Our family has enough of that going
around," she grumbled as they walked toward the back
porch where several wasps were busily constructing a
muddy nest in the corner of the ceiling. Blue struggled
to his arthritic legs and his tail whipped back and forth.
Katie couldn't let the subject drop. "If you haven't

noticed, Jarrod, I don't have time for another man in my life. Believe me, Josh is enough.''

''He's one boy.''

''And a great kid,'' she said automatically as she tugged open the screen door. A jagged tear in the mesh was getting bigger by the day, but she ignored it as she always did. She had bigger worries, but she wasn't about to tell her older brother that she was concerned as all get-out about her son, that it was hard as hell to raise a boy alone, that sometimes it scared her to death. Nope, she'd somehow deal with Josh and whatever challenge he came with. He was worth it.

The interior of the kitchen was sweltering—nearly ninety degrees according to her indoor-outdoor thermometer. Though the window over the sink was ajar, no summer breeze slipped through to dissipate the smells of maple syrup and bacon that hung in the air from the breakfast she'd made hours before. Whining, Blue lifted his nose toward the sink where the frying pan was soaking in greasy water.

''Trust me, boy, you don't want it,'' Katie advised.

Swinging his gaze around what he called ''a thousand square feet of chaos,'' Jarrod asked, ''Where's Josh?''

''At soccer practice. Earlier he was at Tiffany's. He and Stephen have kind of bonded, I guess you'd say.''

''Better than you and Tiffany?''

''Actually, Tiff and I are getting along just great,'' Katie said. ''She wants me to rent out this place and take over hers.'' She explained quickly about Tiffany's offer earlier in the day. ''So Tiffany and I don't have a problem.''

''Real sisters, eh?''

''Half sisters.''

"Close enough." He winked at her and she grinned. "Like you are to me."

"Right."

"So John's getting his wish."

"Not completely, but this ragtag family is finally coming together a little, I think. Tiffany has agreed to be in Bliss's wedding and I *never* would have thought that was possible." There was still some envy on Tiffany's part because Bliss was John Cawthorne's only legitimate daughter, but things were working out.

Katie snagged a peanut from a bowl on the table and plopped it into her mouth. "I would never have thought that Tiffany would agree to be in Bliss's wedding."

"See? Finding a man didn't hurt Tiffany's disposition, did it?"

"Oh, get over yourself. So now men help women's personalities? Come on, Jarrod, that kind of thinking went out with hula hoops."

"I'm just pointing out a simple fact."

"I'm *not* getting married, okay?" Biting her tongue before she said anything she might really regret, Katie took up her scratchy sponge and scrubbed the frying pan so fiercely, she wondered if she'd scrape the Teflon right off the metal. Though she relied on her brothers from time to time, they—especially Jarrod in his current older-brother mood—could be worse than irritating. "My marital status is, as they say, none of your business."

He had the audacity to laugh. "But your car is."

"Touché, brother dear," she said with a sigh. "Want something to drink?"

"Got a beer?"

"Nope. Bottled water, tomato juice and grapefruit juice."

"Thanks anyway. Too healthy for me. I think I'll pass." He grabbed a handful of peanuts and tossed them one by one into the air, catching them in his mouth—a trick he'd perfected before Katie had even entered grade school.

"Thanks for helping out," she said over her shoulder.

"Any time." He was out the door and it slapped shut behind him. Katie rinsed her hands and dried them quickly. Since Josh was at soccer practice, there was just enough time for her to do some research for a story she was investigating—the biggest news story in Bittersweet in years. She found her purse and slung the strap over her shoulder as she breezed out the back door. Someone had to solve the mystery surrounding Isaac Wells's disappearance and she was determined to get the ball rolling. One way or another, her byline was going to be on the story when it broke.

Astride a tired sorrel mare, Luke squinted against an ever-lowering sun. His bones ached from over six hours in the saddle, and sweat had collected on his back. Dust covered his hands and face and all he wanted was a cool shower and a cold bottle of beer. As the horse eased down a steep cattle trail, Luke eyed the rough terrain of rocky cliffs, narrow ridges and scraggly stands of oak and madrona. The place wasn't exactly Eden. Not by a long shot.

He'd spent the afternoon following deer and cattle trails that fanned across the hilly, sun-dried terrain. Thickets of scrawny trees offered some shade, but for the most part the earth was covered with brittle, bleached grass, rocks and a sprinkling of weeds. There wasn't more than five acres of level land, and not much more of rolling hills. Most of the spread was mountain-goat country, with craggy hillsides, narrow ravines and a slash of a creek that zigzagged its way through the canyon floor.

But it was perfect for trail rides and the small cattle drives he planned to organize as part of the working dude ranch he envisioned. Better yet, the eastern flank of the spread abutted a huge parcel of national forest service land that was open for the type of backpacking, hunting or camping he was going to offer to his clients.

He frowned and wondered if, for the first time in his thirty-six years, he would finally find some peace of mind. "Not a prayer," he said to the mare, a game little quarter horse who, he'd been told by Max Renfro, the onetime foreman of the place, was named Lizzy.

Especially not until he found Ralph's grandson or granddaughter. If there was one. Just because Dave had mentioned ten years after the fact that he thought he might have fathered a kid, didn't necessarily mean it was true. Luke could be chasing after the gossamer fabric of an old man's dreams—nothing more.

He clucked to the horse and nudged her sides. They started down the south slope.

A glint of metal flashed in the distance.

"Whoa."

From his vantage spot on the hill, he had a full view of the Isaac Wells place. It had been unoccupied since the old guy had disappeared but it had attracted its share of curiosity seekers despite the lengths of yellow police tape that had been strung across the main gate. According to Max Renfro, the sheriff's department was always having to run someone off the place.

Sure enough, there was a car in the drive—a con-vertible, he realized—and Luke felt an uneasy sensation stir in his gut. He reached into his saddlebag and pulled out a pair of binoculars.

Lifting the glasses to his eyes, he spied Katie Kinkaid, as big as life, climbing over the fence and ignoring not only the police tape but the No Trespassing sign posted on the gate.

Luke's jaw grew hard as he watched her shade her eyes and peer into the windows of the dilapidated old house. Luke had never met Isaac Wells, but his mysterious disappearance a while back was well-known. So what was Katie Kinkaid doing, nosing around the neglected spread?

"She's a snoopy thing," he remarked to the horse, then remembered that she was a reporter of some kind or other. She leaned over to look through one window as if she were trying to see beneath a half-lowered shade, and Luke's gaze settled on her rear end, round and firm beneath her shorts. His mouth turned to sand and he suddenly felt like a schoolboy for staring at her. Who cared if she was wandering around the abandoned farm? It wasn't any of his business.

But the rumors he'd been hearing in the taverns and coffee shops—talk of possible kidnapping, burglary and murder—cut through his mind. What if Isaac Wells had been the victim of foul play? What if he'd been killed and the murderer was still on the loose?

It's not your problem, he told himself and decided he was only borrowing trouble. If there was a culprit involved in the Isaac Wells mystery, he was long gone. There probably wasn't much danger anyway. The whole Isaac Wells mess was probably blown out of proportion, grist for the slow-turning gossip mill in this part of the country. He took one final look at the fiery redhead. She was standing now, one hip thrown out the way it had been earlier and as she turned toward him, he noticed the now familiar pucker of her full lips, the arched eyebrows pulled together in concentration.

He swallowed hard as his gaze skated down the column of her throat to the gap between the lapels of her blouse, to the hint of cleavage he'd seen earlier. He gritted his teeth and looked away in disgust. He wasn't used to the earthy pull of this woman, the desire that singed his mind every time he looked at her. "Come on," he ground out, clucking to the horse and urging her back down the steep grade.

He couldn't worry about Ms. Kinkaid or anyone else, for that matter. He'd learned long ago that he could only take care of himself.

At that particular thought, he scowled. Reaching flatter ground, he pressed his knees into Lizzy's sweaty sides. Though she was tired, the mare responded, her strides stretching as they reached the lower hills where the grade was much gentler and the stables were in sight. Her ears pricked forward and she let out a little nicker at the small herd that had gathered by the weathered fence.

"Yeah, and they miss you, too, Lizzy," Luke said, already feeling at home on this dusty scrap of land. All of the outbuildings needed new roofs, the siding of each was crying out for gallons of paint, and there were few windows that didn't require replacement of at least one new pane.

But he was getting ahead of himself. First he had to find out if Ralph's son had fathered a child around here. It shouldn't be too hard. He'd already started checking birth notices for ten and eleven years back. Tomorrow he'd drive to the county courthouse to check records there and, of course, there was always local gossip—as good a place to start as any.

He cooled Lizzy down and stripped her of bridle and saddle, then set her free in the closest field. With an eager nicker, she joined the small herd gathered near a solitary pine tree. A few half-grown foals frolicked around their more sedate dams while a roan gelding rolled on the ground. His legs pawed the air madly and he grunted in pleasure as brown clouds of dust enveloped his body. Luke smiled. All in all, the horses looked healthy and alert. Good stock. Ten head if you counted the two fillies and one colt.

The cattle were another story. They roamed the hillsides freely and were rangy and lean—not exactly prime beef. But they would do for what he had in mind.

His plan was to start renovations on the main house as soon as the building permits were approved by the county, work through the winter, then start advertising in January. In order to be in full operation this coming spring, he'd have to hire at least basic help—a cook and housekeeper, along with a few ranch hands and a part-time guide or two. Hopefully he'd have his first group of clients in by mid-May. He figured he'd run the first two years in the red but after that, he hoped to turn a profit.

He had to. All his hopes and dreams were tied up in this old place, he thought with a humorless smile.

Years ago, he'd had other visions for his life. He'd thought he'd settle down and raise a family, save enough to buy his own place and live out the American Dream. But things hadn't worked out the way he'd thought they would. His stomach clenched when he thought of his marriage. Hell, what a mess. Seven years of bad luck. Then the divorce. As bad as the marriage had been, the divorce had been even worse.

Well, it was over. A long time ago. Since then, he'd worked his butt off to save enough money to buy a place of his own and this, it seemed, was it. So he'd better make good.

He locked up, then climbed into his old truck. With a flick of his wrist, he turned the key. Tomorrow he'd start by cleaning out each of the buildings and checking on the permits again—just as soon as he'd done a little digging into the past. He figured it wouldn't take long to discover the truth. If Dave Sorenson had fathered a kid eleven years ago, someone around a town as small as Bittersweet would know. It was just a matter of time before he found out.

"Don't do this to me!" Katie cried.

She tromped on the accelerator of the convertible, pushing the pedal to the floor, but the car continued to slow. The engine had died and she had no choice but to roll onto the shoulder of the road.

"Perfect," she grumbled sarcastically. She was nearly three miles outside of town, the sun was about to set and she was wearing sandals that would cut her feet to ribbons before she could catch sight of the town limits of Bittersweet. "Just damned perfect."

The car eased to a stop, tires crunching on the gravel.

Valiantly she twisted the ignition again.

Nothing.

"Come on, come on." She tried over and over but the convertible was as dead as a proverbial doornail and wasn't about to budge. "Great. Just bloody terrific!" She thought of her half brother and his efforts under the hood a short while ago. "Nice try, Jarrod," she grumbled, but couldn't really blame him. He was a private investigator, an ex-cop, and never had been a mechanic. Just because he was male didn't mean he knew anything about alternators or batteries or spark plugs or whatever it was that made a car run.

With a pained sigh she dropped her head onto the steering wheel and whispered, "A cell phone, a cell phone. My kingdom for a cell phone." Sweat ran down the back of her neck and within seconds a lazy bee buzzed and hovered near her head.

Katie drew in a long, deep breath, then gave herself a quick mental shake.

"Okay, okay, you're a smart woman, Kinkaid. When Jarrod worked on this he might have messed up and didn't reconnect a wire or hose properly. It's probably no big deal." She buoyed herself up as she slid from behind the steering wheel and looked under the hood. The same engine she'd stared at earlier in the day sat where it always had, ticking as it cooled in front of her. Everything appeared in order, but then she didn't know up from sideways when it came to cars. Gingerly, hoping not to burn herself or smear oil all over, she jiggled a few wires, poked at the hoses, checked the battery cables and saw nothing out of the ordinary. Not that she would recognize it if it was.

In the distance, beyond the last hill, the sound of an engine reached her ears. "Hallelujah!"

Ignoring all the warnings she'd been given as a schoolgirl, she stepped around the car and raised her hands. On this road she was most likely to come across a farmer or ranch hand, or a mother toting her kids into town.

A battered pickup crested the hill and her heart nosedived. She recognized Luke Gates's truck before it ground to a stop.

"Great," she muttered sarcastically. "Just…perfect." She told herself she should be relieved rather than disgusted, angry or embarrassed. After all, he was a man she trusted. Well, sort of. At least, as far as she knew, he wasn't a rapist or murderer or any other kind of criminal.

He parked just ahead of her car and opened the truck's door. Long, jeans-clad legs unfolded from behind the wheel and leather boots that had seen better days hit the ground. "Trouble?" he asked as he slammed the door shut.

"A little." Katie's heart drummed a bit faster and she mentally berated herself for letting his innate sex appeal get to her. What did she care if he was tall and lean and irreverently intriguing? She'd met a lot of men in her lifetime—*a lot*—who were just as good-looking, rebelliously charming and sensual as this guy.

Hadn't she?

"Looks like a lot of trouble to me."

"I guess. It just died on me," she said as he bent to look under the hood.

"And it was runnin' fine before?"

"No, not really." Standing next to him, her bare shoulder brushing against his forearm, she explained how the car had been giving her fits and starts over the past six months. "It zips along just fine, then something goes wrong. I have a mechanic or one of my brothers fiddle around with it and it finally begins to run again. Or, worse yet, it stops on me and with enough prayer and sweat I manage to get it going again, only to take it into the service station where it purrs like a kitten." She slid the convertible a spiteful glance. "Then the mechanics can't find anything wrong with it." Frustration burned through her veins. "It's what you might call 'temperamental.'"

"Maybe it's just old and worn-out. How many miles you got on her?"

"Two-hundred-and-twenty-some thousand, I think," she said with a shrug.

He let out a long, low whistle. "As I said, she's just tired. Think how you'd feel if you'd gone that far."

"Sometimes it feels as if I have," she grumbled, and frowned at the engine.

"Get inside and try and start it," he suggested.

"It won't go anywhere."

He cast her a look she couldn't comprehend. "Maybe not, but I'll get a better feel for it if I'm watching the engine attempt to turn over."

"Okay. Okay." She climbed into the car, twisted the ignition and heard the engine grind laboriously.

"Again," he ordered and through the crack where the hood was raised she saw his arms reach deep into the cavern that housed the engine. She pumped the gas and turned the key again. Grinding. Slower and slower, then nothing.

Three more times she tried before he slammed the hood down in frustration. "She's dead."

"I knew that much."

He eyed the sky, judging the daylight. "I think I'd better drive you back to town and we can call a tow truck."

"Wonderful," she muttered sarcastically, but reminded herself that at least she wasn't stranded or alone.

She hoisted herself into the passenger side of his truck, an older model with new seat covers and a thick layer of dust. Both windows were open and as Luke steered the rig onto the empty road, late-summer evening air streamed inside, tangling Katie's hair and cooling her skin.

Glancing at her watch, she frowned. "Oh, this is just perfect," she said, unable to hide her sarcasm.

"Something else wrong?"

Why did she feel like an incompetent around him? She wanted to look and play the part of the clever reporter—sassy and bright. Instead she felt like a frazzled woman who couldn't quite get her act together. "I'm supposed to pick up Josh from soccer practice in five minutes."

She folded her arms across her chest in frustration. "Damned machine." Casting her would-be savior a glance, she swallowed her pride yet again. "I hate to ask, but would you mind swinging by Reed Field to pick Josh up? It's pretty close to the high school."

"Not a problem," he said, and she fell back against the seat.

"Thanks. I owe you one."

"Don't worry about it."

But she did. She didn't like owing anyone; especially a stranger she'd barely met. This time, it seemed, she had no choice. Feeling the wind brush against her cheeks, she stared through the bug-spattered windshield and watched as the sun sank behind the western hills to stripe the sky in vibrant shades of gold and pink. All the while she was aware of the man beside her—a sexy stranger with a Texas drawl that seemed to bore right to the very center of her. Angry at the turn of her thoughts, she tapped her fingers nervously on the armrest.

"You okay?" Luke slid a glance her way as he braked for a corner.

She stopped fidgeting. "Fine."

"So what were you doing over at the Wells ranch?"

Every muscle in her body tensed. "You saw me?"

With a quick nod, he turned onto the main highway leading into town.

She had no reason to lie, though the question made her edgy. She'd had no idea she was being observed. Well, a private detective she wasn't. "I thought I'd go check things out," she admitted, feeling suddenly foolish, like a kid caught with her hand in a forbidden cookie jar. "I've been by the place quite a few times ever since Isaac disappeared, but I haven't really pried much—well, not as much as I'd like to."

"Nosin' around for a story?"

"Not just a story," she admitted, trying to contain the excitement she always felt at the thought of uncovering a mystery and being the first to report it. "I think this is the scoop of the century around here." She turned her head to stare at his profile as he shifted down. His face, all hard planes and angles, was a study in concentration. "Where were you that you saw me?"

"At my new place."

"Your new…?" Her throat went dry and she licked her lips as she realized where he was going to live. At the Sorenson ranch. Dear Lord, no. Her heart turned to stone and she had trouble breathing for a second. "Don't tell me you bought out Ralph Sorenson." She could barely say the name. A sick sensation curled in her stomach.

"That's it."

Oh, God. Her fingers clenched into tight fists. Slowly

she straightened them. This was no time to fall apart. "You know Ralph Sorenson?"

"Sure do." He slowed as they passed the sign indicating they'd entered Bittersweet's city limits. A few streetlights had begun to glow as the first shades of evening slipped through the narrow streets and boulevards of Bittersweet. "Ralph helped me out of a jam a long time ago, gave me a job and treated me like a son ever since."

"Did he?" She felt the color drain from her face and her heartbeat thudded through her brain. "I suppose you met his son," she said, trying to sound lighthearted when deep inside she ached.

"Dave?" His smile faded and something dark and dangerous skated through his gaze as he glanced in her direction.

"Y-yes. Dave."

"I knew him," he admitted, his voice suddenly flat. Was it her imagination or did he suddenly grip the steering wheel more tightly? "Helluva guy."

"Is he?" she asked, her own question sounding far away when she thought of the one boy she had loved, the one to whom she'd eagerly given her virginity, the father of her only son.

"Was," Luke said, flipping on his turn signal and wheeling into the gravel lot beside the high school.

Her heart turned to ice at the implication. Luke rubbed his chin as he pulled into a parking spot. He cut the engine and looked at her with troubled blue eyes.

"I thought the news would have gotten back here by now." She felt a chill as cold as Alaska in January and braced herself for words she'd never expected to hear.

"Dave Sorenson died six months ago."

Chapter Three

Katie's world tilted, the underpinnings giving way. All that she'd held true for years shattered, bursting through her brain in painful, heart-slicing shards. *No! It couldn't be. Dave Sorenson was alive.*

But the look Luke Gates sent her convinced her that he was telling the truth, that this wasn't some sort of cruel, hateful joke.

Josh's father was dead.

"Dear God," she whispered, her throat raw, the insides of her nose and throat burning with sudden, grief-riddled tears. "I— I...I didn't know." She cleared her throat and looked away, blinking rapidly against the wash of tears. Her throat was so thick she couldn't swallow, her eyes ached. For years she'd considered trying to find Dave Sorenson and telling him the painful but glorious truth that they had a son—a wonderful, lighthearted boy she'd named Joshua Lee—but she never had. She'd always thought—*assumed*—that there would be time; that the perfect moment would somehow appear for confiding to Josh the fact that his father was a man whose circumstances had forced him to move to Texas; a man who, at the time of Josh's conception, had been little more than a boy himself; a man, who at that tender age, couldn't have been expected to settle down. Then she'd thought, in this silly fantasy, that she'd eventually track down Dave and give him the news. She'd told herself he would be mature and would understand, and that Josh would somehow connect with his father. But...if Luke was telling the truth, it was too late. Josh would never know his father.

"Katie?" Luke's voice startled her.

"It...it can't be." She glanced at him and saw a storm of emotions she didn't understand in his expression. "He was so young—not much older than me." She drew in a long, disbelieving breath.

"I know." His face showed genuine concern. "Are you okay?"

"Yes...fine..." But it was a lie.

"You're sure?" Obviously he wasn't convinced.

"No. I mean, yes." She blinked rapidly, refusing to break down altogether. Inside, she was numb. Shaking. Grieving painfully. But she couldn't let Luke Gates or anyone else know how devastated she felt. This was too deep. Too personal. Dabbing at an escaping tear with the tip of her finger, she stared out the window. "I, uh, knew Dave.... He was in the twins'—my half brothers'—class in high school and he hung around the house sometimes. I liked him and I didn't know that...that he'd..." She swallowed hard, then let out a sigh that started somewhere deep in her heart. "You shocked me, I guess," she admitted, trying desperately to recover a bit when her entire world seemed shaken, rocked to its very core. Forcing an empty, faltering smile, she asked, "What...what happened?" Then, as she looked through the windshield, she said, "Oh, no."

Focusing for the first time on her son's soccer team, a ragtag group of kids in shorts and T-shirts who were coming off the dusty field, she saw trouble. The boys' faces were red, perspiration darkened their hair and grass stains smeared their jerseys. Part of the team was still kicking a ball around, a few others were gathering up their bags and water bottles, but what held her attention was the group huddled around the coach who was helping a sweaty kid who bit his lip as he limped toward the parking lot.

Josh.

Her already-battered heart sank even further.

Luke reached for the door, but Katie was ahead of him, out of the pickup like a shot. "Josh?" she called, waving her arms madly. "Over here!" His face was so red she could barely make out his freckles and every time he started to put some weight on his right foot, he winced, then bit his lower lip. He had one arm slung around his coach's shoulder and he hobbled slowly. Though tears swam in his eyes, his chin was jutted in determination as he made an effort not to cry.

"What happened?" Katie asked when she reached him. Luke had gotten out of the truck and was leaning on a fender.

"Little accident," the coach explained. "Josh and Tom were fighting for the ball and Tom tackled him. Josh went down and twisted his ankle."

"Let me see—" She bent over and eyed the injured foot. His shin guards had been stripped off but the swelling was visible through his sock. She clucked her tongue and when she tried to touch his leg, Josh sucked in a whistling, pained breath.

"Heck of a way to start the season," the coach, a man by the name of Gary Miller, said.

"I can still play," Josh protested.

"Only if the doctor says so." Gary helped Josh to Luke's truck. "I think he should have that ankle X-rayed."

Katie nodded. "We will."

"Where's the car?" Josh asked as he slowly climbed into the bench seat of Luke's truck.

"It's a long story."

"Don't tell me. It broke down again."

Katie's head was beginning to throb. She didn't want to think about what else might go wrong. First the convertible had broken down, then she'd heard the devastating news that Dave had died and now Josh was hobbling, his ankle twice its normal size. "Yep, the car conked out again."

"I thought Uncle Jarrod was gonna fix it— Ooh!" Josh sucked in his breath as he shifted and tried to slide across the seat.

"He did. Sort of. Come on, let's get you to a doctor." She squeezed onto the seat with her son and slammed the pickup door shut.

"I'll call you later and see how he is," the coach said and reached through the open window to rumple Josh's sweat-soaked hair. "It was a great practice until you and Tom got into it."

Luke took his place behind the wheel. "Where to?"

"Cawthorne Acres, I suppose." Katie was already thinking ahead. "My mom's probably there and we can borrow her car."

Luke twisted the key in the ignition. "That's clear out of town."

"I know, but—"

"Isn't there an emergency-care place around here somewhere where we can get that ankle looked at?"

"About half a mile that way," she said, pointing up the street. "But I hate to bother you—"

"No bother at all," he insisted and rammed the truck into gear. There was no reason to argue with him, so Katie guided him to the small clinic and felt pretty useless as Luke carried Josh into the emergency area. She'd been here before, not long ago, when John Cawthorne had collapsed and her mother had been worried that he'd suffered a second heart attack. Fortunately his condition had been diagnosed as heat stroke and he'd survived.

Josh's injury wasn't life-threatening. The worst that would happen was that he'd be in a cast for a few weeks. Yet she hated the thought of him being in any kind of pain or laid up. Katie wiped her hands on the front of her shorts.

"Look, you can go now," she said to Luke, once the paperwork was finished and a nurse had come with a wheelchair to whisk Josh to the X-ray lab. "I'll call Bliss or Tiffany or Mom or someone to come get me."

"No reason."

"But it could be a while. He might have to see a specialist."

Luke eyed her. "Why bother someone else," he drawled, "when I'm here already?"

"You probably have better things to do."

He lifted a shoulder as if his own life were of no concern. "If there was something pressing, I'd let you know."

She was too worried to argue, and while Luke sat on one of the plastic couches and thumbed through a sports magazine that was several months old she fidgeted, paced, and tried not to worry. A jillion thoughts rattled through her head, most of them mixed up with Luke, Josh and Dave Sorenson. How could Dave have died and she not have heard about it? It was true that he and his folks had moved away over ten years before and they had little contact with anyone in Bittersweet, but they'd still owned the ranch next to Isaac Wells's place. Usually, bad news had a way of filtering back to a small town. Katie's heart ached and her head pounded with an overwhelming and desperate grief. What could she tell Josh?

For years she'd kept the name of her child's father a secret. Only she and her mother knew the truth. Even her twin half brothers, Nathan and Trevor, who had known Dave in high school, had been spared the bitter fact that one of their friends had done a love-'em-and-leave-'em number on their half sister. Her hands felt suddenly clammy, her heart as cold as the bottom of the ocean.

"Josh is gonna be all right," Luke said as she passed by him for the thirtieth time. He gestured toward her anxious pacing. "You know, if you're not careful you're gonna wear a patch right through the floor."

He smiled, but it seemed guarded somehow and she wondered about him. From the minute he'd blown into town he'd been a mystery, a man without a past—a tall, lanky Texan with a sexy drawl and, seemingly, no ties. She'd fantasized that he'd held some deep, dark secret that she, as the local reporter with her ear to the ground, would uncover. Instead, he'd dropped a bomb that threw her life into unexpected and unwanted turmoil.

Luke studied her over the top of his magazine. "Can I get you something? A cup of coffee?"

"The last thing I need is caffeine."

"Decaf, then."

"Or maybe a tranquillizer." She knew she was over-reacting, but she was a jumble of nerves today.

His grin widened a bit and the crow's feet around his eyes deepened. "This is probably the place to get one."

"I was kidding."

"I know." He slapped his magazine closed. "I think we should call a tow company for your car."

"Oh...good idea, but I need to be here."

"As soon as Josh is released." He snapped his magazine open again and turned his attention back to the article he'd been perusing. Katie sat down, but couldn't endure the inactivity. Seconds later she was pacing again, her brain pounding with the problem of how she was going to tell Josh that his father was dead. She wanted to ask Luke what had happened to Dave, but thought she had better wait until they were alone, and she felt more in control.

Within twenty minutes Josh was wheeled back into the room. He was wearing a brace on his leg and a woman doctor with short brown hair, wide eyes and round glasses approached. "Are you Josh's mom?"

"Yes. Katie. Katie Kinkaid."

"Dr. Thatcher." The doctor extended her hand and shook Katie's. "I think Josh here is going to live a while longer," she teased. "Nothing appears to be broken, but I'm going to send his X rays to a specialist for a second opinion, just in case. What I see is a pretty severe sprain. He'll need to lie down and elevate his foot for a couple of days. The ankle should be iced, to begin with. I've prescribed some mild painkillers that he can take for the first forty-eight hours or so and I'd like to see him use crutches until the swelling goes down.''

Katie listened and nodded but wondered how in the world she was going to keep an active ten-year-old off his feet. Short of strapping him to the bed, she didn't have many options.

With Luke's help, Josh hobbled to the truck and they drove straight to the pharmacy where they picked up Josh's prescription and rented crutches five minutes before the place closed for the night.

By the time they pulled into the driveway of her little bungalow, night had fallen and the streetlights gave off an eerie blue glow. Crickets chirped softly and from a house down the street music wafted—some piece of jazz that seemed to float on the breeze. Blue, lying on the back stoop, growled his disapproval of the newcomer as Katie unlocked the door and Luke helped Josh up the steps.

''Hush!'' Katie said sharply and the old dog gave off one last indignant snarl. ''Don't mind him, he's getting old and grouchy,'' she said, but fondly patted Blue's head. She snapped on the porch light and the aging dog tagged after them as they entered the kitchen.

Once Josh was in his room and lying on his bed, Katie propped his leg on pillows, then rinsed a washcloth with water in the bathroom. ''I guess you'll have to use this to clean up,'' she said as she handed him the wet cloth and eyed his cramped room. ''You know, Josh, if you agree to keep up with your homework and don't abuse the privilege, I'll bring in the little TV set that's in the kitchen.''

''Really?''

''Mm-hmm. But homework comes first. School's just started, so we don't want to get behind.''

''‘We’ won't,'' he promised with a grin.

''I can take care of that.'' Luke went back to the kitchen and returned to Josh's room with the thirteen-inch TV. Balancing the TV on the top of an already crowded bookcase, he adjusted the rabbit ears and found a baseball game in progress.

''Awesome.''

Luke tossed Josh the remote control.

''Now, you promise to do everything the doctor says and keep up with your schoolwork?''

''Course.'' Josh nodded vigorously. For the first time since they'd picked him up, Josh smiled as he leaned back on his twin bed and immediately clicked the remote control to a different channel and one of his favorite sitcoms.

Blue, eyeing Luke suspiciously, slunk into the room and after circling a couple of times settled on the rug beside Josh's bed. Resting his graying muzzle on his paws, he glared up at Luke as if he were the devil incarnate.

''You be good,'' Katie warned the old dog and he managed one thump of his tail. She turned her attention back to Josh. ''Now, kid, is there anything else you need? How about something to eat?''

Josh's dark eyes sparkled. Already he was getting used to being waited on. ''Pizza?''

''Tomorrow, maybe. *If* we get the car back.''

''Papa Luigi's delivers.''

''As I said, tomorrow.'' She winked at her son.

"Right now, I think I'd better scrounge something up from the refrigerator."

He pulled a long face, which she ignored. "How about you?" she asked Luke. "I'm going to whip up some sandwiches if you're interested."

"You don't have to—"

"Of course I don't. But I do feel like I owe you." He hesitated, then lifted a shoulder as they stepped into the hallway where the door to Katie's room was half open, almost inviting. Inside, a Tiffany lamp burned at a low wattage, reflecting on the windows and spreading a warm pool of light over the lacy duvet and the pink and rose-colored pillows that were piled loosely against the headboard of her bed. The decor was outrageously feminine, with antiques, scatter rugs and frills. Oddly, she was embarrassed that he was looking into her private sanctuary where she worked on her columns, worried over Josh, and dreamed about her career; a room where no man had ever dared sleep. She felt her heart pound a little and when Luke's eyes found hers again, she realized she was blushing.

"So, how about ham or turkey on white bread?" she asked blithely, as if men looked into her bedroom every day of the week.

"Sounds great."

"Good." She walked briskly away from her room and, once she and Luke were in the kitchen, she let out her breath again. Why seeing him so close to her most private spot in the world disquieted her, she didn't know; didn't *want* to know. But there was no doubt about it—this easygoing Texan put her on edge.

He looked awkward and big and out of place in her kitchen. "I'll make the ice bag the doctor ordered," he offered, as if he, too, needed something to do. "Just point me in the right direction."

"Good idea." She handed him the tools he needed, then spread mayonnaise on slices of white bread. He found ice in the freezer, cracked the cubes from a tray and smashed them into smaller chunks with the small hammer she'd dug out for him. Once the ice was crushed, he rustled up a couple of plastic bags, put one inside the other and brushed the ice shavings inside.

"You've done this before," she observed, slapping ham, turkey, lettuce and tomatoes on the bread.

"Too many times to count."

"Do you have kids?" she asked automatically and he hesitated long enough to catch her attention. She'd never thought of him as being married or having children, but then she didn't know much about him. Not much at all.

"Nope. No kids of my own. But I've spent enough time with teenagers to get in this kind of practice. I've worked on crews with kids where we bucked hay, strung fence, roped calves—the whole nine yards. Someone was always getting kicked, or falling off a rig, or being bucked from a horse or whatever." He glanced up at her and she felt her breath stop at the intensity in his eyes. So blue. So deep. So…observant. She felt compelled to look away to break the silly notion that there was some kind of intimacy in his gaze. What was it about him that made her nervous? She was used to men and boys, had grown up with three brothers, yet this man, this stranger, had a way of making her uncomfortable. She pretended interest in slicing the sandwiches into halves. "So you've done a lot of ranching."

"Yep."

"In Texas?"

"All over. Wyoming and Montana for a spell, but mainly Texas."

"And that's where you met Ralph Sorenson?"

He nodded and his eyes fixed on her with laser-sharp acuity. "Years ago." He handed her the bag of ice, and though there were dozens of questions she wanted to ask him about Ralph and Dave and his life, she carried the ice pack, along with a platter of sandwiches, down to Josh's room.

She couldn't help wondering what Luke thought of her and her cramped little home. Filled to the gills with memorabilia from her youth, antiques, and enough books to make her own library, her house had a tight, packed-in feel that bordered on cramped but felt right to her. A string of Christmas lights was forever burning over an old desk she'd shoved into a corner of the living room and her walls were covered with pictures and doodads she'd collected over the years.

To her it was home and, if she moved to Tiffany's house, she'd take every bit of her life—the mementos from her past—with her.

She didn't know but guessed that Luke Gates lived a more austere existence. She imagined he'd be as content to sleep under the stars with a buffalo robe for warmth and a saddle for a pillow as he would in a feather-soft bed with eider-down pillows and thick blankets.

Josh had inherited his mother's need for keepsakes. Posters covered the walls of his room, and model planes hung from the ceiling. His desk was littered with baseball cards, trophies, books and CDs and his floor space was crowded with toys he'd just about outgrown. "You okay?" she asked, seeing that her son was channel surfing, flipping from a docudrama about the police to the baseball game.

"Fine, Mom. Don't worry."

"I'm your mother. It's my job."

"Oh, right." Josh rolled his eyes.

While Blue lifted his head in the hopes of snatching a dropped morsel, Katie handed Josh the plate. "Better than Papa Luigi's," she said. "You've got my personal guarantee."

"Sure."

"Ask anyone in town." She tucked the ice bag around his ankle.

He sucked in his breath and stiffened, tipping his plate and nearly losing a sandwich to the floor and the ever-watchful Blue. "Jeez, Mom, that's cold."

"It's supposed to be."

"I know, but, Mom, it's *freezing* cold."

"That's the general idea," she deadpanned. "It's ice."

"I don't want it."

"You have to. Wait a second." She went to the linen closet in the hall, found a thin washcloth, then wedged it between the bag and Josh's bare ankle. "Better?"

"Lots." He nodded, bit into his sandwich and turned his attention to the little black-and-white TV where a batter was sizing up the next pitch. "Good." She patted him on the head and resisted the urge to overmother him and kiss his cheek.

By the time she'd returned to the kitchen Luke had settled himself into one of the chairs that surrounded the small table she'd bought at a garage sale three years earlier. His long, jeans-clad legs stretched out at an angle to the middle of the kitchen floor and he was sliding his finger down the open Yellow Pages of the phone book. "Tow company," he said to the question she hadn't yet voiced.

"Oh, right. Good idea." She hated to think of her disabled car and the hassle of getting it fixed. She couldn't imagine being without wheels for even a few days and shuddered to think that it might stretch into weeks if the mechanics couldn't find the problem or get the part. On top of the inconvenience, there was the money to consider—extra money she didn't have right now. Again she thought of Tiffany's offer and she realized it was just a matter of convincing Josh. But whether he liked it or not, they would have to move; it only made sense. She set a platter of sandwiches on the table and then poured Josh a glass of milk. Holding the glass in one hand, she paused to pick up a scrap of turkey left on the cutting board, then headed back to Josh's room.

By the time she'd handed Josh his milk, thrown Blue the morsel and returned to the kitchen, Luke was on the phone and instructing the towing company as to the location of her car. "We'll be there in forty-five minutes," he promised and hung up. "All set," he said, winking at her.

Stupidly, her heart turned over.

"All-Star Towing to the rescue," he elaborated.

"Great. Thanks." She scrounged in a drawer and found a couple of napkins that hadn't been used for her Independence Day picnic. Emblazoned with red and blue stars, they gave a festive, if slightly out-of-date, splash of color. "I, uh, appreciate all you've done for me."

"All in a day's work."

"Only if you're into the Good Samaritan business." He smiled and she felt herself blushing for God-only-

knew-what reason. Motioning to the stack of sandwiches on the platter, she added, "Please...help yourself. We believe in self-service in this house."

"Good."

"Is there anything else you'd like—something to
drink? I've got juice, milk and water. Or coffee."

"Decaf?" he asked, lifting a blond eyebrow. "Isn't
that what you said you needed earlier?"

"Yeah, yeah, but I lied." She measured grounds into
a basket, then poured water into the back of the coffee
maker. With a flick of a switch, the coffee was perking.
"I think I need to be turbocharged right now."

"Aren't you always?"

The question caught her off guard. "How would you
know?"

"Seen you around," he said.

"Where?" She was surprised he'd noticed. She
knew she didn't exactly meld into the wallpaper, but
she didn't think Luke Gates was the type of man who
paid attention to most women. He seemed too aloof;
too distant.

She took a seat at the table as the smell of French
roast filled the air.

"I've seen you over at the apartment house with
your sister and a couple of times in town. That convertible of yours is hard to miss."

"It's been a good friend," she admitted. "I hope it
isn't dead for good."

"I'm sure it can be resurrected, but it might cost you
a bit."

"Doesn't everything?" she thought aloud and
reached for half a sandwich.

"I suppose."

The phone rang as the coffee brewed and Katie spent

a few minutes explaining to the soccer coach about Josh's ankle. Gary Miller was concerned and they decided that Josh should forgo practice and games until he'd received a clean bill of health from the doctor. "Here, I'll let you speak with him yourself," Katie offered, and carried the portable phone into the bedroom. Josh talked for a few minutes, handed her the phone again and turned back to his program. By the time she'd returned to the kitchen, the coffee had brewed. She was pouring two cups when the phone jangled again.

"Could you?" she asked as dark liquid splashed into her favorite mug.

"Sure." Luke snagged the receiver. "Hello?" He waited, then said, "Kinkaid residence... Hello...? Hello?" He paused and his eyebrows drew together. "Is someone there?" He paused again. "Hello? Oh, for the love of Mike." He hung up and stared at the phone.

"No one?"

"Oh, there was someone on the line," Luke said, glaring at the instrument as if he could see through the phone to the face of the person on the other end. "But he was put off when he heard my voice."

"Or she."

"Or she," he agreed, rubbing the side of his face thoughtfully.

Katie lifted a shoulder. "They'll call back if they really want me. Probably thought they got the wrong number when you answered."

"Maybe." He didn't seem convinced and his demeanor made her edgy. "You get many hang-ups?"

"My share. Along with solicitations and wrong numbers. Come on, eat. We don't have a lot of time if we're gonna pick up my car." She handed him a cup of coffee, then settled back into her chair.

"I guess you're right." He reached for half a sandwich and they ate in relative silence. It was odd, she thought, to have a man other than one of her brothers sitting across the table in her tiny kitchen. She'd grown up with three half brothers and more than a handful of stepfathers, but she'd never settled down with a man, never felt comfortable with one in her house. There had been other boys and men in her life, of course, before and after Dave. She'd dated on and off over the past ten years but she'd never allowed herself to fall in love; had always found an excuse to break off a relationship before it deepened into something emotionally dangerous.

She'd been accused of being "too picky" by her oft-married mother, or "too flighty" by the twins, and "too bullheaded about that damned job," by Jarrod, but the real reason she hadn't settled down was that she hadn't wanted to. She believed a woman should stand on her own two feet before she started leaning on a man. Any man.

Besides, she had Josh to consider and a career to promote. Just because Luke Gates was interesting didn't mean anything.

He checked his watch and finished a gulp of coffee. "I think we'd better get rollin' if we want to meet the tow truck."

"You don't have to do this," she said, giving him another out. "I have dozens of relatives who would help me."

Luke nodded as he carried his plate to the sink. "I know, but let's just say I like to finish what I start."

She thought about arguing with him, but changed her

mind. For whatever reason, he was willing to help her, and she decided to accept his aid. She dumped the dishes into the sink, told Josh what was going on, then locked the door behind her on the way to Luke's pickup.

As they drove away from town, the night seemed to close in around them. Stars twinkled seductively in the blackened heavens and a slice of moon cast a shimmering silver glow over the countryside. The dark shapes of cattle and horses moved against the bleached grass of the surrounding fields and hillsides and only a few headlights from oncoming cars illuminated the truck's cab as they passed.

Katie hugged the passenger door. Even with the window rolled down, the pickup seemed too small; too intimate. She told herself she was overreacting, but she noticed the position of Luke's hand on the gearshift lever, the way his fingers clutched the knob and how his sleeve was pushed up to his elbow, allowing her a glimpse of tanned skin dusted with gold hair.

So male.

So close.

Don't be ridiculous. He's just doing you a favor, for goodness' sake. There's nothing more to it than that. All her life her silly imagination had run away with her and she'd been forever reining it in. Tonight, it seemed, her fantasy was that Luke Gates, sexy and mysterious, was trying to think of ways to be alone with her. What a joke. Yet she felt her heart pounding in the pulse at her neck, and couldn't ignore the sensual, all-male scents of hay, dust and leather that clung to him.

Get over it, Kinkaid. The last complication you need in your life right now is a man—especially a quiet,

*mysterious stranger you don't have one scrap of solid
information about. Think about Josh. Think about the
Isaac Wells story. Think about your career. And for
God's sake, forget any silly romantic fantasies you
have about this man!*

She bit her lip and, drumming her fingers on the edge
of the window, she stared into the night until they
crested a small rise. Her car, looking abandoned and
lonely, was parked just where she'd left it.

Luke pulled onto the shoulder on the opposite side
of the road. "Let's try it one more time," he suggested
as he helped her out of the cab. His fingers as he
grabbed her hand were warm.

"And what if it starts?" She hopped lithely to the
ground.

"We pay the tow-truck driver and send him on his
way."

"Just my luck—having to pay for service I don't
need." She let go of his hand.

"It hasn't happened yet."

"It's not going to." Crossing her fingers, she unlocked the car and climbed into the dark interior.
"Here goes nothing," she said under her breath and
discovered as she turned the ignition that she was right.
The engine didn't so much as spark. "Satisfied?" she
asked Luke.

"I guess I have to be." He leaned one hip against
the fender and tried not to notice the shape of her leg
as she climbed out of her beater. She slammed the door
shut with a quick movement of her hip and his crotch
tightened. A million questions about her pricked at his
mind, but he ignored most of them. He wasn't interested in her. Just as he wasn't interested in any woman.

He caught the scent of her perfume on the breeze

and wondered what it would be like to kiss her. She was different from the kind of woman who usually attracted him—small and compact rather than tall and slim. He'd convinced himself that he liked a woman who was as quiet as he, thoughtful and soft-spoken, but this redheaded dynamo had changed his mind.

Not that he'd do anything about it.

"You're sure the towing company knows where we are?" she asked, her eyebrows puckering together in concern.

"Yep."

She checked her watch, glanced up the road and frowned. He imagined a dozen thoughts streaking through her mind all at once. "Your last name's Kinkaid," he finally said.

"Uh-huh."

"But your father's John Cawthorne, right?"

"Don't you know the story?" She turned eyes that were as dark as emeralds in his direction. "I thought everyone did."

"I'm new in town."

"But you know that Tiffany is my sister—er, half sister."

"That much I gathered."

"I guess I should be embarrassed about all of this," she confided, as if glad for something to talk about. "The truth is, my family is what you might call 'different'—well, way beyond conventional. I didn't even know I had half sisters until this year." She explained how her father had sired three different daughters with three different women, Bliss being the only legitimate one.

"No way around it, the whole thing was a scandal," Katie admitted, "because rather than break up John's marriage, which would have been horrible, Mom married Hal Kinkaid and told him I was his. The only other person who knew the truth was John.''

''And he allowed it?'' Luke asked, disgusted with the man.

''At least he didn't put up a fight,'' she allowed, obviously trying not to show the little bit of pain she still felt over the fact that her biological father hadn't claimed her for most of her life. ''John didn't want a divorce or to lose Bliss. So...''

''You grew up living a lie.''

She lifted a shoulder and sighed sadly. The breeze caught in her hair, lifting it from her face, and Luke felt a possessive need to place an arm around her shoulders and pull her close, to hold her and comfort her.

''It's not that big a deal now. I never much liked Hal, anyway. He was a jerk, so I didn't cry many tears when he and Mom split up. You have to remember, it was kind of a tradition with my mother to marry a guy for a few years, then divorce him and marry someone else.''

Katie shook her head as if to dismiss the negative sound of her last statement. ''Mom isn't a bad person, just kind of flighty. Impulsive, I guess you'd say, especially when it comes to men. To her credit, though, she always loved John.''

''Even though he was married to someone else.''

''Yeah. Weird, huh?''

''To each his own,'' he said, though he didn't believe it. Marriage was marriage. You didn't step over the line. You didn't cheat. He'd felt the sting of that whip himself and had vowed at the time that he'd never be flogged again. ''So...what about you?'' he asked. ''I thought Kinkaid was your married name.''

"My what?" she demanded. "I've never gotten married, but I see what you thought—because my name is different from anyone else's in my family." She laughed nervously. The subject was touchy.

"Yep."

"I guess you'd say I never met the right guy."

She glanced away as if embarrassed and he mentally kicked himself from one side of hell to the other for the look of pain he'd brought to her pixie-like features. Still, he couldn't give up. There were just too many unanswered questions. "So...what happened between you and Josh's father?"

"Josh's father," she repeated, then cleared her throat and looked away. "He and I... We were just kids." Nervously she rubbed her arms and the sound of a truck's engine cut through the night.

Headlights appeared over the rise and Katie let out a sigh of relief—whether it was because help was on the way or because she'd managed to avoid a painful topic, he couldn't guess. "Thank God," she said, then forced a smile. "The cavalry did make it, after all."

With a squeal of brakes, the big tow truck slowed, then idled in the road while Katie looked up to the driver in the raised cab and explained how her car had died. He was a kid—barely out of high school, it looked like—but he wheeled his big rig around like a pro. Within a few minutes he'd winched the disabled car onto the bed of his truck. Once the convertible was secure, he filled out the paperwork to ensure that Katie's wheels would end up at Len's Service Station.

"I hope this doesn't cost me an arm and a leg," she thought aloud as the tow truck eased onto the road and was off in a cloud of dust and exhaust.

"Shouldn't."

"I've got my fingers crossed." The worry etching tiny lines across her smooth forehead gave him pause. He noticed the pulse beating at the base of her throat and the way the wind snatched at her hair.

For a second the urge to take her into his arms was so strong he nearly gave in. Standing alone at the side of the road with the sound of the truck's engine fading in the distance and the stars flickering in the sky, he was tempted to pull her against his chest and rest his chin on her crown. She was small and warm, smelling of lilacs and honey, and he knew she'd feel like heaven against him.

She glanced up at him with those luminous eyes and he had to set his jaw against the overpowering urge to kiss her until they both couldn't breathe.

The thought struck him hard and he shoved it quickly aside. He cleared his throat. "We'd better get a move on."

"Oh, right." She, as if having read his mind, couldn't get to the pickup fast enough. The entire way back to her house she sat pressed against the passenger door, as if she, too, was touched by the growing intimacy between them, and it scared her to death. She looked like she hoped to bolt the minute he pulled into her driveway.

He switched on the radio, played with the buttons and finally settled for a rock station that was usually more heavy-metal than he liked. They didn't talk much and he tried to ignore her, but his mind was racing down a path that was as dark as midnight; a path he didn't like.

Who was Josh's father?

The kid was ten or eleven. Just the right age.

But it would be too much of a coincidence for Josh

to be Dave Sorenson's son. Too much. There were dozens of kids Josh's age who didn't live with their dads. Besides, Ralph wasn't sure if Dave had fathered a boy or girl or any kid at all, for that matter. Ralph Sorenson's grandchild might be just a figment of the old man's imagination, a pipe dream that he couldn't yet give up.

Still, the thought that Josh Kinkaid might be Ralph Sorenson's grandson burned deep in Luke's brain. Like it or not, he'd have to check out the kid's birth records. He slid a glance at Katie as the lights of Bittersweet glowed ever closer. She leaned against the window of the passenger door and chewed nervously on a fingernail.

As if sensing him watching her, she dropped her hand and Luke turned all his attention to winding through the tree-lined streets of the small town. From what he understood, she'd lived here all her life. It shouldn't be too hard to check out the truth. The knot in his gut bothered him; she'd reacted strongly to the news of Dave's death, with the emotion of someone who was more than just a casual acquaintance.

Was it possible?

Could she and Dave have been high-school sweethearts? Lovers? His fingers tightened over the steering wheel in a death grip as he cruised around the final corner to her house. Hell, what a mess.

He wheeled into the driveway and parked inches from the sagging door of her dilapidated garage. From the open window of Josh's bedroom, Blue gave out a sharp, no-nonsense bark.

"Guard dog," Luke observed, switching off the ignition and trying to ignore the tension that seemed to invade the pickup's dark interior.

"He thinks he is, I guess." Katie managed a smile that was feeble at best. Nonetheless, that slight twitching of her lips touched Luke in a place he'd long forgotten. "My guess is that if Joe Burglar ever did show up, Blue would turn tail and run. Deep inside he's a chicken." She leaned her head against the back of the seat. "But he's loyal and good-hearted. Always glad to see me." She nodded slightly, to herself. "I've had him longer than I've had Josh. Mom gave Blue to me on my sixteenth birthday." She shoved her hair from her eyes. "Most of the kids were hoping for a car and all I wanted was a puppy to love and..." Her voice trailed off as if she'd said too much, as if she'd let a little of her soul slip past her outgoing, breezy, take-the-world-by-storm facade.

"Anyway, Mom gave me this gray bundle of energy with the brightest eyes you've ever seen. He wiggled like mad, peed on the floor and washed my face with his tongue and I...I just fell in love with him. He's been with me ever since." She cleared her throat and slapped her hands on her thighs as if to change the subject. "Well, so much for soppy, maudlin puppy stories. I, uh, guess I should thank you." Turning to face him, her eyes shining with a bit of unwanted moisture, her lips full over a forced smile, she started to speak again. "You've been—"

He lost all control. The resistance he'd so painstakingly constructed disintegrated as quickly as a match striking and bursting into flame.

"Wonderful— Oh!" Without thinking he placed his hands on either side of her face and kissed her with an intensity that he hadn't felt in years.

Her lips were warm and pliant, her skin soft beneath the calluses of his fingers. Her breath caught in a swift, sharp intake and Luke felt a rush of desire, warm and seductive, flow through his bloodstream.

She moaned, then pulled back to lean against the passenger door. He dropped his hands and inwardly called himself a dozen kinds of fool. What had he been thinking? Kissing her, for God's sake! He couldn't, wouldn't be distracted by a woman—any woman. Especially not one who might just be the mother of Dave Sorenson's kid.

"I...I... I don't know what to say.... And that— being tongue-tied, that is—doesn't happen to me very often." She bit her lip and stared at him with wide, forest-green eyes.

"Don't say anything." He grabbed the steering wheel. "I was out of line."

She reached for the door handle of the pickup. "Maybe we both were. I—" she hooked her thumb toward the house "—I've got to go. Thanks. Thanks again." She was out of the truck and up the path to the back of the house as quick as lightning.

He watched her hurry up the steps, her shorts white in the moonlight, her hair bouncing as she ran. At the porch she cast one final, fleeting glance in his direction, then, with a quick wave, opened the door and disappeared into the cozy, cluttered little bungalow.

"Idiot," he growled under his breath as he flicked on the ignition. "Damned fool moron." Throwing his rig into reverse, he rolled back to the street, flipped on his lights and headed toward his rented rooms in the old carriage house.

He thought of her mouth rubbing so sensually against his, and his damned crotch tightened again. What was it about her that got to him?

"Damn." He'd been a fool for a woman before, a

long time ago, and he'd sworn then that it would never happen again.

Until now, it hadn't been a problem.

But then, he'd never met a woman like Katie Kinkaid.

Chapter Four

"**N**inny!" Katie glared at her reflection in the steamy bathroom mirror as she brushed her teeth. What had she been thinking, kissing Luke Gates?

The answer was that she had never let rational thought enter the equation. She'd sensed he was about to kiss her in the pickup, had felt the darkened cab seem to shrink, but she hadn't had the guts, the nerve or whatever-you-wanted-to-call-it to open the damned door and slide out of the truck before his lips had touched hers and the world had changed forever.

Worse yet, she'd spent all night thinking about her reaction, remembering the feel of his hands as he'd taken her face between his palms and gazed into her eyes while his lips had pressed so passionately against hers. Oh, Lord, here she was, thinking about it all over again, feeling tingly inside and stupidly wondering if he'd ever kiss her again. She grasped the sides of the sink for support and mentally counted to ten before letting out her breath.

"Get a grip, Kinkaid," she said to the woman staring back at her in the mirror. "You don't know a thing about this guy." She leaned under the faucet and rinsed her mouth.

Steadfastly she told herself that she wasn't going to be swayed by one intimate gesture. She had too much to think about today, the first being her son.

Josh was still sleeping—the result of watching television until the wee hours of the morning. She'd checked on him, seen that his leg was still elevated, and changed the bag of ice that had long since melted. Blue whined to go outside and Katie obliged, filling his water dish and pouring dog food into his bowl on the back porch. Butterflies and bees flitted through the flowers that grew along the edge of the garage and two wrens flitted to a stop on a sagging bit of her gutter. She smiled to herself and told herself it was only sane that she should move.

Buying this little house had been difficult, a real stretch for her. She'd borrowed the down payment from her mother and convinced the previous owner, an old man who had been moving to California to be with his eldest daughter, to accept a contract with her. No sane banker would have loaned her a dime at the time.

But she'd proved herself by paying promptly each month and this little cottage had been her home ever since. She sighed. Now she and Josh were going to move. She supposed it was long overdue and the repairs that she'd put off—painting the interior, replacing windowpanes, cleaning the gutters and shoring up the sagging garage—would have to be done for the next tenant.

Leaning against a post that supported the overhang of the porch, she smiled as her old dog nosed around the backyard and she thought of Luke Gates—elusive cowboy with the killer kiss. Her whole body tingled at the thought and she pushed herself upright, slapping the post and telling herself that it was time to forget about one stupid act of intimacy. Inside the house, she phoned Len's Service Station and was told that her car was in the process of being checked out by the mechanic. Len would call her back as soon as he figured out what the problem was. "Wonderful," she said with more than a trace of sarcasm as she hung up and imagined she heard the sound of a cash register dinging each time one of the mechanics fiddled with the wires and hoses attached to the engine. For the fiftieth time she promised herself that she would sign up for an auto-mechanic's class offered by the local community college.

But not right now. She picked up the receiver again and quickly punched out the number of her office. Winding the cord around her finger, she stared out the window and waited as the phone ran.

"Rogue River Review," Becky, the gum-chewing receptionist answered in her typically bored voice.

"Hi, it's Katie. I'll be a little late because Josh had an accident. Nothing serious, but it's gonna keep me home this morning." After explaining to Becky what had happened, she was connected with the editor and repeated herself, telling him about her car and Josh's injury. "I'll work here until I get the word on the car, then I'll be in," she promised.

She'd had a second phone line installed months ago so that she could, over the summer months, work from the house while Josh was home for vacation and was grateful that the powers-that-be at the newspaper understood.

She hung up, feeling a little better, grabbed a soda from the refrigerator and settled in at her desk. Hidden in the top drawer was the letter. Was it a fake or the real thing? She reread the typed words she'd memorized since receiving it in yesterday's post.

Dear Ms. Kinkaid,

I've read your accounts of my disappearance with some degree of fascination. Though others have written similar stories, your columns have been the most insightful.

Therefore I decided that you were the person to trust.

I would have come forward earlier, but circumstances have prevented me from doing so. I will contact you again soon.

Sincerely,
Isaac Wells

Katie's heart beat a little faster each time she read the short note. When she'd opened the hand-scrawled envelope yesterday, she'd been stunned. Was it a prank or had Isaac Wells really reached out to her? And why? Why not go to the police or just come home? What "circumstances" had prevented him from returning? If he'd been kidnapped, he surely wouldn't have been allowed to write the missive. Was he running from the law? Or an old enemy? She pulled out a thick file and skimmed its contents—copies of police reports, the columns she'd dedicated to the Isaac Wells mystery, notes from interviews with what little there was of his family and friends.

What had happened to the old guy? Had there been foul play involved? Leaning back in her chair she tapped the eraser end of a pencil to her front teeth as she scanned her own articles for the millionth time.

Wells, who owned the ranch so close to Luke Gates's property, had been a loner. Mason Lafferty and his sister, Patti, were his only relatives living in the vicinity.

He had resided in the area for over sixty years, but had kept to himself, wasn't very friendly. Some people in town thought he was a miser, even a cheat. There was talk of him being involved in some kind of crime, but, as far as Katie could learn, it was all just gossip.

He'd never married, never fathered any children and had lived alone for most of his life. He'd gotten by meagerly, and had struggled for years to keep his scrap of a ranch afloat. But he'd had a passion for old cars and had owned a collection of classic and antique cars that he'd restored himself. He'd hunted once in a while, usually deer or elk. He hadn't been a churchgoer, and had been a solitary man who didn't talk much—a man whom no one, including the few members of his family, really knew. Despite local conjecture, he'd never been in serious trouble with the law.

Why would he take off?

Had be been coerced?

Had he been getting senile and just wandered away?

Or had he left on purpose?

No one, including the police, insurance-company investigators or his family, seemed to have much to go on.

Until now. Katie stared at the note with a jaundiced eye.

The letter certainly could be a hoax. The postmark

was from Eureka, California, which was barely a hundred miles south. Anyone could have driven down the coast and sent it. His signature—the only part of the missive aside from the address on the envelope that was handwritten in ink—looked authentic, but it wouldn't be too difficult to forge.

So, now, what to do?

Katie took a long pull from her bottle of soda. A lot of people had been questioned about Isaac's disappearance. Ray Dean, a local thug who had been in and out of prison several times, was the most current "person of interest" in the case. Ray had recently been paroled, but most of the people in Bittersweet believed it was only a matter of time before he was arrested again for some kind of crime. So how could he be involved? She decided it was time for her to find out.

After letting Blue back into the house, she spent the next couple of hours at her desk writing the story about receiving the letter. She polished the text, then reworked an article about the new school-district administrator and another on the making of applesauce using other fruits and berries to change the color and flavor of an old favorite.

"Not exactly Pulitzer material," she muttered under her breath, because though the community was interested in the warm folksy articles that the *Review* was known for, she preferred something meatier, something with a little flash. When she'd completed her work, she E-mailed the columns to the office, then reviewed her notes on Isaac Wells again.

"Who knows?" she said, snapping off her computer as she heard Josh stirring. Rubbing a crick from her neck, she made her way back to her son's room and found him dozing again. She folded her arms under her breasts, leaned against the doorjamb and watched him sleeping so peacefully. *The sleep of the innocent.*

In repose Josh looked a little more like Dave than was usual. Or maybe it was her imagination working overtime. Ever since learning of Dave's death, she saw flashes of him in their boy. Which was ridiculous. Everyone who met Josh thought he was the spitting image of his mother.

Still, Katie saw the resemblance to his father in the shape of his eyes, the slight bump in his nose, even the way he walked.

And now Dave was gone. Her throat grew thick with memories she'd repressed for over ten years. She'd been young and foolish, anxious to grow up. Dave, just a little older than she was, had had the same wide brown eyes and thick eyebrows he'd given his son. He'd been a quiet boy who had moved from Texas with his mother and father. The first friends he'd made in town had been her half brothers, Nathan and Trevor, two hellions if ever there were any.

Katie sighed as she stared at her son. How could she tell him about his father? That there had been a poignancy, a deep sadness in Dave that had touched her heart? Whereas David Sorenson had been drawn to her wild brothers and their outgoing, tomboy of a sister, she'd been attracted to his shy smile and clever, dry wit. *Oh, Dave,* she thought, *why did you have to die?* And how? She'd never even asked. So stunned by the news, she hadn't voiced the question as there hadn't been much opportunity and she hadn't been sure she wanted to know.

Guilt, an emotion she tried to ignore, pricked at her mind. Dave, while he was alive, had the right to know that he'd fathered a son and, dammit, Josh should have met his father. When Dave and his family had left Bittersweet, she'd told him that her period was late, that there was a chance she was pregnant, but that her monthly cycle was irregular. He'd never called and asked what had happened, and by the time she was certain she was carrying his child, her pride was wounded, her heart broken, and she refused to try and track him down like some pathetic, unwanted woman. Looking back now, she realized she had probably made a mistake.

Her throat grew tight and she told herself that no good came from self-recriminations, that she could mentally beat herself up, but what was done was done. She just had to tell Josh the truth, and, of course, inform Ralph and Loretta Sorenson that they were grandparents.

Easier said than done.

A dozen worries skated through her mind. What if they decided they wanted partial custody of Josh, that this boy was all they had left of their only son? Conversely, what if, upon learning that Dave had fathered a child, they didn't want to deal with Josh, and felt that seeing him was too painful a reminder of their late son? What if they didn't believe her, thought she was lying, or worse yet, was trying to scam them because they were a wealthy family that, after Dave's death, had no heir?

Just as she chided herself for borrowing trouble, Josh stirred and blinked. "Mom?" he asked around a yawn. He stretched one arm over his head.

"How ya feelin', bud?"

He wrinkled his nose. "Not great."

"How about breakfast—or lunch? It's nearly noon."

"Whatever."

He started to climb to his feet and winced. "Ouch."

"Hey. Use the crutches."

"I just gotta go to the bathroom," he complained and hopped on one foot down the hallway.

Don't nag him, she reminded herself as he managed to shut the bathroom door behind him. *He's gonna be grumpy for a while. He's in pain, but he's got to do for himself.* Rather than overmother him, she went to the kitchen and finished her cola. She'd just tossed the empty bottle into a sack on the back porch when she heard the bathroom door open, then the sound of Josh hopping to his room. He muttered something under his breath that she probably didn't want to hear.

Blue whined at the back door and while she held it open, she heard the uneven cadence of crutches hitting the floor as Josh hitched his way down the hall. She was wiping the counter when he paused at the archway leading to the dining room. "Is the car okay?" he asked, leaning forward on his crutches in order to scratch the old hound behind his ears.

"We can only hope. The mechanics at Len's seem to be baffled." She held up both her hands, showing him that her fingers were crossed.

Blue grunted in pleasure.

"I think we should get a new one."

"Do you?" Josh had been pushing for a new car for the past couple of years. "And give up the cool convertible?"

Rolling his eyes theatrically, he nodded. "It would be cool if it wasn't a billion years old. I think we need something like a Corvette or a Porsche or...or a Ferrari."

"Oh, sure. Or maybe a Jaguar or—"

"A BMW."

"In your dreams," she said, flashing him a smile.

"Mo-om!"

"Back to the real world, bud. What can I get you for breakfast?"

"We *need* a new car."

"You get no argument from me on that one. I just have to figure out how to pay for it." She tossed her sponge into the sink. "If you want me to make you something to eat, speak now or forever hold your peace."

He bumbled his way across the kitchen and half fell into the chair Luke had occupied the night before. "How about a double-cheese bagel?"

"You're in luck. There's one left." She reached into the cupboard and while opening the plastic bag with one hand, she pointed a knife at his bad ankle. "Keep that raised, okay?"

"Okay," he grumbled and hoisted his foot onto the seat of a second chair. His hair was rumpled and he was still wearing his soccer uniform from practice the day before.

"We'll have to figure out a way for you to take a shower," she said as she sliced the bagel and slipped both halves into the toaster.

"*I'll* figure it out."

"Okay, okay. Whatever." She bit her tongue to keep from saying anything more and scrounged in the refrigerator until she found a tub of cream cheese.

"So why was that guy with you last night?" Josh asked and she looked up sharply to find him staring at her with curious eyes.

"You mean Luke."

"Yeah. Why was he here?"

"He rescued me when the car broke down." The

toaster popped. Quickly, as she slathered the bagel halves with cream cheese, she ran down the details of the night before and only left out the fact that Luke Gates had kissed her. That was one little fact that no one would ever know. It had been a mistake. A big one. She wouldn't be surprised if Luke was as embarrassed about it as she was—if he even remembered.

She placed the bagel halves and a glass of orange juice on the table in front of Josh.

"So why did he hang out? Why didn't you call Uncle Jarrod or Uncle Trevor or—"

"I offered," she interrupted. "But I guess Luke just wanted to see it through and make sure I was okay."

"Humph." Josh bit into his bagel and she let the subject drop.

The telephone rang sharply. Katie snagged the receiver before it had a chance to jangle again.

"Ms. Kinkaid?" a gravelly voice asked.

"Yes."

"This is Len down at the service station. I took a look at your car and I've got some bad news."

"What?" she asked, feeling a headache starting to pound at the base of her skull.

"You really need a new engine, or at least to have this one rebuilt."

"No." She felt a sudden weight on her shoulders. Even though she'd told herself she was prepared to hear the worst about her car, she'd held out a slim hope that the old convertible could somehow be resuscitated.

"'Fraid so. The rings are shot, the distributor cap needs to be replaced, the cylinders are only working at about thirty percent of capacity...." Len rattled off a list of repairs that made her tired. In her mind's eye she envisioned hundreds of dollars flying out of her wallet just the way they did on cartoon shows. "So," he said, and she imagined him scratching the silver stubble that forever decorated his chin, "looks to me like you might want to scrap her out and start over. For the same amount of money you could get a car a few years newer and probably a helluva lot more dependable."

"I—I'll think about it," she said and hung up slowly.

Josh's eyebrows lifted with an unspoken question.

"That was Len at the service station," she said, deciding not to let this one last piece of bad news bring her down. "Looks like we're going to have a funeral."

"What?"

"The car's officially dead."

Josh's face split into a wide grin. "So we're gonna get a new one?"

"Maybe," she said. "Yeah, probably." How, she wasn't quite sure.

"All-l-l-l ri-i-i-ight!"

"But the most important thing is, we're going to move."

"Move?" he repeated, suddenly serious. "Where to?"

"Tiffany's house."

"No way." Josh looked at her as if she'd just said they were going to be living on Jupiter.

"Yes, way. They're moving to a farm J.D.'s family bought—the old Zalinski place, so Tiffany wants me to be the manager of the apartments in exchange for living there free. We'll be closer to the main part of town and the school. We'll rent this place out and yes, I think we'll be able to afford a new car—just not a BMW."

Josh's smile fell away and his eyes thinned suspiciously. "Wait a minute. Doesn't the guy who was here last night live over there?"

"Yep." She'd thought about Luke residing right next door and she didn't like the rush of anticipation she felt when she considered how close they'd be. "But he won't be renting there for long. He's got a ranch outside of town."

"Good," Josh said as he kicked open the screen door with his good foot so that Blue could saunter outside and lie in his favorite spot in the shade of a rhododendron bush near the back steps. "'Cause I don't like him. I don't like him at all."

Katie bristled a little. "Why not?"

"I don't know. It feels weird when he's around."

That wasn't surprising, she supposed. Josh probably sensed that she was interested in Luke. At that thought she froze inside. She was *not* interested in him. Not really. It just had been so long since a man had shown her any attention, since she'd let a man flirt with her. Remembering Luke's kiss, she touched the tips of her fingers to her lips, then realized that her son was staring at her.

Quickly, fearing he might read her mind, she reached for the phone again. Cradling the receiver between her shoulder and ear, she dialed the number of John Cawthorne's ranch. "I'm going to see if I can borrow Grandma's car 'cause I've got some errands to run this afternoon. Will you be okay here alone for a couple of hours?"

Josh lifted a shoulder. "I'm not a baby anymore."

"I know, I know, but you're only ten—"

"Almost eleven." He stuffed the end of one of the bagel halves into his mouth and Katie heard the sound of someone picking up the phone on the other end of the line.

Her mother answered with a quick, "Hullo."

"Hi, Mom," she said, feeling warm inside at the sound of Brynnie's voice. "It's Katie. I've got kind of a crisis." Then, hearing her own words, she said, "Don't have a stroke, it's not serious—not really, but the car is in the shop again."

"I thought Jarrod fixed it yesterday."

"He tried, but as a car mechanic he makes a great private investigator."

"Oh."

"Anyway, it looks like I'm going to have to go car shopping soon because Len thinks it would cost more to fix the convertible than it's worth. Josh is laid up— a sprained ankle—and I need to run out and do a couple of things, so I was wondering if I could borrow your car."

"Of course you can!" Brynnie didn't hesitate for a moment. She might have had lousy taste in men and had more husbands than a cat had fleas, but she was a good mother and had always put her children first in her heart. Katie had never doubted how much she was loved. "I'll bring it down and sit with Josh for a while."

"But aren't you going crazy, what with Bliss's wedding plans and all?"

"Bliss has it all handled, believe me." Brynnie chuckled and coughed a bit. "Never been married and she's carrying this off like a pro. As many times as I walked down the aisle, I was rattled each time, let me tell you. Now, is Josh all right?"

Katie slid her son a glance. "I think so. His pride might be more bruised than his ankle." Josh, who was reaching for his crutches, didn't seem to hear her comment.

"Tell him Grandma's coming over and I'll take him on in Hearts or Pitch or whatever card game he wants."

"I will," Katie promised.

"Good. Now— What?" she asked, obviously turning away from the phone as her voice faded for a few seconds. "Oh, Katie, wait a minute, your father wants to talk to you."

Katie was still uncomfortable hearing John Cawthorne referred to so casually as her father. As much as she loved her mother, she couldn't forget that Brynnie had kept the truth from her until this past year; that Brynnie let her live a lie, even given her another man's surname.

"Katie?" John Cawthorne's voice blasted over the phone. "What's this I hear about your car givin' up the ghost?"

She went through the whole story again while Josh finished his breakfast, then hobbled into the living room. As she was ending her tale, John interrupted, "We've got lots of rigs out here. If you can drive a clutch, you can have the Jeep. It's just sitting in the garage collecting dust."

She didn't want John Cawthorne's or anyone else's charity. "I just need to borrow something for a couple of days."

"Fine, fine, but there's no sense putting yourself out much. Brynnie'll drive the Jeep into town, visit with Josh and I'll come pick her up later. Now, what's this about Josh hurtin' himself playin' soccer? You know, I told you that game was more dangerous than football. No pads. No protection."

She talked with him for a few minutes, heard for the

dozenth time about the pros of football, which was played at the same time of the year as soccer, and how a fine, "strappin'" boy like Josh should get into a decent sport. She hung up, wondering if borrowing the car was worth hearing all the advice. As much as she disliked Hal Kinkaid—a surly, quiet man who seemed to forever carry a chip on his shoulder—at least he didn't butt into her life. In fact, he'd never shown much interest in her at all.

Growing up, Katie had felt neglected and had knocked herself out trying to get Hal's attention. She'd been flamboyant in high school, part of the "wild crowd" who drank and smoked, though she'd drawn the line at drugs. She'd flirted outrageously, gained an ill-gotten reputation and, of course, lost her virginity to Dave. At the thought of her one and only lover, she felt a pang of grief. In retrospect, getting pregnant was the best thing that had happened to her. She'd settled down, suffered the indignities and slurs about being an unwed mother when it wasn't quite as fashionable as it was today, but given birth to the greatest kid in the world. She glanced into the living room where Josh was flopped on the couch with his ankle propped on the overstuffed arm. Nope, she wouldn't have changed anything about her life. It was just too darned good. Even if she did have to put up with John Cawthorne's opinions on every subject in the world.

When her mother came over to drop off the car, Katie hoped to speak to her in private, tell her about Dave. All in all, Brynnie was the only person in whom Katie could confide.

And what about Luke? Are you going to tell your mother that for the first time since Dave Sorenson, you

*enjoyed kissing a man, even fleetingly wondered what
it would be like to make love to him?*

She swallowed hard at the thought. Making love to
any man was out of the question right now. She had
too much to do to get involved with anyone. Even if
she had the time, Luke Gates was the last man in the
world she could dare trust.

And yet…she couldn't help fantasizing about him a
little. After all, what would it hurt? It wasn't as if she
would ever get the chance to make love to him.

"Thank God," she whispered and realized that a
sheen of perspiration had broken out all over her body.

"Oh, honey, I hope you're not getting yourself into
the kind of trouble you can't get out of." Worry
pinched the corners of Brynnie Cawthorne's mouth as
they walked through the overgrown vegetable garden
at the side of Katie's house.

"I'll be fine."

"But a letter from Isaac Wells?" Brynnie bent over
and picked a plump cherry tomato from a scraggly
vine.

"Or someone who wants me to think he's Isaac."
Katie lifted her hair off her neck as the sun warmed
her crown. "I just wanted you to know what was going
on before the story was printed in the paper. I took a
copy of the note for me and one for Jarrod, then I'll
drop off the original at the police station."

"I don't like the sound of this."

"I know, Mom, but this could be my big chance."

"Just be careful, okay? You're a mother." Brynnie
slid the sunglasses that held her hair away from her
face onto her nose.

"I know, I know, and there's something else I wanted to talk to you about." Katie's enthusiasm drained.

Brynnie took a bite from the tiny tomato. "Shoot."

"Luke Gates knows the Sorensons. He said…" Her throat tightened and she looked away. "He said that Dave is dead."

Brynnie froze. "But he's only about thirty."

"I know, I know." Katie shook her head and blinked back tears. "I didn't get a chance to ask what happened, but I will." She sniffed and looked away from her mother. "I can't believe it. I always thought there would be time to talk to Josh, to tell him about his dad, have them meet." Her voice cracked. "Oh, Mom, I really blew this one."

"Are you sure? This could be a mistake." Brynnie threw an arm around her daughter. "Maybe Luke got his facts wrong."

Katie sighed and fought tears. "I doubt it, Mom. Luke Gates doesn't strike me as the kind of man to spread idle gossip. I think… Oh, God, I think Dave's gone." She took in a long, deep breath. "And someway I've got to tell my son."

"Hold on a second, will ya? Don't rush into anything. This could all be a mistake."

"I doubt it," Katie said. "But I thought I'd ask Jarrod to look into it for me, find out what happened and then…" She shuddered inwardly. "And then I'll talk to Josh."

"This won't be cheap," Bliss Cawthorne said as she rolled out the blueprints she'd drawn for Luke on a long low table in her small office. "But I think it incorporates everything you wanted in the most cost-efficient manner.''

Luke stared down at the drawings and nodded, but he had trouble concentrating. Ever since being with Katie the night before, he'd thought of little else than the fact that he'd impulsively kissed a woman for the first time in years. He prided himself in always being in control, in taking charge of the situation, in avoiding the pitfalls of getting involved with any woman.

Worse yet, Katie just might be the mother of Dave Sorenson's kid. If, indeed there was a child at all.

''So...I enclosed the area between the two existing buildings for the dining hall and added an exterior as well as an interior stairway.'' From the old blueprints and a quick look at the ranch house, Bliss had drawn a new set of plans according to his specifications and the latest building codes. And the blueprints looked good.

Bliss Cawthorne, Katie's other half sister, was an interesting woman. Sophisticated and bright, with blond hair and blue eyes, she spoke and held herself well. Yet there was an earthiness to her, a down-home charm that was appealing.

Manicured nails slid across the pages as she explained how she'd created a large kitchen within a small amount of space, enclosed an area between the two buildings that would become an oversize dining room and dance hall when the tables where pushed aside, then incorporated three more bedrooms and accompanying baths on a second level. It would cost him every dime he owned. A big gamble. But then he'd been a gambler all his life.

"Looks good," he admitted. Finally, a place of his own.

"I think it'll work."

"I appreciate you doing this so fast." He'd only made the request ten days ago and even though Bliss was planning her wedding, she'd found the time, energy and imagination to draw up exactly what he had in mind.

"Had to get it done before the big day." She smiled, showing off perfect white teeth that he suspected had once been braced. "It's this weekend."

"So I've heard," he replied. "The talk of the town."

"Bittersweet doesn't have much to gossip about." She rolled the plans into tubes and snapped them closed with rubber bands. "Well, except for my family. I guess we keep the rumor mill in business." She blushed a little as she slapped the plans into his open palm. "If you'd like to come, it's this Sunday at the church in the square and we're having a reception afterward at the Reed Hotel just out of town." She grinned up at him and seemed to sense his unease. "I know that this is sudden, but you are my client and Mason and I would love it if you'd attend."

No way, José. "Thanks, but I don't think I'll make it." He knew the invitation was just because she felt obligated to hand it out. Besides, he wasn't interested.

"If you change your mind, the wedding's at seven and the reception will probably last all night."

A bell over the door to the office tinkled and Luke looked up to see Katie, dressed in a white-and-blue sundress, dash inside. "Bliss, I wondered— Oh." For a moment the red-haired locomotive stopped dead in her tracks. "Hi," she managed, recovering herself as she spied Luke and a rosy color invaded her cheeks as it had her half sister's a heartbeat earlier. Her eyes held his and in a second he remembered the kiss—the damned touching of lips that had kept him awake all last night. He'd thought of her, fantasized about her, then dreamed of making love to her. He'd woken up on fire and had taken the longest cold shower of his life.

"Get the car fixed?" he asked and she shook her head, fiery red curls brushing her nape in a movement he found ludicrously sensual.

"Nope. You were right, it's dead." She hooked her thumb to the window overlooking the parking lot. "I'm borrowing one of John's rigs."

"So you two know each other?" Bliss asked thoughtfully.

"Luke helped me out yesterday," Katie explained, giving her half sister the blow-by-blow of her evening.

Bliss's forehead had wrinkled as Katie finished. "But Josh is okay—the ankle is all right?"

"He'll be fine. For the moment he's enjoying being king of the roost."

"Good, good." Folding her arms across her chest, Bliss asked, "Okay, so now that I know Josh will survive and the car won't, why don't you tell me what you think you were doing poking around Isaac Wells's place? I thought it was off-limits to everybody but the police."

Katie lifted a shoulder. "I know, but I was hoping to find something—some sort of clue, I guess, to what happened to him."

"I thought that was the sheriff's department's job."

"Yeah, but I was...well, hoping to look at it with

different eyes—a woman's eyes, a reporter's eyes—that I might see something everyone else had missed.'' She was excited now, talking rapidly, and it gave Luke some insight into how much she loved her job. Katie Kinkaid, ace reporter.

"Isaac's been gone for months," Bliss reminded.

"I know, I know, but—" Katie hesitated, then looked as if she'd decided that confiding in her sister and Luke would be all right. Her cheeks flushed and a smile pulled at the corners of her full mouth. "I want the story. Period. I'm tired of writing about bridge-club meetings and covering the school-board agenda."

"You want something with some mystery to it. Some adventure." Bliss nodded, as if she'd heard it all before.

"At least." Katie looked away and Luke noticed the column of her throat, the way it disappeared into the tangle of bones between her shoulders. She was sexy as hell and didn't seem to know it.

He wondered about the men in her life, then quickly shoved that wayward thought aside. What did it matter whom she dated, whom she kissed, who had experienced the rush of making love to her? His jaw tightened and he fought a ridiculous envy of those unnamed men. All that he cared about was whether or not Dave Sorenson had fathered her child over a decade ago.

"Well, I'd better be shovin' off," he said. "You'll bill me, right?"

"You can count on it."

"Bliss did some work for you?" Katie asked, as if eager to know what he was doing in her half sister's office. Luke noticed her eyelids crinkle at the corners as if she was trying to put two-and-two together.

No way out of it now. "Bliss drew up some plans for me for the ranch house. I'm going to expand it."

"Oh."

"So you already know that he owns the Sorenson place," Bliss added and Katie again felt that dull ache in her heart, the one that reminded her Dave was dead.

"I heard."

"And I heard that you might be moving into Tiffany's place," Bliss said.

Luke froze. Katie was going to live next door to him?

"I'm thinking about it."

"That's what Tiffany said when I bumped into her this morning."

"I've already talked to Josh and he's game, so I guess I'll rent my place and move in whenever Tiffany and J.D. settle into the farm that they're turning into a winery. I was on my way next door to the insurance office to give Tiffany the news but I wanted to stop by here and see how the wedding plans are going."

"Hectic," Bliss replied. "This is my last day of work—" she pointed a long finger at Luke's blueprints and skewered him with her blue gaze "—so if you want any changes, they'll have to wait for a couple of weeks until I get back."

"They're fine," he assured her and reached for the handle of the door. "Thanks."

"You're welcome." Before he could yank the door open, Bliss added, "I was just trying to talk Luke into attending the wedding and reception."

"Oh, you should come." Katie turned and gave him her thousand-watt smile. "It's going to be the event of the summer."

"I'm not usually one for 'events.'"

"Well, think about it. Just drop by the reception, if you'd like," Bliss invited and he inclined his head.

"I just might." He left feeling that he'd somehow been manipulated by the two sisters, but he didn't much care. He wouldn't attend the wedding, but, hell, he might as well check out the reception.

But it had nothing to do with the fact that Katie Kinkaid would be there, he told himself. Absolutely nothing.

Chapter Five

"You think this is authentic?" Jarrod asked as he eyed a copy of the note Katie had received from Isaac Wells.

Dressed only in frayed cutoff jeans, he toweled his hair and stood dripping on the rocky shore of the Rogue River. His house, a small single-story cabin of shake and shingles, overlooked this wild stretch of water and had been his home for nearly ten years. Jarrod, solitary by nature, lived alone here with his dog and seemed to like it just that way. No women to bother him. No children to care for.

"I wish I knew," Katie admitted. "It would make things a whole lot easier."

"What did the police say?"

"Just that they'd look into it."

A half-grown black Lab bounded up and Jarrod bent down to pick up a stick. "Here ya go, Watson," he said, hurling the stick into the water. The dog jetted into the swift current and caught up with the bobbing piece of wood.

"Do you think it's a hoax?"

"Could be." Jarrod scowled and squinted as the sun lowered over a ridge of hills to the west. Overhead a hawk slowly circled in the hazy blue sky. "But why?" He shoved his hair out of his eyes and chewed on his lower lip. "I don't like it. Something's not right."

"What do you mean?"

"Why would Isaac Wells—or even an imposter, for that matter—want attention from you?"

"Publicity?"

"A man who spent most of his life as a recluse?" Jarrod's eyes followed the dog as he galloped out of the river and, with the prized stick in his mouth, shook the water from his coat. "Tell me you're not going to print it."

"Too late."

"Not smart, sis." His eyebrows slammed into a single, intense line. "You might be playing right into his hands."

"Whose? Into whose hands? Ray Dean's?"

"I wish I knew," Jarrod said.

"Well, maybe we'll finally find out."

"Be careful, Katie. One guy's already missing and don't even think about messing with the likes of Ray Dean if he's involved—and even if he isn't. The guy is a criminal, remember that." Jarrod's eyes held hers for a second. "I wouldn't want anything to happen to you."

"It won't. I'm always careful," she said flippantly. "I just stopped by because I thought you'd want to know."

Jarrod flung the wet piece of wood back into the river.

"I do." His scowl was so dark she nearly laughed.

"Better crack this case quick," she teased, "or I might just beat you to it." She checked her watch and sighed. "Look, I've got to get a move on. I've got another errand to run before I go home. Mom's hanging out with Josh and I said I'd be back by five." With a wave she was off and she refused to let Jarrod's warnings give her pause. He was just in a bad mood because this was one case he hadn't been able to solve. The deputy she'd spoken with at the sheriff's department hadn't been any happier with her. He'd taken the note and asked her if she'd touched it, which, of course, she had, though she'd been cautious as she'd figured someone would check it for fingerprints.

"Curiouser and curiouser," she whispered to herself as she drove away from Jarrod's hermit's abode in John Cawthorne's Jeep. At a fork in the road, she turned toward the hills and angled away from town. As she passed Isaac Wells's ranch she thought fleetingly of the mystery surrounding him, but didn't turn off until she reached the Sorenson place. Her heart thudded with painful memories as she wheeled through an open gate where wildflowers and brambles grew in profusion. The smell of dust, dry grass and Queen Anne's lace hung in the late-summer air as the Jeep bounced over the ruts and potholes of a lane that was once familiar to her.

How had she let the years roll by without once trying to contact Dave, to tell him about Josh? Why had she let pride—always her enemy—come between her and the truth? She swallowed back a lump in her throat as she angled the Jeep around a bend in the lane and the

Sorenson cabin came into view. A rambling single-story with a loft, it sprawled between thickets of pine and oak.

Wearing only worn jeans that looked as if they might fall off his hips at any second and a pair of weathered rawhide gloves, Luke was straining against a wayward post in the fence near the barn, trying to push it into an upright position. His booted feet were planted solidly in the dry earth, one muscular shoulder braced against the graying post. Jaw set, lips pulled back with effort, he glanced in her direction, then gave one final shove. The post slowly inched upward and Luke, muscles straining, sweat rolling down his face and back, moved one leg and kicked a pile of stones into the widening hole at the post's base.

Katie felt a jab of disappointment that he wasn't glad to see her, then swept that wayward emotion aside. Feigning disinterest in his sun-bronzed chest with its mat of gold hair, she pretended not to notice how those curly, sun-kissed sworls arrowed down to his navel to disappear in a gilded ribbon past the worn waistband of his jeans.

Her heart fluttered and her stomach did a slow, sensuous roll as he straightened, crossed his arms over his chest and she noticed the striated ridges of his flexed shoulder muscles. Perspiration glistened on his chest, face and arms; dust clung to his skin.

She climbed out of the Jeep and managed a smile that felt as frail and phony as it probably appeared. Just being on Sorenson ground gave her pause. "Hi."

"The convertible's still not workin'?" He kicked the remainder of the stones into the hole, then tested the post by trying to move it with his hands. It held and he grunted in satisfaction.

"No... And Len seems to think it's a goner." Lifting a shoulder, she tried to sound cheerier than she felt. "I guess I'm in the market for new wheels."

"Humph." He yanked off his gloves and stuffed them into a back pocket. "Somethin' I can do for you?"

Her heart pounded and her throat went dry. She remembered his hands on either side of her face as he'd kissed her, the desire that had burned through her body. Clearing her throat, she looked away. "Thank you again for helping with the car...it's been acting up a lot. I don't know what I would have done if you hadn't come along."

"It was nothing. Really. Don't think anything of it."

She managed a smile and glanced around the outbuildings. "So this ranch was the Sorensons'."

"That's right."

"And you said you knew Dave."

Luke nodded slowly, his eyes narrowing. "Since I was about twenty when I went to work for his old man. I was hell on wheels, in trouble all the time, and Ralph took a chance on me. Gave me a job. That's how I met Dave."

"You became friends?"

"For the most part, when he was around," Luke said as he walked toward the ranch house. Katie fell into step with him. "He joined the army a little while after high school, became career military."

"What happened to him?" Katie asked as they reached the shade of the wide front porch.

Luke frowned. "I'm not sure anyone knows all the details, but he was killed this past year in a freak accident. Helicopter crash during routine maneuvers."

Katie's blood turned to ice. She closed her eyes and held on to the rail by the steps to steady herself.

"Ralph and Loretta took it pretty hard," Luke said.

"I don't blame them." She ran a trembling hand over her forehead. "Lord, what a blow."

"I'm sorry."

She swallowed hard and sagged against the rail. Dozens of memories, yellowed with age, their edges softened as the years had passed, swam through her mind. "So am I," she said roughly, then cleared her throat.

"You knew him well?"

Better than anyone, she thought, then realized that wasn't the truth, either. Dave had kept to himself, for the most part. As naive as she'd been all those years ago, she'd sensed that he was holding back, that even during their lovemaking there had been a part of him he'd kept hidden and remote; a part she would never understand. "I'm not sure anyone really knew Dave," she admitted. "As I said, he didn't live here all that long."

"A year or two, the way Ralph talks about it."

"Yeah, about eighteen months, I think."

"He involved with any girls back then?" Luke asked, and she stiffened.

"I, uh, I don't think he dated much. Why?" She couldn't help but ask. There were questions in his eyes she didn't understand, didn't want to trust.

"Ralph seemed to think he might've had a girl-friend."

"He could have," she hedged. Though tempted, she wasn't about to tell this sexy stranger that she'd been involved with Dave Sorenson. Not until she'd spoken with her son. Josh deserved the truth. All of it. "So...tell me about your plans."

She needed to change the subject. She'd dwelled enough on the subject of Dave Sorenson. She'd mourn her first and only lover in private and then confide in her son. Josh might hate her for keeping the truth from him, might never forgive her for not allowing him the privilege of knowing his father, but she couldn't keep Dave's death from him.

Luke hesitated for a second, as if he had more questions, but he eyed her, tugged on his lip and lifted a shoulder. "Let me show you around."

He opened the door and led her into the main house, a building she'd been inside only twice before, long ago, and both times in the middle of the night, with Dave holding her hand and leading her through the darkened rooms.

It hadn't changed much. From the looks of the curtains, she imagined that they were at least twenty years old; the furniture, too, felt as if it had been in the house for two decades. A couch with wooden arms and feet, tables nicked and scarred, a leather recliner that was worn in the arms and where a man's head had rested.

"The entire place will be remodeled," he said as they walked through a small eating area and into the kitchen. He showed her how he planned to push out walls and connect the main house with what had once been the detached garage and bunkhouse. That area would be more rustic, with bunk beds and shared baths, while in the existing house the attic would be expanded into bedrooms with private baths and a back stairs that led to the main hall that could be used for dining or dancing or general recreation.

"If things work out, I'll expand the stables in the

next year or two," he said, leading her down a short hallway and past the door to Dave's room. She felt a sliver of pain pierce her heart again but ignored it as he opened the door to the master bedroom, an expansive room big enough for a king-size bed and an armchair or two. A stone fireplace, dusty and missing a few rocks, filled one corner and a mouse scurried quickly into a hole in the mortar. Long horns were still displayed above a thick mantel, and from one of the exposed beams of the ceiling a wagon-wheel chandelier hung from a wrought-iron chain.

"In time this'll be my living quarters," he said with a crooked smile. "I was going to make it the only guest suite in the place, but decided I didn't want to bunk with the hands." He walked to a window and cranked it open. A soft summer breeze slipped into the room, carrying with it the scent of roses and honeysuckle.

"It'll be nice." She was already envisioning the room as it would be. With a few dollars and a lot of elbow grease, the hardwood floors would gleam, clear-paned windows would give a view of the garden and beyond, to the fenced fields where the hills rose sharply and trees dotted the fence line. In her mind's eye she saw volumes filling the now empty bookcase near the fireplace and warm coals glowing in the grate on a cold winter's night.

"Why did you decide to settle in Oregon?" she asked as Luke opened a door that led from the bedroom to the backyard.

"Ralph and I had a deal. I worked for him for ten years and he kept half of my salary—invested it in some of his real estate. I was supposed to end up with a small spread of his outside Dallas, but he really wanted to get rid of this place, which is quite a bit larger.'' Luke eyed the craggy hillsides. ''I needed an excuse to get out of Texas. This was it.'' He turned his attention back to her and she felt the weight of his gaze, hot and steady, against her skin.

''Why did you want to leave Texas?''

His lips tightened just a fraction, as if he didn't like the intrusion into his personal life. ''It was time. I lived there most of my life.''

She sensed there was more to his story, but that no amount of prying would get it out of him. Luke Gates was a private man with a past he preferred to keep to himself. A secretive man. The kind to avoid.

They walked to the front of the house, past the overgrown rose garden and a sagging clothesline. Luke frowned as he eyed the grounds. ''It's gonna take a lot of work.''

''But it will be worth it, don't you think?'' Katie asked, some of her enthusiasm returning.

''I hope so.''

''Oh, sure. The area is primed for this kind of thing. Are you going to let your guests brand and rope and whatever else it is a cowboy does?''

''That's just the routine stuff. I'm planning to have trail rides that last from eight hours to four days. Some will be the real thing—roughing it up in the mountains complete with pack horses and a mess wagon. But I'll have the more deluxe groups as well, where caterers will be set up along the trail. Food, drink, and entertainment provided. The only thing the guests will have to do is ride. Their tents, cots and sleeping bags will be set up for them while they're out riding. When they return, they can relax around a gourmet meal and I'll even include portable showers to wash the dust off.''

She was impressed. This had obviously been his dream for a large part of his life.

"For the people who want to stay down here on the ranch, we'll not only do the regular work, but we'll have horse races during the day and hayrides at night. They can swim in the river, or raft or canoe if they want to and in the winter—well, not this year, but hopefully next winter—I'll organize ski trips to Mount Ashland or hunting expeditions up in the hills."

"So you'll be open year-round."

"Mmm." He nodded and eyed her speculatively. "This isn't an 'official' visit is it?"

"'Official'?"

"You're not up here scoutin' up a story for your paper?"

"Not today." She offered him a smile. "Believe me, when I interview you for the *Review* you'll know it."

"Good."

She glanced away. "I just wanted to thank you again." *And to find out what happened to Dave Sorenson.* And now she knew—the sad truth. Her heart began to ache again and she knew she should leave this ranch. There were too many ghosts from her past still wandering through the old house. And of course, there was the other problem that came in the form of a rangy Texan who played havoc with her mind—whether she wanted him to or not. "I'd better be off. Josh has probably driven his grandma crazy by now."

"How is he—your boy?"

"Better, I think," she said with a grin. "He's getting a little cranky and my mom always said that a bad mood is a sure sign that the patient is getting better."

"Your mother sounds like a wise woman."

She thought of Brynnie and all her husbands. "Some

people might disagree on that one. She seems to get married at the drop of a hat.''

''But you don't.''

''Me?'' she said, startled. ''Well, no. I, uh, tend to think marriage is more of a commitment than Mom does.''

''Is that why you didn't marry Josh's dad?''

She felt a needle of warning, the way she always did when the subject of Josh's paternity came up. ''I told you we were just kids.''

''Even so, most men want to do what's right.''

''Most boys don't,'' she replied automatically, then felt a twinge of guilt. ''It was complicated.''

''Does he see Josh often?'' Luke asked, and Katie's heart hitched painfully.

''No.'' She considered telling Luke the truth; after all, he'd known Dave, but what good would come of it? First she had to talk to Josh, then the Sorensons. And then, her family.

Luke, as if sensing the subject was too tender to discuss, asked, ''Can't you stick around a few more minutes? Since you're already here, I thought you might want to see the rest of the place.''

''I would. Very much,'' she admitted boldly as the offer, softly seductive, hung in the air between them. It was true. Katie was tempted; she'd enjoy nothing better than to get to know Luke Gates with his slow, sexy drawl, bedroom eyes and past that had yet to be unraveled. She thought of their one shared moment of passion, that unguarded instant in time when she'd felt his lips on hers, tasted the salt on his skin, experienced his flesh pressing hot against her own. ''But I'd better take a rain check.'' Her gaze held his and she saw in his blue eyes a flicker of something darkly dangerous and ultimately erotic.

"I'll hold ya to it," he said, and her insides turned to jelly. He was too close, too unclothed, and too damned male. But she couldn't just let sleeping dogs lie.

"I really do have to go pick up Josh right now, but maybe I'll see ya around. At Tiffany's. Or Bliss's wedding reception."

"I don't think so." But he hesitated.

"Well, I'll look for you anyway," she said, surprised that she was intentionally flirting with him. Hadn't she told herself a thousand times over to avoid him, that he was all wrong for her, that there was something about him no sane woman would trust?

"I don't think I'll show."

"Your loss." Somehow she managed to turn on her heel and walk to the Jeep without feeling like she was fleeing. But her fingers were shaking and her palms sweating as she jabbed her key into the ignition. "You're an idiot," she told herself not for the first time, as the engine fired and she twisted the steering wheel. With what she hoped looked like a carefree wave out the window, she was off in a cloud of dust and exhaust. "Stay away from him, Katie! For once in your life, be smart!" She glanced in the rearview mirror and along with a vision of her worried eyes she saw him standing watching her, his feet apart, his long, jeans-clad legs stiff as they met at his slim hips. His arms were folded over his bare chest and his jeans hung low enough to show off the bend at his waist.

Katie's throat went dry and she knew right then and there that she was in trouble. Deep, deep trouble.

Chapter Six

Every muscle in Luke's body ached. He'd spent ten hours setting fence posts and cleaning out the stables. He smelled bad and probably looked worse, though the woman behind the convenience-store counter hadn't appeared to notice as she'd counted out his change when he'd stopped to buy a six-pack of beer, a bag of chips and a copy of the local paper.

He pulled into the driveway of the carriage house and parked near the garage. As he grabbed his copy of the *Review* and his sack from the store, the Santini family, dressed to the nines, emerged from the back door of the main house.

Tiffany had her purse in one hand and her other was wrapped around Christina's wrist. Wearing a long, shimmering blue dress she was giving orders to her family, commands Luke heard through the open windows of his pickup. "Now, listen, I don't want any more fights,'' Tiffany said, leveling her gaze at her son as her small family gathered on the back porch. ''You're a lot older than Christina and fighting with her is ridiculous.''

The little girl, pleased with the turn of the conversation, smiled broadly, then, behind her mother's back, stuck out her tongue at her brother.

Stephen yanked at his tie, looked about to say something but just rolled his eyes instead.

If Tiffany noticed any part of the exchange she ignored it as J.D. locked the back door. ''Now, come on, I just talked to Aunt Katie. She and Josh need a ride.''

''Still no car?'' J.D. asked. He seemed every bit the lawyer in what looked to be an expensive suit and neat tie.

''Not for a few more days. If I were her, I'd go out of my mind. The good news is that Josh is off crutches and that the phone calls he was getting have stopped.''

''What phone calls?''

''Oh, some kind of prank, I think. He'd answer and no one was there.''

''Probably kids.'' J.D. shook his head but every overworked muscle in Luke's body tightened. He hadn't seen Katie in a couple of days, not since she'd been out to the ranch.

Tiffany had shepherded the family down the back steps and onto the dry grass of the lawn when she spied Luke climbing out of his truck. ''Oh, hi!'' The worried knot between her eyebrows disappeared as both kids dashed for J.D.'s Jeep. ''It's a madhouse as usual around here. If we make it to the wedding on time it'll be a miracle,'' she said with a laugh. Her eyes skated down his dusty, sweat-stained T-shirt and worn jeans. ''I thought—I mean, didn't Katie say that you were going to Bliss's...'' She blushed and he figured out the rest for himself.

''I think she expects me to show up at the reception.''

''You should!'' Tiffany enthused.

''I told Bliss I'd think about it.''

A horn blared and Luke spied Stephen behind the steering wheel of J.D.'s rig. A broad smile creased his face.

''Stephen, stop!'' Tiffany said, shaking her head at her son. She turned back to Luke. ''We really do have to run,'' Tiffany said as J.D. managed to get his soon-to-be stepson to move to the back seat as he was still a few years too young to drive.

Luke waved and headed up the stairs. He tried not to think about Katie dressed up and looking for him at the reception, nor did he want to dwell too long on the thought of a couple making vows. He'd been down that road himself and had ended up being burned. Big time. Good luck to Mason and Bliss. He wanted no part of it.

The carriage house was stuffy and hot, so he cracked the windows, opened a beer and settled into his recliner with the paper. The headline on page one caught his attention: Wells Mystery Deepens. Katie Kinkaid's name was on the story. ''Great,'' Luke growled, taking a long swallow from his bottle. His eyes skimmed the article and his jaw hardened. ''Damned fool woman.''

There was no doubt about it; she was trying her best to get herself killed.

It's none of your business, Gates. None.

''Hell.'' He attempted to read the rest of the paper, but his mind kept straying back to Katie and her stubborn fixation on becoming some kind of hotshot ace reporter. In Bittersweet, Oregon. Fat chance. No wonder she wanted to jump feetfirst into this Isaac Wells mystery.

He drained his bottle, then slammed it down on a nearby table. Try as he might, Luke couldn't forget the fact that she was getting crank calls and weird letters.

Dog-tired and irritated as all get-out, Luke slapped the copy of the *Rogue River Review* onto the table and shoved himself to his feet. Knowing he was about to make a huge mistake, he kicked off his boots and stormed into the bathroom.

He yanked off his T-shirt and dropped it onto the floor. What the devil was Katie thinking? Why did she insist upon stirring up trouble? Muttering under his breath about hardheaded career women who had more guts than brains, he twisted on the shower faucet and stripped out of his jeans.

In the past two days he'd half expected her to show up at his ranch again, half wanted it. Anytime he'd heard a rig slow at the end of the lane, he'd felt an unlikely rush of adrenaline, experienced a clenching in his gut, only to end up disappointed when she didn't appear.

Whether he wanted to admit it or not, there was something about that little spitfire of a woman that got under a man's skin—well, at least his skin.

"Man, you've got it bad, Gates." Disgusted with that particular thought, he stepped under the shower spray and sucked in his breath. Hot water splashed against his chest and ran down his torso. As he scrubbed the dirt, sweat and smell of horse dung from his body, he told himself that Katie Kinkaid was off-limits. Way off-limits. She was the kind of woman who could turn a man's head around, and he needed no part of that. None. And yet...

Annoyed, he scrubbed until the dirt under his fingernails had washed away and all the lather that swirled down the drain was white. Why did he care what Ms. Kinkaid did? It wasn't as if she was someone special in his life. As a matter of fact, she wasn't in his life at all. Heretofore he'd helped her out of a jam with her car and her kid, and had made the mistake of kissing her. She'd shown up on his doorstep asking about Dave. That was it. So what if she wrote articles about hermits who disappeared? Who cared that the man had decided to contact her? It wasn't any of his business.

Oh, yeah? What if she's the mother of Dave Sorenson's kid? What then? It sure as hell is your business.

And he was bothered by Katie's involvement in this Isaac Wells mess. The situation bordered on the bizarre. What if the old man was involved in something criminal or sinister? The police had been questioning Ray Dean, a local hoodlum who'd been in and out of prison for years. Though no connection had been made, there was speculation in town that the two men had known each other.

A lot of people had thought Isaac Wells was dead. Maybe even murdered.

Yeah, then who wrote Katie the letter?

That was what bothered him. Was the letter the real thing or some kind of grand hoax? Either way, he was worried.

Angrily he dried his hair with a towel, stepped in front of the foggy mirror and swiped at the glassy surface until he could see his reflection well enough to scrape off his five-o'clock shadow and run a comb through his hair. He'd suspected from the moment Katie had invited him that he would attend the wedding reception, but it galled him to think that he had no will where that woman was concerned. One curve of her lips, a tiny sparkle in her eye, a mocking lift of her eyebrow and he found himself doing things he'd sworn to avoid.

"Damn." He dressed in a white shirt and black slacks, then fingered a bolo tie only to discard it and slide into his best pair of boots. By the time he walked outside it was dusk and the filmy clouds gathering over the moon were beginning to thicken. The air was hot and sultry without the slightest hint of a breeze, and yet he sensed a storm was brewing.

As he walked to his truck, he eyed the old Victorian house. It seemed strangely empty. No lights glowed in the windows, no kids ran in the yard, no angry guitar chords wailed from one of the upstairs rooms. Boxes were stacked on the porch—evidence that the Santini clan was moving out.

And Katie Kinkaid would be moving in. That thought made him edgy and restless. Living less than a hundred feet away from her was much too close. Though she probably needed a man to look out for her, he wasn't a candidate. As he climbed into his truck he tried to take solace in the fact that he wouldn't be here long. As soon as the electricity and phones were connected, he'd set up housekeeping at the ranch.

Oh, yeah? And then what? Are you just going to forget her and the fact that she's wading into dangerous waters? Are you going to ignore the fact that you'd like nothing more than to kiss her until her knees went weak, peel off her clothes and make love to her until dawn? And what about the fact that Josh just might be

Ralph Sorenson's grandson? What the hell are you going to do about that?

His fingers tight on the wheel, he drove through town, past the church where Bliss Cawthorne had become Mrs. Mason Lafferty, and on to the old Reed Hotel. A tall three-story building with a Western facade, narrow windows and the original weathered siding, the Reed Hotel had once been a stagecoach stop. Now, after some remodeling and additions, it was the most elegant and historic inn anywhere near Bittersweet.

He handed his keys to a kid who didn't look old enough to drive, but was eager to park the truck, then headed inside. As if it were Christmas instead of early September, thousands of tiny lights winked in the branches of the trees and shrubbery that flanked the front porch. Again, he told himself, he had no business being here—none whatsoever—and yet he climbed the few steps to the open double doors.

Music filtered from within and he didn't have to pause at the front desk; he just followed the tinkle of laughter and buzz of excited conversation to a ballroom that was filled to the brim with the citizens of Bittersweet. A small band was playing a lively tune and couples were already swirling around the floor.

He spotted Katie instantly. In a long blue dress with her red hair piled onto her head, she danced with a guy Luke didn't recognize. Long-legged, with hawkish eyes and a smile that looked as phony as a three-dollar bill, Katie's partner held her close. Too close. As if she were his personal possession. And Katie was eating it up. She talked and laughed, tilting her head back and flirting outrageously with the stranger. Her cheeks were flushed, her green eyes sparkling, her smile positively radiant. Luke's gut twisted with something akin to jealousy and he silently swore.

When offered a glass of champagne by a waiter dressed like an old stagehand, Luke accepted the drink and downed it in one long swallow. The room was crowded, the music a little loud, the room surprisingly stuffy and hot. With two fingers he pulled at his collar and told himself his claustrophobia was way out of line.

Mason and Bliss danced past, she in white silk and lace, he in a black tuxedo. He twirled her off her feet and she laughed gaily, as if she hadn't a care in the world, as if she were completely and truly in love.

The thought sat like lead in Luke's stomach and he snagged another glass of champagne from a tray near a fountain that spouted gallons of the stuff. Hearing Katie's laughter rising above the buzz of conversation, clink of glasses and notes from a dance band, he sauntered outside to a veranda where there was a little respite from the heat.

Several people had gathered on the flagstones, talking and smoking, holding drinks or resting their hips against the stone railing and looking over the creek that splashed behind the hotel.

Two women strolled onto the patio and stood far enough away that he only caught snatches of their conversation.

"Can't imagine what happened to him," one of the women was saying. She was short and round, with hair starting to turn silver and long, well-kept fingernails that rummaged through the contents of her purse.

"So you don't believe the letter is real?" her companion, a wasp-thin woman with harsh features and more makeup than she needed, asked.

"The letter that was printed in the paper? Naw." She found a pack of cigarettes and shook one out. "If you ask me, Lois, Isaac Wells is gone for good."

At that point Mason strode onto the patio and spying Luke, offered a smile.

"Aren't you supposed to be cuttin' the cake, or toasting the bride or somethin'?" Luke asked as they clasped hands.

"Needed a break." Mason tugged at his collar and Luke noticed the sweat sliding down his neck.

"I hear Bliss has designed a new house for you. That you're going to open up a dude ranch at the old Sorenson place."

"That's the plan." Luke sipped his drink. He wasn't much good at small talk, but felt comfortable with Lafferty; there was something about him that seemed sincere. Beneath the expensive tux was a real, solid man, a fellow rancher who felt a kinship with the earth. The kind of man Luke trusted.

"I'd like you to show me around sometime when work gets under way."

"Come on out, anytime," Luke offered, then asked a question he'd been tossing about all day. "I heard you were related to Isaac Wells."

"Yep."

"What do you think happened to him?"

"Wish I knew." Mason rubbed his chin. "I'm afraid it might become one of those unsolved cases around here, just like the Octavia Nesbitt thing a few years back."

"Nesbitt?" Luke asked. The name was familiar.

"Tiffany's grandmother. Years ago she was robbed—her jewelry taken from her house, even her damned cat stolen. The case was never solved and made everyone nervous. Leastwise, that's what Bliss and her father tell me.''

"But no one was hurt?" Luke asked.

"Nope. This is different that way." Mason's eyebrows drew together. "Can't help but wonder whether old Isaac is dead or alive."

"There you are!" Bliss, breathless, caught up with her new husband. "Hiding?" Her blue eyes sparkled with a teasing light.

"From you?" he asked. "Always."

"Such a charmer." She clucked her tongue and to the delight of the two women on the far end of the patio, Mason swooped her into his arms and kissed her as if he'd never stop. One woman fanned her face, the other turned away, hiding a smile. Luke grinned. He felt the passion between the just-married couple, knew what it was like to want a woman so badly he ached.

When Mason finally lifted his head, Bliss appeared breathless. "Well," she finally said, her cheeks flushed to a rosy hue, "I'd love to steal away to the bushes with you right now, Mr. Lafferty, but we have duties to attend to."

"Too bad," Mason drawled.

Bliss touched him lightly on the nose. "If you're lucky, I'll give you a rain check."

"I'm gonna hold you to it, Mrs. Lafferty."

They linked fingers and she pulled him back into the interior of the old hotel.

Luke finished his drink, then stared through the windows and spied Katie dancing. She was grinning and looking as if she were having the time of her life. He wondered what kind of trouble she was getting herself into. First the letter—be it a hoax or the real thing— then the phone calls to her house where no one answered. They could just have been someone dialing the wrong number, but he couldn't shove them out of his head.

Not that he could forget much about Katie Kinkaid. As the two women drifted back into the ballroom, Luke leaned against the rail and glared down at the darkened ravine. Lights from the hotel reflected on the tumbling water of the creek and he thought he saw a lone man, a black figure, slip behind a thick copse of trees.

The hairs on the back of his neck lifted in warning, even though he told himself that he'd imagined the shadow, or, if there really was someone hiding in the undergrowth, it was probably just some kid sneaking booze from the reception or stealing away from his parents' wary eyes. Luke squinted hard into the darkness and strained to hear a sound—a snapping twig or muttered oath or anything to convince himself that he hadn't imagined it.

Watch it, Gates, you're getting paranoid. Still, he studied the night-darkened banks of the creek. The suspicious part of his mind considered vaulting over the rail and following his instincts, tailing whoever it was and finding out if he was up to no good.

"I thought I saw you sneak in." Katie's voice startled him.

Luke glanced quickly over his shoulder. She was standing only inches from him, her tiny, flushed face angled up to look at him. Her green eyes sparkled and he wondered if she wasn't the most intriguing woman in the universe.

"I suspected that you might decide to put in an appearance after all." Her lips curved into a smile of silent amusement, as if she could read his mind and found his thoughts laughable.

"I think you invited me," he replied, turning and placing his body between hers and the stranger in the shadows—if there was one. A thin sheen of perspiration added an alluring glow to her skin, which was already smooth as silk.

"That I did," she said flirtatiously, and Luke remembered seeing her in another man's arms, how at-home she'd seemed, how lighthearted and free. She interrupted his thoughts when she asked, "So...how about a dance?"

He hadn't been asked that particular question since high school. "I'm not much of a dancer."

"That makes two of us. Come on." As if she expected him to come up with some kind of excuse, she grabbed hold of his hand and pulled him into the warm room where couples were gliding around the dance floor. Rather than protest, he went with her into the ballroom. He felt safer inside even though there was probably no danger lurking in the gloomy shadows by the creek. It was just his imagination working overtime.

A song from the big-band era was playing. He'd heard the tune before, didn't know its name, and didn't have time to speculate. Katie fell into his arms as naturally as if she'd been born there. She didn't seem to mind that his dancing was limited. He hadn't lied. He'd had a few dance lessons in physical education when he'd been about twelve and scared to death of the opposite sex; then he'd experimented a little in high school and at rare social events while he'd been married to Celia.

"See?" Katie said, looking up at him with eyes as green as a forest. "This isn't so bad."

"Could be worse," he admitted and wondered why it felt so right to hold her.

"A lot worse."

As if of their own accord, his arms tightened around her. She felt small, warm and pliant as she rested her head against his shoulder. Music and laughter swirled around them. The lights dimmed and Luke's heart pounded. He imagined kissing her again, melding his lips over hers and sliding his tongue between her teeth; imagined slipping his hands beneath her dress and how her skin would feel as he peeled the blue folds of silk from her body.

Tiffany and J.D. glided past. Tiffany's head was thrown back and she was laughing gaily, as if she had the world by its proverbial tail. In a glimmer she spied Katie and winked at her half sister, as if the two women shared a private joke.

"Mind if I cut in?" John Cawthorne's voice surprised him. "I'm making a point of dancing with each of my daughters." Luke stepped aside, ended up with Brynnie in his arms and watched as the father of the bride made a big display of dancing with his third daughter. He'd already had a turn with Bliss, who had seemed radiant in her father's arms—as well as with Tiffany, who had danced stiffly, no smile upon her face. Now Katie fell into step with her newfound father as if she'd been a part of his family for years.

"He loves them, you know. Each one," Brynnie said as she and Luke paused for a glass of champagne. "All the hard feelings that existed between the girls and him, well, let me tell you, it's taken its toll. Trying to put this scrappy family together has been hard on him."

"And on his daughters," Luke added.

"Oh, my, yes. Even Katie." Brynnie sipped slowly. Her face was flushed and her fading red hair, precariously curled onto the top of her head, was starting to fall. "Here, would you mind holding this?" She handed him her glass, extracted a bobby pin from her crown and held it between her lips as she expertly tucked the falling loops of hair into place again. "There we go." She pushed the bobby pin to the spot where it belonged, securing her tresses, then took her glass from him. "What I wouldn't do for a smoke," she admitted, "but I'm trying to quit, what with John's condition and all. I suppose you know that he had himself a heart attack."

"I'd heard," Luke admitted, still watching John and Katie move easily around the dance floor.

"That's what started all this—him and me getting together and his obsession with making us all one big happy family." She glanced up at Luke. "I'm not a gambling woman, but I'd bet my life that our family's a little bit like Humpty-Dumpty—darned near impossible to put together. At least, not as fast as he'd like it to. Emotions take time to heal.... Oh, listen to me. This is a wedding, for goodness' sake, and here I am gettin' maudlin." She blinked rapidly, sniffed, and swept a beringed finger under her eyes. "It's so silly. I guess I just want John to be happy."

"He looks like he is," Luke observed as the music ended. Katie looped her arm through the crook of her father's elbow and they maneuvered through the knots of people clustered around the ballroom floor.

"I hope so," she said fervently as John and Katie approached. John and Brynnie moved off.

"So what did Mom tell you?" Katie asked. "I saw you two with your heads together."

"She was just giving me some background on the family."

"Such as?" she asked as his arms surrounded her again.

"Your mother seems to think there's no hope of bringing your family together." He held her tight and got lost in the scent of her perfume.

"Maybe not, but I think it's time to bury the hatchet and get on with our lives. Bliss is married now, has her own life with Mason and his daughter, Dee Dee— that's her, dancing with her father." She pointed to Mason and a girl of about nine or ten, he guessed, as they danced together. Dee Dee was embarrassed, but Mason swung her off her feet and she couldn't help but laugh. "Anyway, so Bliss is happy and now Tiffany and J.D. are going to tie the knot, so why dwell on the past? Don't get me wrong—John and Mom should never have carried on an affair while he was married. Though, come to think of it, if they hadn't, I wouldn't be here, would I?" She grinned and the reflection of a thousand tiny bulbs in the chandelier overhead shone in her eyes.

"And that would be a shame." Luke brushed a lock of her hair off her cheek and saw her smile slowly fade as she stared at him. The pulse at the base of her throat jumped a little and he was lost in her. He forgot the dozens of people in the room, was alone and intimate with her as the world around them slipped away.

"A...a big shame," she said, trying and failing to lighten the mood. She avoided his eyes for a second and he forced himself to think of something, anything other than holding on to her and never letting go.

"So what about you? Both your half sisters are getting married."

"I have my career," she said automatically and sensed her blood heat. Being this close to Luke, feeling the pressure of his fingers on her back caused her head to swim. Oh, Lord, how had she gotten this close to him?

"And that's the most important thing in your life."

"Second. Josh is first." That was a given, but she didn't want to discuss her son; not with this man who spoke little but asked questions that delved far too deep. Changing the subject was simple. "So, I guess you and I will be neighbors in a couple of weeks."

"More than neighbors," he said, and stupidly her heart took flight as the leader of the dance band announced that the musicians would be taking a break.

"More?"

"You'll be my landlady."

"Oh." She let out her breath and laughed. "Good. It'll give me a little bit of power, won't it?"

His smile was off-center and sexy as all get-out. "A little. But I'll be movin' out myself soon."

"I suspected as much," she said and mentally gave herself a shake when she heard the note of disappointment in her voice. "Come on, it's time you met some people around here." She guided him through the throng where they not only spoke with her half sisters, and Mason and J.D., but she introduced him to her half brothers and three quarters of the town. While he seemed to recognize a sprinkling of the guests at the reception, Katie knew them all.

"It's hard to believe there are this many citizens in the town," he whispered to her as she located Josh, who was ignoring his crutches in favor of hanging out with Stephen and a couple of other boys.

"I should go and talk to my son," she said, but hadn't taken a step in Josh's direction before Brynnie caught up with her.

"Come on, come on," she said, tapping Katie's shoulder. "We've got dinner in the dining room and it'll go to waste if we don't eat it."

"In a minute—"

"Now or forever hold your peace."

"I think we'd better not cross my mother," Katie said with a teasing grin.

"Good idea," Brynnie remarked as she beelined toward her twin sons and hustled them in the direction of the buffet.

They dined on salmon, prime rib and venison, though Katie's appetite was nil. She was too keyed up, being with Luke. Touching him and smelling the faint odors of leather and musk that clung to him caused her heart to flutter, her mind to spin, and, apparently, her stomach to shrink. She played with her food, barely eating a bite, sipped a little more champagne, and after the meal, danced to a couple of songs. She then stood beside Luke as Bliss and Mason cut their five-tiered cake and fed each other enormous pieces that left smudges of frosting on their faces. Mason kissed the icing off Bliss's cheeks and she repaid him by swiping a dab of the white confection onto his nose.

The crowd laughed and Katie glanced up at Luke, who managed a smile.

"Silly, huh?"

"But fun," he conceded, staring so deeply into her eyes that she had to swallow hard and her mouth lost all moisture. "I... I...uh, need to talk to Tiffany," she said to break the spell, the pure madness that seemed to be a part of the night.

Sometime near eleven, Mr. and Mrs. Mason Lafferty ran out the front door of the hotel and, while being showered with birdseed, ducked into a long white limo that idled near the front steps. As the guests waved and shouted, the newlyweds roared away. Katie felt a faint twinge of envy, then told herself she was being a romantic twit. She was glad that Bliss and Mason were together, thrilled that Tiffany had found J.D. to become her husband as well as a stepfather to Stephen and Christina. What was right for her half sisters didn't necessarily mean that she wanted the same thing. She couldn't. She didn't dare let her heart be broken again.

They lingered for a while, dancing, talking with friends and sipping coffee as the crowd thinned. She wandered onto the veranda but Luke grabbed hold of her arm.

"Let's stay inside."

"Are you kidding? It must be a hundred degrees in here." She winked at him and tugging on his hand, dragged him outside. "Don't tell me you're afraid to be alone with me, Gates."

"That's not it—"

"Good."

Ignoring the look of unwarranted consternation that twisted his features, she walked across the flagstones and leaned over the rail. From far below, the sound of the creek tumbling over stones and exposed roots reached her ears.

"Tell me about the letter you got," he said, resting a hip against the stone railing and folding his arms over his chest. He stared down into the canyon, his eyes narrowing as if he were searching for something. Or someone. "The one that's supposed to be from Isaac Wells."

"I take it you read the article in the *Review*."

"Every word."

"That's what I like to hear," she teased, then added,

"Really, there's not much more to say. I received the note, gave the original to the police and wrote the article. I don't know if it's phony or real." She turned her palms upward. "I guess time will tell."

"Could be dangerous," Luke mused aloud, though his gaze was still searching, his eyes narrowed against the darkness that escaped the wash of light from the hotel's security lamps. "A nutcase."

"You sound like Jarrod."

"Just be careful."

She lifted a skeptical eyebrow. "You think I'm in some kind of danger?"

"I don't know that you're in danger, Katie, but, yeah, it could be trouble."

"Maybe." A needle of fear pierced her heart. How many times had she told herself just the same thing?

"It doesn't worry you? You're a mother and—"

"And what I do shouldn't worry *you*," she interrupted as her anger suddenly flared. Who was he to insinuate that she was messing up her life? She couldn't control her tongue. "If I didn't make it clear before, let me assure you I don't need another brother, okay? Three half brothers add up to too many—way too many when it comes to giving advice about my life." Turning quickly and seething deep inside, she headed toward the French doors. The last thing she needed—the very last thing—was a man telling her what to do.

Before she'd taken three steps he grabbed her elbow, spun her around and kissed her so hard she didn't know what hit her. She gasped as hot, demanding lips crashed over hers and strong arms surrounded her waist, dragging her close. She started to protest, to push away, but his hands splayed against the exposed skin of her back and a tingle of excitement sped through her blood.

Don't do this, Katie. Don't kiss him. This was what was dangerous—emotionally dangerous. Not the Isaac Wells case.

But she didn't stop and the sound of wanting that reached her ears came from her own throat. Oh, Lord, what was she thinking?

With all her strength she pushed away. "Is—is that what you do?" she asked, drawing in a shaky breath and hating herself for how weak she was when it came to him. "When a woman gets into an argument with you, do you always grab her and kiss her just to make her shut up?"

"Most women don't get me so riled up," he admitted.

"Don't they? Well, good. That's very good. For you. Because these Neanderthal, 1950s B-movie tactics are...are..." Damn the man! He was actually smiling, amused by her reaction. Her fists balled in frustration.

"Are what? Effective?"

"I was going to say boorish, or antiquated, or at the very least, rude and entirely unacceptable!"

He laughed then. Threw back his head so that his blond hair brushed the collar of his shirt and he laughed.

"This is not funny!" She almost stomped her foot, then decided she'd look even more adolescent than she felt. "Good night, Luke. The evening has been... entertaining, but I think I'd better leave now."

"And back off from a fight?" he challenged.

Though she knew she was being goaded, she couldn't stop herself. Like a trout spying a salmon fly on a hook, she rose swiftly to the bait. "I'm not backing off from anything, Gates. If you don't know anything else about me, you should at least figure out that I'm dogged, not afraid of too much, and never, never duck an argument.'' She was about to say more when Josh, who had somehow rediscovered his crutches, hobbled onto the patio and Katie, wondering if her skin was as inflamed as it felt, told herself to count to ten and cool off.

''Is it okay if I spend the night with Stephen?'' he asked.

''But you're still recovering.''

''I'll be good. Promise.'' Josh flashed her his most engaging smile just as Stephen, eating a piece of wedding cake, sauntered outside. His hair was unruly, his tie was dangling from his neck and he licked a spot of icing from the corner of his mouth.

''Why doesn't Stephen come over to our house?'' Katie asked, trying not to remember that Luke was standing only inches from her, that he kissed her like no other man had ever kissed her, that she didn't know quite how to handle her wayward emotions whenever he was near.

'''Cause we're gonna camp out in the backyard.''

Tiffany and J.D. joined the group. J.D. was carrying an exhausted Christina, whose usually springy curls were as droopy as her eyelids. Her head was nestled against J.D.'s shoulder and she yawned broadly. ''I take it you've already heard?'' Tiffany asked, nodding toward the boys.

''Sounds like they've already cooked up plans.'' Katie eyed her son and his crutches. ''He really should come home and elevate the foot and—''

''Aw, Mom…I'm okay.'' To prove his point, Josh lifted both crutches in the air and walked without so much as a limp. "I'm better. A lot better. Besides, it's almost our house, isn't it?"

"Not quite," Katie said, but shrugged. "It's all right with me if you're sure—" She looked at Tiffany who nodded. "I'll see he takes care of that ankle and in the morning, if he's up to it, he can help Stephen pack his room."

"He doesn't have his pajamas—"

"Don't need 'em," Josh said.

"But I don't want you sleeping in your church clothes. I'll stop by the cottage and pick up anything you need."

"I said I *don't* need anything," Josh insisted.

"He's probably right," Tiffany agreed. "We have double of just about anything he could want. He can have something Stephen's grown out of."

Josh threw Katie a look that begged her to give in.

"If you're sure," she said to Tiffany.

"Positive."

"Okay. I'll call you in the morning." Katie planted a kiss on her son's cheek and he made a hasty retreat on his crutches. Tiffany and J.D. ushered the kids through the ballroom and out a side entrance. As Katie watched them leave, she realized that she'd just lost her ride. "Oh, wait," she called after them. "I need a lift home...."

Luke grabbed her again. "Don't worry about it," he said as she turned and saw the smoky blue of his eyes.

"But—"

"I'll take you home, Katie. It would be my pleasure."

Chapter Seven

In her driveway, Luke braked and cut the engine of his pickup. Katie reached for the door handle. Once before, she'd been in this very truck with the night closing in on them and had felt the sheer intimacy of the moment as he'd kissed her. She didn't want a repeat of that incident. Or at least, she tried to convince herself that she didn't. "Thanks for the ride."

"Maybe I should come in and see that everything's okay."

Her heart nearly stopped. She heard the ticking of the engine as it cooled and the jingle of his keys as he pulled them from the ignition.

"Okay? What wouldn't be okay?" she asked, buying time. Part of her was tempted to invite him in, to take a chance; the other, more sane portion of her mind warned her that she was only asking for trouble. Begging for it. The kind of trouble she didn't need and couldn't deal with. This man was linked to Ralph Sorenson, Josh's grandfather. "For what?" she asked, shoving her shoulder against the door while trying to ignore her elevating pulse and dry mouth. *Come on, Katie, let him in. What would it hurt?*

"I'm not sure. But it's just a feeling I've got that something isn't right."

"Anyone ever tell you you're a worrywart?"

"A few people," he said and climbed out of the cab.

Blue gave a soft bark as Katie inserted her key into the dead bolt and discovered the door unlocked. "That's odd," she said, dropping her keys into her purse. Frowning to herself she walked into the kitchen. "I'm sure I locked it."

"You remember doing it?"

"No…" Flipping on the kitchen lights she tried to think over the rapid beating of her heart. Blue's toenails clicked on the linoleum as he greeted her with a wagging tail and lowered head. "It was real crazy," she said, dropping her purse on the table as she scratched Blue behind his ears. "We were running late. Josh had trouble with the knot of his tie and then had a fit about having to use the crutches and the next thing I knew, Tiffany was knocking on the back door." She shook her head, trying to clear the cobwebs. "I don't remember, but I always lock it. It's habit."

Luke's gaze was thoughtful. Worried. Katie felt suddenly awkward. "Would you like…some coffee or soda or…anything?" Why did the question sound so lame?

"I'm fine." Jaw set, he strode through the kitchen and into the living room to her desk. Without asking, he pushed the Play button on the answering machine.

"Hey, wait! You can't—"

The machine clicked as someone hung up.

Katie's stomach curled and the hairs on the back of her neck rose. "Who was that?"

"That's what I'd like to know." Luke scanned the desk area. "Just about everyone you know was at Bliss's wedding tonight, right?"

"Of course, but—"

"So who would have expected you to be home?"

"No one," she thought aloud, her skin crawling at the thought that someone might actually be watching her. "You think it might have something to do with the letter?"

"I don't know. It could be just a mistake, a wrong number, but it might be a crank—either this Wells character or someone looking for him." His gaze fastened on hers. He was stone-cold sober. "But your door was unlocked. Someone could have been in here."

Her knees threatened to give way at the thought.

She laughed a little nervously. "I can't believe—"

"Sure you can. Now take a look around. Does anything seem out of place?"

Walking slowly through her few cluttered rooms, she eyed her belongings, touched a few pieces of furniture and saw nothing out of the ordinary. Everything was just as she and Josh had left it when they had rushed out of the house and into J.D.'s Jeep. She would have sworn that, out of habit more than anything else, she had locked the door behind her.

"Nothing seems to be missing or out of place," she told Luke.

"You're sure?"

"Yeah. Pretty sure."

"Would your dog have allowed anyone inside?"

"Probably, but I don't really think anyone was here," she said, though she had a severe case of the creeps. Thinking that an intruder, a stranger, had been in her house—in Josh's room, for crying out loud—caused a chill in her blood as cold as all November.

"Maybe you should call the police."

"And tell them what? That I left the door unlocked? That I think someone was in here, but nothing is missing or out of place, that someone has been calling and hanging up? What could they possibly do?"

"Stake out the place?"

"On what? Your hunch? Just because I got a letter from Isaac Wells?"

"Yes."

She almost laughed. "Even in a small town like Bittersweet, the police have better things to do."

Scowling, he paced to the front window and stared through the plate glass to the yard. Even with the glow of the streetlamp at the corner, it was dark. "I suppose you're right."

"I know I'm right. There's nothing anyone can do."

"Sure, there is," he said, slowly turning to face her. "I can stay here."

"What?" *Was he out of his mind?* "Here? No way." She couldn't believe her ears. Although a secret little part of her was pleased, the other saner, more rational side of her nature was scared to death.

"On the couch."

"I don't want a bodyguard!" she snapped, throwing up a hand. "I can't believe we're having this conversation. It's…it's ridiculous."

"I don't think so." He was firm, his jaw set, his gaze steady. He looked like a man who wouldn't be swayed. But the thought of him in the house alone with her, even on the couch, was unnerving. "I'll be fine. Blue's here with me."

"What if the guy has a key?"

"A key? Wait a minute. I don't think there is a guy, and if there was, why would he have a key to my house?"

"Don't you have one hidden outside for Josh?"

"Yes, but—" She felt the color drain from her face. Was it possible? "You're spooking me, Gates."

"Just trying to get you to see the possibilities."

She went to the back porch, skimmed her fingers over the ledge above the door and found the key. "Still here," she said, holding it up for Luke's inspection. The metal glinted in the glare of the single bulb burning over the door.

"Good. Bring it inside."

"No one was here," she insisted as she tossed the key into a kitchen drawer and met him in the archway to the living room. "You're borrowing trouble."

"Maybe."

"You can't stay here."

"Why not?"

A million reasons. I can't trust myself around you. I don't know you. Having you in my house is more emotionally dangerous than anything. "I hardly know you."

As if he could read her mind, he grinned—a wide, sexy smile that did considerable damage to her self-control. "Maybe this is a way to get to know me better."

"I'm not sure I want to."

His eyes said he didn't believe her. "I'll stay on the couch. Believe me, your virtue is safe with me."

"My 'virtue'?" She couldn't believe what she was

hearing. "My *virtue?* Are you crazy, or what? You think I'm worried about my inability to say no to you?" If it wasn't so near the truth, it would have been funny.

"Something like that, yeah."

"Of all the conceited, self-centered, egotistical ideas I've ever heard... Hey, what do you think you're doing?" she demanded, following him down the short hallway to her bedroom. He shoved open the door and strode inside as if he'd done it all his life, as if it were his damned right!

Her heart was in her throat as he strode to her sleigh bed in the center of the room. "Luke, you can't—"

He threw back the covers, grabbed a pillow, then reached for the blanket folded over the foot of her bed, an antique quilt her great-great-grandmother had pieced from scraps seventy-five years earlier. "I'll be out there," he said, his smile disappearing as he hitched his chin toward the door, "in the living room. You stay in the bedroom."

"But—"

"Don't argue." To her surprise he reached forward, grabbed hold of her arms, yanked her close and kissed her hard. She opened her mouth to protest and his tongue slid past her lips and beyond the barrier of her teeth. Steely fingers clenched her forearms. She tried to concentrate, to find the words to disagree with his high-handed tactics, to tell him exactly what he could do with all his good intentions, but she was lost.

A small moan escaped his throat and her heart pounded expectantly. His tongue touched hers, explored the roof of her mouth and a thrill, hot and wanton, swept through her blood. She told herself she was being foolish, that she shouldn't let him touch her, but

she couldn't stop herself. She heard the zipper of her
dress hiss open, felt the cool air touch her back where
the silky fabric parted, experienced a rush of desire as
the tips of his fingers, callused and blunt, brushed
across her skin.

A thousand warning bells rang through her mind as
he kissed her cheeks and eyes and throat, but she ignored them all. Her neck arched as her head lolled back
and his lips found the shell of her ear.

Don't! Don't! Don't! Her mind screamed as her legs
buckled and Luke caught her, sweeping her off her feet.
This is madness! Katie, use your head! But the alarms
ringing through her head couldn't chase away the wonder of the feel of him, the heat of his body, the smell
of sweat and musk that lingered on his skin. He placed
her on the bed and slipped her dress over her shoulders.

"I—I don't know about this," she whispered, but
her words caught in her throat. Kneeling next to the
bed, he leaned forward. His lips brushed the tops of
her breasts and an ache deep within the most feminine
core of her began to pulse.

"Me, neither." His tongue skimmed her breastbone
and her skin turned to fire. Nudging the silk bodice of
her dress even lower, he kissed her breasts where they
bulged above her bra. Inside her, something dark and
painful broke. She closed her eyes as the dress slid
down, exposing her to the warm lamplight.

Don't do this, Katie! Don't.

Desire, long slumberous, rose and seeped through
her veins. His breath was warm, the scent of him arous-
ing. With gentle fingers he edged one breast from its
confines. Her nipple puckered in anticipation. As he
placed his lips over the hard little nub, she drew in a

swift breath. His tongue encircled her nipple until he began to suck slowly, seductively.

Katie's fingers slid through his hair and she fought the urge to cry out as his teeth tugged and pulled and one of his hands pushed her dress past her ribs to her waist. She was breathing fast and hard, her body quivering inside.

"Katie," he whispered, his voice rough as he lifted his head. "I—"

"Shh."

"Oh, hell." The muscles of his face tightened as he battled between good intentions and self-control. "I— I think we should stop. While I still can."

Disappointment welled inside her as he gently pulled the dress back up and over her breasts. His gaze, still bright with passion, touched hers. "I'll be in the living room."

She fought the urge to mew in protest, to beg him to finish what he'd started, to make love to her all night long, and she watched in fascination as he straightened, turned his back to her, and with long, swift strides crossed the room and closed the bedroom door behind him.

Hot tears starred her lashes. Whether the tears were from embarrassment, regret or just plain frustration, she didn't know or care to analyze. She slapped them away with her fingers and told herself she was every kind of fool known to womankind. What had she been thinking, letting this man—this virtual *stranger*—into her home, into her bedroom and darned close to into her bed? "Oh, Kinkaid, you're really losing it," she chided herself, then decided not to dwell on what had happened between them. He was here, on the couch, presumably to help her and that, as they said, was that.

She pulled off her dress, hung it haphazardly on a hanger, then tossed her favorite nightgown over her head. She needed to wash her face, but that would mean walking into the hallway. "So what?" she growled under her breath. Just because Luke was in the house, didn't mean she couldn't do what she had to do. The man wasn't going to intimidate her, for goodness' sake! This was her house. Her life. She snagged her bathrobe from a hook on the closet door, flung her arms into the sleeves and cinched the belt snugly around her waist. She crossed the hall, slipped into the bathroom and went through her nightly ablutions with one ear cocked to the door.

Luke didn't disturb her. A few minutes later she crawled into bed, pulled the covers to her neck and wondered how she'd get one second of sleep knowing that he was just down the hall. Blue, who had padded into the room when she was in the bathroom, circled and dropped into a sleeping position at the foot of her bed. "Good dog," she said around a yawn and he thumped his tail. Sighing, she closed her eyes and the exhaustion of the day took hold. She was asleep within minutes.

A sharp pain in his neck drove Luke to consciousness. He blinked, focusing on the small living room, and realized he was in Katie's house.

The smell of coffee drifted from the kitchen and as he lifted his head, Katie, her hair wound into a knot atop her head, her face scrubbed free of makeup, peeked around the corner.

"Good morning," she said, her eyes sparkling in the dawn light.

"Mornin'."

"Some bodyguard you turned out to be." She giggled and he should have felt irritated by her ribbing, but he managed a thin smile.

"You're safe, aren't you?"

"Yeah, but I don't think it's because of you."

"Well, then, you're wrong. I chased away all sorts of evil types last night."

"Did you?" She laughed and ducked back into the kitchen as some bell rang.

He got up from the couch, rubbed the kinks out of his neck and back, then ambled into the kitchen where she was busy tossing slices of bread into an ancient toaster.

"Breakfast?" Katie asked him.

"You don't have to—"

"No trouble," she insisted with a lift of one shoulder. "Consider it payment for protecting me. Ham and eggs okay?"

She didn't know that he'd stayed awake until dawn, only falling asleep when he'd felt certain that there was no one skulking in the night to threaten her. "Great." He couldn't help noticing the long, graceful arch of her neck, the feminine slope of her shoulders and the nip of her waist where her robe was tied. Beneath the soft velour fabric her hips shifted as she twisted to look at him.

Her eyes caught his for a second and she blushed, a fetching pink hue that climbed her throat and colored her cheeks. In a flash, he was reminded of kissing her breasts. He'd thought of little else all night and had fought the urge to return to her bedroom, press his lips to hers until she couldn't protest and make love to her over and over again. His crotch tightened. "If you don't mind, I'd like to step through the shower."

She hesitated for a second, then said, "Sure. There're extra towels in the hall closet."

"Thanks." In less than two minutes he was under the spray of the showerhead, silently damning himself for his wayward thoughts and the hardness in his crotch. What was wrong with him? Every time he looked at Katie Kinkaid, he wanted to start kissing her and never stop.

It had been just too long since he'd been with a woman. Way too long. He let the hot water work out the kinks in his muscles, washed as best he could, toweled off and dressed. As he opened the bathroom door, he heard Katie's voice.

"I know it's tough, especially for you, but it's something we all have to face, Tiff. Whether you like it or not, John's your father and you have to deal with him. Just like I do." There was a pause, then she added, "Yeah, I know. Okay, I'll start moving stuff over in a few days. I've still got Dad—er, John's Jeep. The convertible is officially dead. Len at the gas station is going to try and sell it or scrap it out and I'll find something else soon. But while I've got John's rig, I may as well start moving." There was a short pause, then she added, "Just let Josh know that I'll pick him up by noon. Thanks again."

She was replacing the receiver when he entered the kitchen. Her face was drawn in concentration until she saw him and grinned. "Well, well, Mr. Gates," she teased, "don't you clean up nice."

"Do I?"

"Here." She handed him a cup of coffee. "Now, sit." At the table were two place settings complete with orange juice, toast, ham, eggs, and hash brown potatoes.

"Yes, ma'am," he drawled in his best Texan accent and she laughed, the sound as musical as wind chimes in a summer breeze.

They ate and talked as Blue sat on the floor at Katie's side, his brown eyes following each morsel that she forked into her mouth. Every once in a while, she'd toss the dog a tidbit and he'd deftly catch the treat with a snap of his jaws.

It felt comfortable and right in the cozy kitchen. In her fluffy bathrobe and slippers, Katie was innocently seductive, expressive with her hands and eyes as she talked about her job, her son, her ambitions and her family.

"So it's all rather complicated," she admitted as she poured the last cup of coffee. "All those years I'd grown up with and tolerated my half brothers, never dreaming that I'd end up with not one, but two half sisters." She grinned, showing off the sexy overlap of her teeth. "Kind of weird, when you think about it. How about you? Any siblings?" She munched on a bite of toast.

"Nope." He shifted uncomfortably in his chair.

"So where are your parents?"

He felt his eyebrows quirk and drained his cup. "My mom took off with some other guy when I was two and my old man was killed in Vietnam when I wasn't much older."

He noticed the color drain from her face. "I was kicked around between a couple of aunts and pretty much raised myself."

"I—I'm sorry."

"Nothin' to be sorry about." He saw the pain in her eyes and refused to let her pity him. "Trust me, it was harder on them than it was on me. I was in and out of juvenile homes for a while until I met my wife.''

"Your...wife?'' she repeated, stunned.

"Ex-wife.'' He shoved his chair back. "I've been divorced for years.''

"Oh.'' She forced a smile that didn't seem genuine and tiny lines deepened between her eyebrows.

"It's over, Katie. Been over a long time.'' Why he felt compelled to explain, he didn't understand. "We didn't have any kids together and the last I heard, Celia had divorced her second husband and was on her way to marrying a third—not that I care. I don't even know where she's living now.''

She seemed troubled and he felt something tug at his heart. Katie Kinkaid, for all her tough-as-nails-investigative-reporter inclinations, was soft inside, couldn't stand to see anyone hurt.

He went to her chair, reached under her arms and drew her to her feet. "Thanks for breakfast,'' he said, bending down so that the tip of his nose brushed hers.

"Thanks... Thanks for staying here last night.'' Katie could scarcely breathe. His hands, big and possessive, held her on either side of her rib cage. One corner of his mouth lifted into that smile she found so damnably sexy.

"My pleasure, Ms. Kinkaid.''

"Mine, as well.'' Cocking her head to the side she looked up at him, heard a deep, heartfelt groan develop from somewhere around his lungs, then gasped as he pulled her roughly to him and pressed hard, insistent lips against hers.

In a heartbeat her blood was rushing through her veins, her bones began to melt and she sagged against him, only to be released quickly. She nearly lost her

balance and glanced up to find his eyes a smoky blue.
"I gotta go," he said.

"Y-yes."

With another quick kiss to her cheek, he turned and
walked through the back door. Katie was left with her
heart pounding wildly, her thoughts tumbling discon-
certingly and a new hunger burning deep in the most
womanly part of her. She dropped into her chair and
held her head in her hands as she realized that she was
starting to fall in love with a man she barely knew.

"Don't," she warned herself, and Blue gave out a
bark of agreement.

But she feared it was already too late. Much too late.

A few days later Luke stared at a copy of Josh Kinkaid's birth certificate. Luke smoothed the official paper open on the scarred maple table that had come with
his apartment in the carriage house. The name of Josh's
father was missing, but the birth date was perfect. With
a little math, Luke figured Katie had gotten pregnant
about a month to six weeks before Dave Sorenson had
left Bittersweet.

It wasn't proof positive, of course; she could have
had another lover, but Luke had the painful sensation
that he knew for certain that Josh Kinkaid was Ralph
Sorenson's only grandchild. His jaw tightened and he
wondered where the feeling of satisfaction he'd antic-
ipated in figuring out this mystery was. He was about
to earn the money he'd been promised, about to give
an elderly man a ray of hope before he died, about to
betray a woman he thought he could all too easily fall
in love with.

At that thought, he started. He wasn't falling in love!
Hell, at best what he felt for Katie Kinkaid was lust.

And what did it matter if he let Sorenson know the truth? The man had a right to meet his grandkid, didn't he? Of course he did. Luke kicked out his chair, grabbed his hat from a peg near the door and walked outside to the landing where the sultry evening air was so thick it seemed to weigh against his skin.

Somewhere over the mountains, thunder rumbled and he thought about his livestock at the ranch. He'd better check on the horses and cattle, then return to town.

To Katie.

His gut clenched when he thought of leaving her that morning in her bathrobe. He'd wanted to stay, to carry her back to the bedroom and finish what he'd started on the night of Bliss Cawthorne's marriage. It had been five or six days since then, and the image of her lying on the bed, the shimmering blue gown peeled down to her waist, her gorgeous breasts exposed and crowned with rosy nipples, had haunted him. Day and night. He'd cruised by her house since then, telling himself that he was checking to see that no one was lingering in the shadows of her cottage, that no intruder was hell-bent on breaking in, that he was only checking on her.

And he'd called. Asked her about Josh's ankle and if she'd had any more hang-ups, or if she'd changed the locks. She'd told him in no uncertain terms that it wasn't really any of his business, but he knew that it wasn't his concern that bothered her; it was the unspoken current that existed between them, the passion that they both tried to ignore, that caused her tongue to lash out.

He could break down and knock on her door. Use the same excuse he'd used the other night, about the potential prowler. And they'd end up in bed; they wouldn't be able to stop themselves. But he knew it was a sham, a pretense to see her again.

Trying to convince himself that he'd been overreacting—that no one had been observing them at the hotel the night of the Lafferty wedding, that nothing in her house had been out of place and no one had broken in, that the phone calls she'd received were just a rash of wrong numbers—he climbed down the outside staircase.

The main house was nearly empty; a moving van had carted off most of Tiffany Santini's belongings the day before. Boxes, crates and sacks were piled on the back porch and the windows were dark. Soon, Katie and Josh would be moving in. It calmed him somehow, to think that she'd be near. Sure, there'd be hell to pay because he knew himself well enough to realize that he'd use any reason to get close to her, any excuse to get her into bed with him.

"Damn it all to hell." What was it about that woman that made him want to protect her one minute and make love to her the next?

As he crossed the dry, yellowed lawn he noticed that the sky was dark, thick with swollen-bellied clouds that blocked the sun. He made his way to the truck just as the first fat raindrops began to fall. Inside the cab it was hot, breathless. He opened the windows, shoved the rig into reverse and squinted as rivulets of rain slithered through the film of dust that covered his windshield. He wouldn't think of Katie right now; but sooner or later, he'd have to deal with her.

"I don't believe you." Josh, half lying on the rumpled sheets of his bed, stared at his mother with wide-eyed disgust.

Katie cringed. "It's true. Why would I lie?"

"But you did. You lied."

"And now I'm telling you the truth," she said, dying a little inside. "Dave Sorenson is...your father." She sat on the edge of the bed and opened the yearbook from her days in high school. "I'd always thought there would be more time. That when you were older... Oh, Josh, I made a horrible mistake." Her voice was thick, her throat nearly closed. "Your dad and I..." How could she explain a short-term love affair to a boy who wasn't yet eleven? "We were just kids and he moved away. By the time I knew I was pregnant with you, he was already gone and, I think, dating some other girl in his new town." She pointed to Dave's senior-class picture. He looked so young, so boyish, and yet he'd been her first love. "I'm sure he would have loved you a lot, but he never knew about you."

"Because you lied."

"Yes." She bit her lip and fought the urge to break down and sob like a baby. "Yes."

"You should have told me."

She felt as if she'd been stabbed through the heart. Of course she should have. "I know."

He swallowed hard and folded his arms over his chest. Thrusting out his chin, he demanded, "Are you gonna send me to him or is he comin' here, or what?"

"No," she said, summoning every bit of courage she could muster. "He can't. Not anymore. He died...a few months ago, I guess...and I didn't know it. He was in the military. There was a helicopter accident while they were on maneuvers and...and he didn't survive."

Josh gasped and his face, tanned from the summer sun, turned a sickly chalky shade. Tears filled his eyes.

"I don't believe you," he said again.

"It's true."

"How do you know?"

"A friend...he told me." For the first time she considered the fact that Luke could have been mistaken or lied, and she mentally kicked herself for not checking it out herself. She was a reporter, for God's sake. She knew better than to take someone's word. She spent days double-checking sources and yet this time, she'd taken Luke's story about Dave as if it were Gospel from the Bible.

But he wouldn't have lied.

"You shoulda told me. Told him about me," Josh said.

"As I said, I'm sorry, Josh." She sniffed as tears drizzled down her cheeks. "So sorry."

"Why didn't you?"

"I—I couldn't. It was wrong. Bad. I wish I could change things, but I can't. I..." She sighed and fought the urge to break down altogether. "I just can't. Not now."

He blinked and looked away toward the window that was open just a crack. Outside, thunder rumbled over the hills and rain began to drip down the windowpanes. Blue growled from the living room. With a swipe of one hand Josh wiped the tip of his nose and as Katie touched him he shifted, using his shoulder as a shield, silently shunning her.

They were only inches apart but the distance between them seemed vast. Unbridgeable.

"Josh—"

"Leave me alone."

"Honey, please—"

He hopped to his feet, winced from the pain in his ankle, then skewered her with eyes filled with hatred.

With a condemning finger pointed at her nose, he whispered his newfound mantra: "You shoulda told me." His voice cracked and Katie's heart shattered into a million pieces.

"You're right," she admitted, standing and wanting so badly to fold him into her arms. Here in his room where model airplanes, books, CDs and magazines had begun to be packed into boxes for the move. Boxes of memorabilia that his father had never seen. A soccer trophy winked in the harsh light from the overhead fixture—a trophy Josh had never shared with his father. How had she been so selfish? She'd denied her son his right to know his own dad. Just as she'd been denied the knowledge of her biological father. "You're right, Josh. I made a mistake," she admitted, "but I can't change anything now. I can only let you meet your other grandparents—your father's parents. They want to see you."

"Just leave me alone." His chin inched up in rebellious defiance and his cheeks were wet from his silent tears.

"Listen, Josh—"

"I said, leave me alone." He snagged up the yearbook and Katie told herself she had no choice but to let him sort through his feelings, whatever pain she'd inadvertently hurled at him. She swallowed hard. "Think about it."

"I don't want to talk to anybody!"

"Okay, okay, I'll let you be," she said, knowing he needed time to adjust to the bomb she'd just set off in his life. "But Grandma's coming over and—"

"I don't want to see her," Josh insisted, reaching for the remote control and clicking on the small television set to a decibel level guaranteed to shatter glass. "I don't want to talk to anyone."

"You might. Later."

He glared at her with red-rimmed eyes that were filled with silent, deadly accusations. His chin wobbled and his back stiffened in some vain attempt at manhood.

"I'll be in the living room. When Grandma gets here I'll send her in."

"No."

"Josh—"

His lips compressed and she held both hands up as if to fend off an attack. "Okay, okay, bud, I'll give you some time alone, but I think we should talk this out."

"I don't want to talk to you or Grandma or anyone."

"We'll see." She walked out of the room and jumped as the door slammed behind her. Clearing her throat she headed for her desk and told herself it would all work out. Of course, Josh was hurt, disappointed and angry. Of course he wanted to scream and cry and mourn for a father he'd never known.

She sank into her desk chair and sighed, stirring her bangs.

And of course, he was right. She should have told him the truth. Years ago. But she hadn't. Now, it seemed, they would all have to pay the price.

Chapter Eight

"Of course, Josh is upset," Brynnie said, rummaging in her purse for a pack of gum that, it was advertised, would cut down her need for a cigarette. She tossed her keys, eyeglass case, coin purse and wallet onto Katie's table before she found the gum. "Who wouldn't be?" She opened the pack and shook out a stick. With a longing sigh for a smoke she'd sworn to give up, she plopped the gum into her mouth.

Katie swiped at the counter haphazardly with her sponge. "I should have told him about Dave. No. Reverse that." She rinsed the sponge at the sink. "I should have told Dave about Josh." Wiping her hands on a towel hanging over the handle of the oven she glanced down the hallway. "He's been in there over an hour."

"Give him time," her mother advised.

Katie bit her lip. She felt worse than awful. Sometimes she thought that as a mother she'd failed miserably. This was one of those times.

Brynnie eyed the few boxes that were stacked in the corner. "I've got an idea. I'll help you load these into the Jeep and you can take them over to the new place."

"Even though Tiffany and J.D. moved out the other day, I think they still have some things they want to do to the place before I call it home," Katie said, though her half sister had told her that the house was just about ready and had encouraged her to start moving. "Besides, I can't leave Josh now."

"Of course you can." Her mother wasn't swayed. "Do you really think it makes any difference to him if you're here or a few blocks across town?"

"But if he wants to talk—"

"He can wait. Besides, I'm here. I know the scoop."

"It's my job."

"I'm his grandmother and I've dealt with this kind of thing a lot." Brynnie managed a smile as she popped her gum. "Besides, I kind of owe you one, don't I?"

"Why?"

"For letting you think that Hal Kinkaid was your father." Two spots of color appeared on her cheeks. "I, uh, should apologize to you for that little fib."

"I think it was more than a 'little fib,' but it doesn't matter right now. It's water under the bridge," Katie said, waving off her mother's concerns.

"You didn't think so at the time."

Katie managed a half smile. "Well, come on, Mom, you have to admit that of all your husbands, Hal was the least…'memorable,' for lack of a better word."

"You mean boring."

"That, too." Katie rubbed her arms at the thought of her surly, overbearing namesake. He was a steady worker, but found absolutely no joy in life. "I never knew what you saw in him."

"Neither do I. Not now." Brynnie motioned to the boxes. "Go on, Katie, take these over to the house. Give me a couple of hours alone with my grandson."

Katie hesitated. "If you think it'll work."

With a wink, Brynnie slowly nodded her head. "Guaranteed."

"Okay, okay." Katie walked down the hall to Josh's room and rapped on the door with her knuckles. Her mother was just a step behind. "Bud?" Katie called through the panels.

"Go 'way!"

So Josh was still in his foul mood. Despite his order, Katie opened the door a crack. "No reason to be rude."

He didn't look her way but she could read the I-don't-want-to-talk-to-you expression on his face.

"I'm gonna run some boxes over to the new place, but Grandma's here, okay?"

"I can stay by myself."

"Not while I'm anywhere in the vicinity," Brynnie said. "I never give up a chance to play darts or Hearts or Scrabble with my favorite grandson."

"I'm your only grandson," he grumbled, but a dimple creased one cheek—a dimple Katie hadn't seen since she'd told him about his father.

"Then that makes you extra special, doesn't it?" Brynnie edged into the room and looked over her shoulder. "Go on," she mouthed to Katie as she took a seat on the foot of the bed. "Now, kiddo, what'll the bet be?"

"I dunno."

"I know. If I win, you'll come over and mow my

lawn, but if you win, I'll take you and a friend over to the water park next weekend.''

"Really?" Josh sent his mother a glance that said he knew he was being conned.

"Of course." Brynnie looked up, caught Katie standing at the crack in the doorway and gave her a curt little wave.

"Okay, okay, I can take a hint," Katie said, relieved that her son seemed to be jollying out of his bad mood. "I'll see you both later."

She packed the Jeep with boxes, coats from the front closet and a few sacks from the kitchen, then drove to the old Victorian house she would soon call home. It felt odd, somehow; she and Josh had lived in the cottage for all of his life. But it was time for a change.

She parked in an open spot by the garage, noticed that Luke's pickup was missing and kicked herself when she felt a pang of disappointment. "Forget him," she whispered under her breath as she started unloading boxes and carrying them into the old house. It seemed empty and cold. Fresh paint, a soft gold color that Tiffany had let Katie pick out, covered the walls and the wood floors gleamed, but the furniture was missing, the hanging pots, the dried herbs and the children's artwork stripped from what had been Tiffany's once-cozy kitchen. No black cat slunk through the shadows and without the wail of Stephen's guitar, the patter of Christina's busy feet or Tiffany's soft laughter, the house was little more than a tomb.

"Cut it out," she reprimanded and busied herself by carrying box after box into the house and leaving it in the appropriate room. She'd finished her last trip and was actually hanging coats in the front hall when she heard the back door open.

Her heart nearly stopped.

"Hello?" Luke's voice filled the empty space.

"In here." Her pulse jumped a bit as he came into view—tall and rangy, in jeans and a faded denim shirt with its sleeves shoved to the elbows, his hair windblown. He brought with him the scents of rainwater and horses.

"Movin' in?" he asked, his blue eyes intense.

"The first load." She shut the closet door and suddenly felt tongue-tied. "I, uh, I'll move the big stuff in a couple of days. My brothers have offered to help with the furniture and appliances."

He glanced around the empty rooms. "Your boy here?"

"At home with Grandma." A pang of regret sliced through her heart at the thought of Josh and his reaction to the news that the father he'd never known was dead.

As if he read the pain in her expression, Luke said, "Wait here, I've got an idea."

"For what—?" she asked but he'd already turned on his heel and was striding toward the kitchen. A second later the screen door banged shut behind him. Curious, she couldn't help but follow the sound and walk into the kitchen where she looked through the window and watched as he dashed through the raindrops to the carriage house, then took the stairs to the upper floor two at a time. A few seconds later he reappeared carrying a bottle of wine and two glasses. She watched as he jogged across the yard and entered the house with the smell of fresh rain clinging to him.

"I think we should christen the place," he said, removing a corkscrew from his pocket and piercing the foil over the cork with the tool's sharp tip. "Come on," he encouraged, as if witnessing skepticism on her face.

"Let's do it right. In here." As he started uncorking the bottle he led her into the parlor where bay windows, draped in gauzy curtains overlooked the front yard and a marble fireplace loomed against the opposite wall. The cork popped. "Here, you pour. I'll be right back."

"What now?" she asked, but watched him leave again and didn't argue. There was something enchanting about spending some time alone with him here.

Careful, you'll only get yourself into trouble, her mind warned as she tipped the bottle and the rich, dark Merlot streamed into the two stemmed glasses.

"I wouldn't have thought of you as having anything like these," she observed, holding up one of the goblets and twisting its stem between her fingers as he returned carrying chunks of firewood and kindling. He leaned over the grate and cast a glance in her direction. Over his shoulder he muttered, "Castoffs from the divorce."

"Oh." She didn't want to be reminded that he'd been married once. Not tonight. "I just meant that you seem more like a guy who drinks beer."

"Sometimes. Whatever suits the mood." He looked over his shoulder again, his eyes a deep, glittering blue. "I think it's good to mix things up, don't you?"

"Of course."

"Good." He turned his attention back to the fire and she noticed the darker streaks of blond where rainwater had run from the top of his head and the way his neck, at its base, spread into strong shoulder muscles that disappeared beneath the collar of his shirt.

She remembered seeing his bare chest and muscular back and at the thought her pulse elevated and she fought the urge to run. This was too close, too intimate. He was squatting, the worn heels of his boots above the carpet as he leaned forward. His jeans were low on his hips, his waistband gaping at his spine, but, unfortunately, the tail of his shirt never moved, remained tucked while he struck a match against the sole of one boot and lit the fire. She realized that being alone with him was darned close to emotional suicide, that her fascination for him was running far too deep, and yet she couldn't resist staying with him.

With a spark and a crackle, flames began to devour the dry kindling and wood. Smoke billowed into the room. "Dammit," he said, reaching quickly above the hungry, snapping flames to open the flue. "I forget some people close these things." The chimney began to draw. "You didn't know that my plan was to asphyxiate you, did you?"

She laughed as he straightened, dusted his hands together, then cracked one of the windows. "Better?"

"Much."

"So much for being suave and debonair." He sat on the floor next to her and accepted a glass.

"That's okay. I'm not into the sleek-and-sophisticated type."

"Lucky for me." He offered her a crooked smile that drilled right to the core of her. "How about a toast?"

"A toast? I can't wait to hear this."

"Here's to you, Katie Kinkaid." He touched the rim of his glass to hers and looked deep into her eyes. "May you find your happiness here and may you always be safe."

Her heart nearly crumpled and her throat grew thick, but she managed a frail smile. "And here's to you, Luke Gates," she said, again nudging his glass with hers. "Man of mystery, cowboy and Bittersweet's newest entrepreneur. May the ranch be a raving success."

"It will be." He grinned crookedly, his gaze still holding hers as he took the first sip. Katie's heart thrummed, her throat was as dry as a desert and she sipped from her glass, feeling the red wine slide down her throat more easily than she'd expected. She shouldn't be doing this; the room was much too intimate, the atmosphere seductive.

Firelight played in Luke's hair, reflecting in his eyes and gilding his skin. He stretched out, boots nearly touching the marble hearth, one elbow propping his shoulders upright.

"Tell me about yourself," he suggested.

"Not much more to tell." She took another swallow. "I think you know most of the high points."

"Do I?" One of his eyebrows arched and her stomach rolled over. He was so damned sexy, so raw and male. As he drank from his glass she watched his Adam's apple move and she found the involuntary motion decidedly seductive. What was wrong with her? Why did she always see Luke Gates as a raw, sexual man; not just someone she wanted as a friend. "How about the men in your life?"

"'The men'?" she repeated and smiled. "The dozens of men?" When his smile faded she shook her head. "The truth of the matter is, there just haven't been many."

"There was Josh's father."

Dave. Her heart twisted a bit. "He was a long time ago. I was in high school."

"And since?"

"I've dated a little. Nothing serious. I had Josh to think about, to protect, and of course, my job. I…I told myself I couldn't get involved with anyone, I had too many responsibilities and maybe it was just a defense mechanism, but the truth of the matter is that no one interested me.'' *Until you.*

''Most women want a man to be a father to their kids.''

''I'm not most women,'' she said, lifting her chin defiantly.

''I noticed.'' His eyes locked with hers and in that instant she knew she would make love to him. It was inevitable, like the ebb and flow of the tide. The wine was beginning to warm her blood and the intimacy of the room enfolded her in a soft, seductive cocoon. Raindrops sparkling with firelight trailed down the windowpanes and she felt as if she and Luke were the only two people on earth. She licked a drop of Merlot from her lips and his gaze followed her movement.

Slowly he took her glass from her hand, set it along with his in a corner near the fireplace, then stretched out beside her on the carpet and wrapped his arms around her. She turned her head up expectantly but wasn't prepared for the onslaught on her senses as his lips met hers, his tongue delved between her teeth and a rush of desire as hot as lava sped through her blood.

This time there were no excuses, no interruptions. His tongue and hands were everywhere and without a thought she kissed him back, her arms drawing him closer still, her mind swimming with erotic images as he pressed wet, warm kisses onto her eyes, her neck, her shoulders. He stripped her clothes from her body, leaving her naked, her skin shimmering with perspiration before the fire. And she, too, worked at the buttons of his shirt, tore open the waistband of his jeans, pulled hard and heard a sexy series of pops as his fly gave way.

His body was lean and sinewy, sleek muscles visible

through skin that was tanned except for a strip of white over his buttocks. Golden hair covered his chest and his manhood, which was strong, erect and ready.

His fingers caressed her, his lips and tongue exploring each intimate crevice and curve. She tingled inside as she, tentatively at first, and then with more confidence, touched him and heard him moan with deep, hungry pleasure.

She didn't think about the consequences as he rolled atop her, didn't consider recriminations. She arched as he placed his big, callused hands on either side of her rib cage, his fingers splaying around her ribs, his thumbs rubbing her nipples seductively. His hair fell forward, streaked gold and red by the firelight as he bent forward and kissed the tip of each breast. The world began to tilt. He pushed his tongue through the valley of her sternum; then, with his lips, climbed each mound and lingered, laving and sucking at her nipples. Desire, dark and insistent, curled deep inside her, and brought with it a moistness, a wild yearning she hadn't felt in years.

"Katie," he rasped, lifting his head as her fingers dug into the hard, sinewy muscles of his buttocks. "Sweet, sweet Katie."

She opened her mouth to speak but couldn't form a word.

"Is this what you want?"

"Yes." She didn't hesitate. It had been so long. Too long. Winding an arm around his neck, she pulled his head down to hers and kissed him, her mouth open and waiting, her body quivering with a passion she'd feared she'd lost.

His knees parted her legs and he looked one last time into her eyes before he thrust into her as if he'd wanted to make love to her all his life. She gasped as he entered her, holding tightly to the arms planted on either side of her head, and as he withdrew and entered again, rose to meet him. She held his gaze as their bodies joined, moved her hips to his rhythm, felt the sing of anticipation in her bloodstream. All her doubts fled, all her worries disappeared and she was lost in the single purpose of loving this lone, tough man.

Faster and faster he moved and she could scarcely breathe, gasping in short, sharp bursts that matched the crazy beating of her heart.

"Katie," he cried, throwing back his head as he spilled himself into her. "Katie!"

She clung to him, her body convulsing, her universe shattering deep in her soul. He fell against her, breathing hard and holding her close as he rolled to the side.

Tears welled deep in her eyes and he leaned over and kissed each eyelid. "Regrets?" he asked, his expression clouding.

"Relief."

"Good." He held her close, in strong arms that made her feel safe and secure, and she closed her eyes, knowing that the moment would soon end, but making it last for as long as she could. He sighed across her hair and she snuggled close. She wouldn't believe that making love to Luke Gates was anything but wonderful.

A few days later Katie was still thinking about making love to Luke, wondering if it would ever happen again as she carried a box of pots and pans onto the back porch. She stacked the box on top of the growing pile of assorted crates and cartons that waited for Jarrod, Nathan and Trevor on the back porch of her little cottage. Sweat drizzled down her nape and forehead. She mopped her brow, then swiped at a cobweb that dangled from the rafters of the roof. The rainstorm of a few nights before was long gone and the temperature had soared into the nineties again, proof that summer wasn't ready to give up its searing hold on the Rogue River Valley.

The yard was patchy and yellow, the leaves on the trees just starting to turn gold with the promise of autumn. She'd miss this place, she thought, as she squinted against the sun and watched Blue sniff in the shrubbery for a squirrel or bird hidden deep in the foliage. The old dog moved his head to look at her, wagged his tail, then turned back to smelling the underbrush.

But it was time to move, she decided. Things were changing. Josh on the threshold of adolescence, was dealing with the new changes in his life—about his father's death and accepting a grandfather he hadn't known. Brynnie had gotten through to him. Within a few more years he'd slowly be pulling away from his mother.

Katie had already run an advertisement in the "For Rent" column of the *Review's* Classified section. It was time to move on in many ways.

She went inside her sweltering kitchen, turned on the tap and holding her hair away from her face, drank from the faucet. She swiped the back of her hand over her mouth, then walked to Josh's room. With a rap of her fingers, she called through the door. "Need any help in there?"

There was a pause. Her hand was on the doorknob when he answered. "Nope."

"Jarrod and the twins will be here soon."

"I know."

She wanted to reprimand him, to tell him to try and stop punishing her; but she bit her tongue and decided to give him some space. For the past few days—ever since Katie had told him about his father—Josh had been upset and sullen, offering her the juvenile equivalent to the cold shoulder.

Katie had tried to broach the subject of Dave several times since she'd first told her son about his father, but Josh had retreated into disgusted silence and had spent his time either at school or with his friends. When he was at home, he kept to his room, watching the small television, playing video games and generally indulging his bad mood. But, the good news was that he was off crutches for good; the doctor had called the Monday after Bliss's wedding with a report that the specialists who had read his X ray had found no indication of fracture in his ankle and physically he was solid again.

And today was different. They were moving and she'd forced Josh into a halfway-decent mood. He'd even offered to help her pack up her desk. A small olive branch, but one that she'd quickly accepted.

Their lives were changing in other ways. As of this day, Katie would live next door to Luke.

Which was another problem.

She'd seen Luke several times since the late afternoon when they'd made love. Each time, he'd been cordial and warm, a sexy, affectionate smile creasing his jaw whenever they'd run into each other. But he hadn't called and hadn't so much as touched her again.

It was almost as if something had come between them, an invisible barrier she didn't understand. She filled another cardboard box with memorabilia from her kitchen, piling in knickknacks and pictures, cookbooks and a few pot holders.

She heard the truck before she saw its rear end back into the drive. As it slowed and parked several feet away from the garage, she heard her half brothers' shouts.

"Start with the big things—washer and dryer," Jarrod ordered as he climbed out of the cab. "And don't forget the refrigerator."

"As if I'd let them forget anything." Katie stepped onto the back porch as her twin brothers leaped past the two steps and barreled into the kitchen. "But don't worry about the refrigerator. It stays with the place."

"Good. Just point us in the right direction," Nathan told her. His hair was a dark brown, stick straight and flopped over a high forehead beneath which intense hazel eyes bored into her.

She followed her brothers inside and from the archway in the kitchen looked down the hallway to where Trevor was already unhooking the hoses to the washing machine that was wedged into what was euphemistically called a "laundry closet."

Jarrod pushed open the screen door and frowned at the torn, jagged mesh. "I think I made some wild promise about fixing this," he said, sticking a finger through the hole.

"That you did." She winked at him. "And just because I'm moving doesn't let you off the hook, you know. This is still my house and you made a promise."

"Consider it done."

"Oh, sure. Promises, promises," she quipped blithely.

"Hey, are we gonna get some help in here?" Trevor, the more hotheaded of the twins, yelled.

''Duty calls.'' Jarrod was already halfway there. ''Hey, kid. How about giving your uncles a hand?''

Josh, hearing the commotion had poked his head out of his room. Upon spying Katie's half brothers, he joined in and forgot to cast his mother a disparaging glance before he helped unhook the dryer. Katie mentally crossed her fingers that he'd forgive her.

As the men handled the bigger items—the beds, couches, tables and chairs—Katie kept filling boxes from the few cupboards that she hadn't already cleared out.

''I can't believe how much junk you've got,'' Trevor observed on one trip to the truck. ''Can't you get rid of half of it?''

''Didn't have time for a garage sale.'' She carried a kitchen chair to the loading area at the rear of the big truck. ''Besides, I don't like living as spartan as you.''

''Easier that way.''

Nathan laughed. He handed an end table to Jarrod who was standing inside the truck. ''Yeah. Trevor thinks that a person can get by with a bedroll, a mess kit, and a television.''

''Don't need much more,'' Trevor said, his hawkish features identical to his brother's. The difference in the twins was in their temperament. Nathan was steadier and levelheaded while Trevor was the hothead, always ready for a fight.

They finished loading and the house was nearly empty. Jarrod, Nathan and Josh rode over to the new place in the truck while Katie, with Trevor in the passenger seat and Blue in the back, followed in the Jeep.

''This is gonna be weird,'' Josh said, once they'd parked and everyone began unloading the furniture.

Josh commandeered Stephen's old room while Katie set up her home office in Christina's bedroom.

Josh was right; it felt strange to see her bed and bureau in Tiffany's old room and stranger still to look out the window at the carriage house where Luke Gates lived. As she instructed her brothers on the placement of chairs, tables and lamps in the parlor, she noticed the ashes in the grate, testament to her afternoon of lovemaking with Luke. Their two empty wineglasses stood next to the once-full bottle of Merlot on the hearth.

Images of making love with Luke, of his corded muscles gleaming in the firelight, shot through her mind.

"Looks like someone had themselves a private party," Trevor observed as he and Nathan carried in a bookcase.

"That it does." Quickly Katie reached down, picked up the goblets and bottle, and hoped the back of her neck didn't look as warm as it felt.

Trevor didn't let up. "I wonder who—"

"Hey, pay attention!" Nathan, who was holding one end of the bookcase, wasn't in the mood for conjecture.

"Just put it there, to the side of the window," Katie said, and silently counted her lucky stars that the conversation was dropped. She carried the evidence of her evening with Luke into the kitchen and hoped Trevor's curiosity was sated. She didn't want to think about Luke and what had happened between them. Not now. Nor did she want to explain it to anyone. Especially her half brothers.

She had too much to do.

An installer from the phone company came and hooked up the telephone and fax line while she was organizing the kitchen. In the midst of the pure chaos of wadded newspapers on the counters and floors, dishes in every available space and cupboards half filled, the easygoing man worked on the outlets, kept up a steady stream of conversation about his grand-children and managed to install three phones.

Once they were installed, she found her courage along with Ralph Sorenson's phone number and she dialed. One ring, two, three and so on. No answer. No answering machine. She hung up disappointed, but told herself she'd try again.

A few minutes later Tiffany and J.D. came over and they, along with Katie's half brothers, finished putting things in order. Christina was confused, but contented herself in chasing a nervous Blue through the house and Stephen and Josh holed up in Josh's new room. Though Stephen was three years older and in high school, he didn't seem to mind hanging out with his younger half cousin when they weren't in school.

"It looks different," Tiffany said as she eyed the parlor and foyer. "And yet the same."

"It'll take some getting used to."

"For all of us." Tiffany showed Katie a file she'd left in the front-hall closet. Inside was information on the house, rental agreements, application forms and ex-tra sets of keys. "I'll get you started and show you how this works," she said, "but it's not all that tough once you get the hang of it, and you can always call me."

"Hey, now that the phones are hooked up, how about ordering pizza?" Trevor called down from the second floor.

Katie grinned. "You think you deserve to be fed?"

"At least. It wouldn't hurt if you stocked the refrigerator with some beer, too."

"Okay, okay. You guys are in charge of the kids. Come on, Tiffany, let's run down to Papa Luigi's and figure out what we need for this crowd."

"Pepperoni!" Josh yelled.

"With double cheese," Jarrod added.

"Naw, get the all-meat special." Trevor was reaching for his wallet. "An extra large and—"

"I'll take care of it," Katie said. "It's on me." She ignored Trevor's offer of money and found her purse wedged between half-filled boxes on the kitchen counter. As she and Tiffany headed outside, Katie glanced up at the upper story of the carriage house, the place Luke temporarily called home. How would it be to live so close to him, to know that he was only a few short footsteps away? She thought again for a second about making love to him on the parlor floor and decided she couldn't dwell on the future or what, if any, kind of relationship she had with him. Only time would tell.

"I was wondering when I'd hear from you again. How's it going out there?" Ralph Sorenson's voice was loud, and filled with anticipation.

Luke had steeled himself for this phone call—a call he hadn't wanted to make. "It's going," he replied, hedging. "Renovations on the ranch house have started and I should be moving out to the spread in a month or two."

"So what about the other? Have you found out if Dave had a kid like he hinted at?"

Luke heard the note of eager enthusiasm in the older man's voice, could almost see Ralph's aging fingers curl, white-knuckled around the receiver. "I'm not certain yet," Luke admitted, "but I've got a couple of leads. Good ones. As soon as I know for sure, I'll let you know."

"It means a lot to me," Ralph said. "It's all I have left of my boy."

"I know. I'm working on it. Trust me." Luke heard the old man sigh and felt like a heel. How had he gotten himself roped into this mess? He turned the conversation to the weather, the price of feed, a new virus that was infecting cattle herds in west Texas—anything but the topic of David Sorenson's child. Stretching the telephone cord so that he could look out the window to where Josh Kinkaid and Stephen Santini were playing one-on-one at a basketball hoop hung on the garage, he leaned his shoulder against the window.

The older kid was winning by a lot, but Josh, even though he still hobbled a little, wasn't a slouch. Luke hated the thought, but he would bet dollars to doughnuts that the kid was Dave's. His age was perfect, and Katie acted so oddly—like she couldn't wait to change the subject—whenever the question of Josh's paternity came up. She'd also been blown away when she'd learned about Dave's death—had turned white as a sheet. Hell, what a mess.

But he couldn't prove it. He suspected only one person knew the truth.

"I'll call in a couple of days," he promised and hung up. It was time for a showdown with Ms. Kinkaid. As soon as her half brothers and the Santini clan cleared out, Luke would have to confront her.

For a second the image of her lying beneath him, her eyes wide and verdant green in anticipation, her lips parted in passion as he made love to her, flashed through his mind.

His gut clenched.

He'd never felt so completely satisfied in his life as he had with her; and he'd never felt so guilty for seducing someone. Katie Kinkaid was different from any of the other women he'd had in his lifetime. Very different. And that was a problem. A big problem.

Chapter Nine

That night, after most of the stuff had been packed away, Katie opened the door to Josh's room and smiled as she saw him spread-eagled across the bed, snoring softly, dead to the world. Her heart swelled as she brushed a wayward lock of hair from his forehead, leaned down and kissed his smooth brow. He had been warmer to her today, as if he was getting over the shock of realizing that she had lied to him, as if he were finally forgiving her. *Thank goodness.* She didn't know how much more of the cold shoulder she could take. As she left the room she snapped off the TV and lights, then softly closed the door behind her.

In the next room over, her new office, she rearranged some files on her computer, edited an article on the new Santini winery and vineyards, and went through her notes on Isaac Wells. It had been over a week since she'd received the letter, and she'd never been contacted again. The police had told her nothing and she was starting to believe she'd been the target of some kind of hoax, though she couldn't begin to think why. "Live and learn," she said, frowning and catching a glimpse of her pale reflection, blurred over the words of her article in her computer monitor.

A truck roared into the drive and Katie's heart jumped. The engine died as she opened the blinds and peered through. Luke's truck was parked near the garage, the glow of a security lamp reflecting on its hood. Stretching as he climbed from the cab, he strode across the backyard. His expression was stern, his demeanor that of a man with a mission. Her pulse jumped of its own accord.

He cast a quick look at the house and upstairs to the lighted window. Katie's throat caught. She couldn't look away. He didn't so much as smile, and quickly disappeared from view beneath the roof of the porch. Her porch. Oh, God, he was coming to see her.

Katie was down the stairs in a flash, her bare feet skimming the wooden steps and hallway into the kitchen. She opened the door and found him in the shadows, as taciturn and unfriendly as she'd ever seen him. "Something's wrong," she guessed.

"You could say that."

Her heart went wild. "Come in, come in. What is it?"

Once inside, he grabbed one of the chairs positioned around the table and straddled it. Folding his arms over the back, he stared up at her. Dread did a slow crawl up her spine. In a moment of intuitive divination she knew what this was about.

"I want to talk about Josh's father."

"I figured as much." Her voice sounded strangled, even to her own ears. "Why?"

"It's time."

She wanted to argue, to tell him it was none of his business, but the truth of the matter was out. Now that Josh knew his parentage, there seemed no reason to lie. "I don't see why it could possibly matter to you," she began, rubbing at a spot on the counter with one finger, "but you may as well know that Josh was Dave Sorenson's son. We…we knew each other in high school, got involved and then, just before he left, I got pregnant." Her cheeks burned and for a second she thought she might break down altogether, but she managed to keep her voice steady and look Luke in the eye.

"You never told him that he had a son."

"Nope." She shook her head and couldn't hide the regret in her voice. It seemed Luke was determined that she face all her demons. Tonight. "I should have. For Dave. For Josh. I…I was young and stupid and naive and hurt. I had explained to Dave before he moved away that there was a chance that I was pregnant, but he didn't seem concerned and then, when I knew for sure, I found out that he'd already hooked up with another girl in Texas. I guess I had too much pride to run after him and give him the news he didn't want to hear—that he was going to be a father." She drew in a long, shaky breath. "So the only person I confided in was my mom. No one else knew and she kept my secret. I didn't even tell Jarrod who Josh's dad was and I felt badly about it, because Jarrod saw me through some pretty dark hours. Stood by me and didn't ask any questions or give me any lectures."

Luke raised an eyebrow, silently encouraging her to continue.

"I'm not making excuses. I should have told Dave the truth. I thought I was protecting my son and myself, but really—I only ended up hurting Josh." She managed a thin, frail smile. "I made a mistake. A big one."

"Everyone does." Surprisingly, he didn't seem to judge her.

Folding her arms under her breasts, trying to maintain some semblance of poise, she fought tears. "So, cowboy from Texas, what does it matter to you?"

"I already told you that I knew Dave. Worked for years for Dave's father, Ralph."

"Uh-huh." She didn't like the way this was heading.

"And you know I bought my place from him." Luke seemed as tense as she. His shoulders were rigid, his eyes watching her every move.

"Maybe you should tell me what I don't already know." She was careful. Wary. Where was the warm man to whom she'd made love only a few days before?

"As I said, I didn't buy the place with cash, really. I worked for him, he withheld part of my paycheck with the understanding that I'd one day use that money as a down payment on a place outside of Dallas. However, that didn't work out and he offered me full ownership out here instead. It was a deal I couldn't pass up."

He'd told her all this before, but nothing he'd said so far explained the rigid set of his jaw or the lines of silent anger that bracketed his mouth. "So?"

"He asked a favor of me before I headed west."

Here it comes. "What kind of favor?" she asked, not really sure she wanted to know. Her pulse thundered through her brain.

"Ralph asked me to do some checking when I came into town. Before his death Dave had mentioned that he might have fathered a child back here and Ralph wanted to locate that grandchild if he had. That's why I came over here tonight. To get this all out in the open. It's been a secret too long.''

Katie's chest was as tight as if it had suddenly been strapped in steel bands. ''I had already decided to talk to the Sorensons,'' she said, though she still felt cornered, as if tracking hounds had been put on her trail and she had no place to run to, her back against the face of a sheer cliff. ''But first I had to talk to Josh.''

''He didn't know?''

She shook her head and felt beads of sweat collecting at her nape and forehead. ''As I said, no one did. Whenever the subject of his father came up, I told him that the man was in my life for a very short period, then gone, that I didn't know much about him anymore. I promised to tell him the whole story some day, but, for the most part, I hedged. I didn't want Josh to hear things about a father who had left him before he was born, and I thought that if I kept the guy anonymous, and if there was no speculation, no gossip, it would be okay. Of course, that was a mistake. People talk and kids are cruel.'' She swiped her bangs from her eyes. ''You have to understand I was little more than a kid, myself. I'd been teased all my growing-up years because my mom was forever getting married and divorced. It seemed like everyone else's family was stable and mine was this…this chaotic mess.

''I know now that it wasn't true. All families have their little secrets.'' She laughed at the irony. ''And of course, I had no idea that the man who was supposed to be my father, wasn't. My mom lied to me, too. I would have *died* if I'd guessed that I was the product of a…an illicit affair. That I would be called 'illegitimate.' It was bad enough as it was, and I was determined that I wouldn't put my kid through the same kind of pain."

She leaned a hip against the kitchen island and glanced out to the backyard where moonlight was casting the dry grass in soft shades of silver. "Anyway, of course it was probably worse for Josh to not tell him the truth, but I was young and convinced I was doing the right thing. The trouble with a lie is it feeds on itself and keeps growing. Any time the subject came up, I evaded the issue and told myself he was too young to understand. I thought there would be plenty of time. It wasn't as if Dave had shown any interest in my possible pregnancy, anyway. But then you landed in town with the news that Dave was dead and I...I couldn't stand it. I knew I had to level with Josh. I finally talked with him a few days ago."

"How did he take the news?"

"He was stunned. No. *Horrified* would probably be a better word. Then, once the disbelief subsided, he was angry—I mean, really angry with me." She swallowed hard and reached into the cupboard for a glass. "Can't say as I blame him. I was mad that my mom lied about who my father was, but at least I had the chance to meet him and decide for myself how much I wanted John Cawthorne in my life. Josh has no options. I took them away from him." She flipped on the tap, filled her glass and drank to quench the dryness at the back of her throat.

"You did what you thought was best." Luke's voice was low, a balm.

"Yeah, and it blew up in my face." She lifted her glass. "You want some?"

"Naw, I'm fine." Getting to his feet, he went to her

and wrapped solid arms around her torso. "You can't beat yourself up for this."

"Oh, no?" Turning to gaze up at him, she saw the sweet seduction in his eyes, heard his sharp intake of breath as her breasts brushed against his shirt.

"Nope." His gaze slid down her face. "Besides, we have other problems."

"Do we?"

"Mmm." His arms tightened, holding her close, and she was pulled snugly to him, her breasts flattening against his chest, her hips pressed intimately to his. Gazing into her eyes, he lowered his head to hers. "This," he said, his breath warm against her face, "is a much bigger issue." His mouth slanted over hers and her blood turned to fire.

So this was the way it would be with him, she realized. Each and every time they touched, passion would ignite. Her arms wound around his neck and he lifted her off her feet. When he started for the stairs, common sense ruled. "We can't," she whispered, struggling to get down. "Not with Josh here."

Luke's eyes were the color of midnight, but instead of releasing her, he carried her outside, across the moon-washed lawn and up the stairs to the carriage house. "If he wakes up, we'll know," he assured her as he kicked open the door and crossed the hardwood floor to the bedroom. He paused long enough to flip the lock behind him, then laid her on the bed and kissed her as if he would never stop.

"So I thought we could have lunch and catch up," Bliss suggested a few days later. Katie, working at the office, balanced the receiver between her shoulder and ear.

Bliss, home from her short honeymoon, was calling from her cell phone and still sounding breathlessly in love. She and Mason had just gotten back to Oregon and were living at Cawthorne Acres, the ranch John Cawthorne had called his own until his marriage to Brynnie. Brynnie had insisted he give up ranching for fear of his having another heart attack and he'd reluctantly sold the ranch to Mason and Bliss. John and his wife would move into town as soon as Brynnie's house was remodeled to suit them. Meanwhile, Bliss and Mason shared the place with them.

"Sounds great." Katie stretched the cord of her phone around the computer monitor glowing on her desk and reached into a drawer for her pen. Her cubicle, or "office," as it was sometimes referred to, was situated in the middle of a huge room that was divided by soundproof barriers that didn't quite do the job. The conversation of other reporters, the clacking of computer keys, even noise from the street filtered through the maze of desks.

"Let's meet at Claudia's at one and I'll call Tiffany to see if she can join us."

"I'll be there," Katie promised, making a note to herself. She had an interview with Octavia Nesbitt, Tiffany's grandmother and president of the local garden club, this morning; then she wanted to talk with the police department and Jarrod about the Isaac Wells case.

Each day, she'd riffled eagerly through her mail, hoping for another missive from the mystery person, but there had been nothing at work or at home. She'd even checked her mailbox at the cottage, on the off chance that the mail hadn't been forwarded. No such luck.

"Face it, Kinkaid," she grumbled to herself, "you've been led down the garden path." Lately, it seemed, her life had been bedlam. The move had been exhausting, but finally, most of her possessions seemed to have found new places of their own. Josh's ankle was fine and he was back at soccer practice, but the car was still a problem; she'd gone to the local dealer and hadn't been able to locate a used vehicle that suited her. Nor did there seem to be the perfect car in the "Autos for Sale" part of the classified advertisements in the paper. She was still using her father's Jeep, and though John assured her that it was better she be driving the rig than it be gathering dust in the garage, she wasn't comfortable without her own set of wheels. Her convertible, if not all that reliable, had been an old friend. She punched out Jarrod's number with the eraser end of her pencil and prayed that she wouldn't have to leave a message if he was out.

Her oldest half brother had the decency to answer on the fourth ring.

"Hello?" His voice was curt, all business.

"It's me," she said. "I just wanted to thank you for helping with the move."

"No problem. And I will fix the screen door at the cottage. I promise."

"Good. I'll hold you to it. Now, what's new with the Isaac Wells case?"

"Ah, the real reason you called."

She grinned. "You always could read me like a book."

"Why don't you tell me about Mr. Wells, Katie. You're the one getting the letters."

"Letter. Singular. No more."

"Good. You know I don't like you involved in that

mess," he admitted, not for the first time. "Stick with writing about the schools, and recipes and obituaries before your name is in one."

"Very funny."

"I'm serious, Katie. You know the police have been talking to Ray Dean and he's bad news."

Katie knew everything there was to know about Ray Dean, his estranged wife and their two sons. Ray was a criminal, convicted of theft, burglary and suspected of being involved in other crimes that had never been solved. But he'd never been caught with a weapon or had anything to do with violent crimes. Nothing like kidnapping. Or murder.

"Just tell me you'll keep me posted," Katie nagged and heard her brother swear under his breath.

"I don't know what good will come of it."

"Only give my career the biggest shot in the arm of its life."

"Didn't I stupidly promise that if I find out anything," he said reluctantly, "I'd let you know?"

"I believe the exact words were that you'd give me 'an exclusive.'"

"You got it."

"Great," she said without a lot of enthusiasm, as time was ticking by and she was afraid this case might just end up as an unsolved mystery.

For the next few minutes they talked about the twins, their mother and Josh, then hung up. Grabbing her recorder, notepad, and purse, she flew out the door to where her father's Jeep was parked. The rig was hot, having sat in the sun all day, and Katie made a mental note to find another vehicle. She hated being obligated to anyone, even the man who had sired her.

Katie spent the next two hours interviewing Octavia

Nesbitt. With honey-gold-colored hair that was teased to stand away from her small head, oversize glasses, and a big, toothy smile, Octavia was one of Bittersweet's leading citizens. In three-inch heels she was barely over five feet and Katie had never known her not to be dressed as if she were going to the opening of a Broadway play. At eighty, Octavia had the energy of a thirty-year-old, and she wasn't satisfied until she'd walked Katie through her house—the old Reed estate—and had given her a guided tour of her rose garden and greenhouse.

They drank tea during the interview and after the cups were drained, Octavia read the tea leaves that had settled in the bottom of Katie's porcelain cup.

"You're involved in an affair of the heart," she observed, lifting a penciled eyebrow above the top of her thick glasses. "And this man is very special to you."

Katie blushed to the roots of her hair. "Anything else?"

"Mmm." Her brow knitted and her lips puckered. "I can't make it out, but I'd say there was danger in your future."

Katie's heart nearly stopped, then she shook her head as she reminded herself she didn't believe in such nonsense as reading tea leaves, or palms or any other spiritual mumbo-jumbo. Still, the odd sensation stuck with her as, after the extended interview, she explained that she was meeting her half sisters for lunch and Octavia told her to say hello to Tiffany. "Darling girl," she said. "The apple of my eye, and her children...so dear. But her mother is such a proud woman—wouldn't take any help from me when she was raising Tiffany. Insisted on doing it on her own. Kind of a martyr, if you ask me. But...eventually Tiffany will get her trust fund and Rose will just have to accept it. Well, enough of that…'' Her eyes twinkled behind her glasses. ''I can't tell you how pleased I am that she's marrying J.D.''

''She's happy, I think.''

''As well she should be.'' Octavia clapped her be-ringed hands and looked skyward. ''She deserves it. Now—'' her owlish eyes fell on Katie again as they walked to the Jeep ''—you be careful.'' She touched Katie lightly on the arm. ''Whatever it is you're getting yourself into, it's perilous.''

''I'll be fine,'' Katie assured her, but left with an uneasy, nagging sensation that wouldn't let go of her. So what if the older woman saw danger in the bottom of a porcelain cup? ''There's nothing to it,'' she told herself as she drove through the lazy streets of Bittersweet. ''Nothing.'' Reading tea leaves was just the older woman's way of passing time.

But she saw that you were involved with Luke.

''Lucky guess,'' Katie assured herself as she wheeled into the restaurant parking lot. She locked the car and half jogged to the front door of the little cottage that had been converted into an eatery. Filled with antiques, books and ferns, Claudia's was known for its special soup of the day and cozy, intimate atmosphere.

Tiffany and Bliss were already in a corner booth, chatting as if they'd been friends forever instead of wary siblings who'd only recently discovered that they were related. Over the course of the summer, Tiffany had warmed to Bliss and the animosity that she originally had felt toward John Cawthorne's only ''legitimate'' daughter had all but disappeared. Slowly, the walls holding them apart were crumbling.

''We had a fabulous time,'' Bliss was saying as Katie slid into the booth and sat next to Tiffany. ''I've been to Hawaii before, but Mason hadn't and—'' she sighed dreamily, her honeymoon still fresh in her mind ''—it was different, being there with someone you love. We want to go back there when we can spend more time. Hi, Katie.''

''Sorry I'm late.''

''Not a problem. I took a chance and ordered you an iced tea.''

''Thanks. So what were you talking about? Your honeymoon, right?''

Tiffany winked at Katie. ''I'm trying to get all the details from her.''

''Come on, spill 'em,'' Katie encouraged. ''I hear Hawaii is way beyond romantic.''

Bliss's cheeks turned a soft rosy hue. ''It is. We snorkeled and rented a catamaran, and took long walks along the beach. Maui was breathtaking. You're in a mountain jungle one minute and in a resort on the beach the next.''

''I'd love to go there,'' Tiffany said wistfully.

''Why don't you?'' Bliss reached into her purse and came up with a handful of brochures and slapped them onto the table. ''Take it from me, it's the perfect place for a honeymoon.''

''With Stephen and Christina?'' Tiffany thumbed through a brochure with a picture of a couple lying on the sand beneath a palm tree and staring at an aquamarine surf.

''No way. They can stay with me,'' Katie offered, then turned to Bliss. ''You didn't take Dee Dee, did you?''

''Not this time, but we plan to the next.''

''See. You can do the same,'' Katie told Tiffany as a waitress dressed in khaki slacks and a black T-shirt served them the iced tea. "Oh, jeez, I haven't figured out what I want," Katie said, opening her menu while her half sisters ordered.

She settled on a French-dip sandwich, while Bliss ordered a Caesar salad and Tiffany chose a fruit plate and a bowl of soup. Bliss insisted Tiffany keep the information on Hawaii and Tiffany slipped the pamphlets into her purse. Conversation never lagged. Lunch was served and they ate and caught up, laughed and talked about everything and nothing. Katie felt a warm glow inside; as much as she'd loved her half brothers growing up, she'd always wanted and needed the intimacy only a sister could inspire.

"Your grandmother says hi," Katie said to Tiffany, explaining about her interview with Octavia. "She's an interesting woman."

"Beyond interesting," Tiffany observed. "Did she give you a cup of tea, then read your fortune?"

"Yep." Katie grinned. "How'd you know?"

"She's done it to me for years. Let me guess.... She saw romance in your future, right?"

"Yeah."

"What else?"

Katie thought of Octavia's concerns about danger, then decided to dismiss them. It was all nonsense, anyway. "Not much."

Tiffany lifted a disbelieving brow. "That's odd. She usually comes up with two or three predictions. It's...her passion."

"Now there's a good topic," Bliss said. "Passion. Why don't you fill us in on this romance you've got going with Luke Gates."

Katie nearly choked on a swallow of iced tea. "I don't think I'd call it a 'romance.'"

"Looked that way to me. At the reception." Bliss nudged her plate aside. "Convenient that he lives in the carriage house."

"'Convenient'?" Katie repeated.

Folding her arms across her chest, Bliss pinned Katie with her incredibly blue eyes. "Isn't it?"

"I don't know if 'convenient' is the right word," Katie hedged, "but, yes, since you're asking, I like him. That's about it. There's really not much more to tell."

Tiffany rolled her large eyes. "Who are you trying to kid?" Sending Bliss a conspiring glance, she said, "Katie's been interested in him since he first came into town."

"I remember," Bliss agreed, showing off a dimple as she grinned at her youngest half sister. "You were certain he was involved in some kind of mystery."

"My imagination tends to lean toward the melodramatic."

"Part of your charm," Tiffany said.

"Then, at the reception, Mason and I both noticed that you were very interested in him and that the feeling is mutual," Bliss commented.

"He's an interesting man," Katie admitted, determined not to reveal too much, though it was out of character for her.

"That's it? Just 'interesting'?" Bliss asked with a laugh. "Come on, Katie."

"Okay, okay, a *little* more than 'just interesting.'"

"A lot more," Tiffany guessed. She dabbed at the corners of her mouth with her napkin. "And now you're living right next door. If you ask me it's pretty handy for a romance."

Katie's eyes narrowed. "If I didn't know better I'd

guess this was a plot set in motion by two kindhearted, if tunnel-visioned sisters who want me involved with a man." She pointed her finger at the half sister seated on the bench beside her. "If I remember correctly, *you* were the one who suggested I move into the main house."

Tiffany giggled. "Guilty as charged."

"Okay, okay," Bliss interjected. "Tiffany might have gotten you to move into the house, but *I* had nothing to do with it."

"Don't look at me." Tiffany shook her head. "I don't play Cupid. I just needed someone reliable to take care of the renters."

"I would hope so." Katie brushed the crumbs to one corner of her plate. "Because you've got your hands full as it is. When are you and J.D. going to get married?"

Tiffany's gaze slid away. "Soon."

"How soon?" Bliss insisted. "You said something about this fall."

Tiffany bit her lip and leaned over the table. "Our plans have changed a little. I think we might just drive to Reno and elope."

"No!" Bliss's eyes were round with dismay. "You have to have a wedding."

"I agree." Katie had always considered herself practical, but she had enough of a romantic side to think that there should be a little pomp and circumstance, white lace and satin, a wedding cake and flower girls.

"I did the big-wedding bit before. Remember, I was married to J.D.'s older brother. It's like we're already family."

Bliss was having none of her arguments. "But you

need a special day, an event, a rite of passage to start your life with J.D.''

Tiffany leaned back in the booth as the waitress brought their check. "We'll see."

"Really, Tiffany—"

"Look, Bliss, there are other complications, as well," Tiffany said, then, hearing the edge in her voice, she sighed.

"Oh." Bliss cleared her throat and Katie got the message.

"You mean you're not going to have the big church wedding because you don't want to deal with John."

"What would I do, have him give me away?" Tiffany asked, her lips pursing. "That's a joke, isn't it, since he never even claimed me for over thirty years."

Bliss's chin hardened. "Have Stephen give you away. Leave Dad out of it."

"Too late." Tiffany tossed her napkin on the table and reached for the check. "John's already asked to pay for the wedding, just like he's been my father all along." She lifted a shoulder and shook her head. "Maybe if this were my first wedding, maybe if there had been more time since I'd connected with him and accepted him as a father figure of some kind, if not a real dad, then maybe this would work. As it is, I think it's best if J.D. and I scoop up the kids and steal away in the night. When we return a few days later, we'll be married."

"There is an edge of romance to that," Katie allowed.

"Well, it's your decision." Bliss reached across the table and squeezed her half sister's fingers. "Don't mind me. I just learned at an early age to speak my mind, even when I know that discretion is the better part of valor and I should be shot for being so blunt.''

"Forgiven," Tiffany said with a wave of her hand.

"Good, then consider a big wedding."

"I'll think about it," Tiffany promised.

They split the check and Katie headed back to the office. For the next forty-five minutes she worked on her story about Octavia Nesbitt and decided not to mention the tea leaves.

She checked her E-mail and regular correspondence, hoping that someone had answered her "For Rent" advertisement for the house she and Josh had called home for over a decade, or, on the off chance that Isaac Wells had tried to reach her again. No such luck.

By four o'clock, she'd met the following day's deadlines, endured a late staff meeting and left work. Josh was at soccer practice and another mother had offered to drive him home, so Katie had an hour or so alone in the house, an hour she could use to clean and put away odds and ends.

She'd introduced herself to all of her tenants and was particularly fond of Roberta Ellingsworth, known as Ellie, an older woman who lived in a unit downstairs. On the second day Katie had been in the house, Ellie had brought her a home-baked pie and a cluster of asters, then promptly offered to watch Josh whenever Katie needed a hand. All in all, living in the old Victorian manor was beginning to feel like home.

Except for the fact that Luke lived nearby. Being this close to him was unnerving. And exciting. To her disconcertment she found herself looking out the window, watching his comings and goings, waving as he passed by a back window and dreaming of making love to him.

Don't trust him, she told herself when she found herself fantasizing about him again. *You barely know him. He could have a dozen women in a dozen different towns.*

Chapter Ten

"That does it," Ralph Sorenson said, his voice shaking with emotion. "Loretta and I will be on the next flight to Oregon. I've got to hand it to you, Luke. I didn't have much faith in you when you took off, didn't think you'd really put your heart and soul into finding Dave's son, but you did it. And don't think I won't remember that I said I'd pay you."

"I think you should slow down a minute," Luke interjected, trying to tamp down the older man's enthusiasm. "I said that Katie Kinkaid told me that Dave was Josh's father. She told her son as well, but I think you should hold off coming out here until the dust settles."

"Hold off? For the love of Pete, why?"

"To give everyone time to adjust."

"Like hell, boy. I'm seventy years old. It's up to the Man Upstairs how much longer I'll be walkin' on this planet and I don't see any reason to slow down. By next month I could be six feet under.''

Luke doubted it. Ralph, though no longer a young man, was as spry and healthy as most men ten years younger.

''Why don't you just give me the boy's phone number and I'll call him up?''

''Wait a second.'' Luke's head began to pound. ''How about the other way around? I'll have Katie and Josh, if he's up to it—call you.''

''Why wouldn't he be up to it?'' Ralph demanded.

''He's ten, for God's sake. Give him a break, would ya?''

''I guess you've got a point.''

''Good.'' Luke wasn't convinced that the old man was actually listening to reason, but he had no other options. ''I'll let you know how this all turns out.''

''Do. Loretta and I... Well, we don't get along much. Been separated for years. When Dave died we nearly divorced, but we're hangin' on by a thread right now, Luke, and that thread is Dave's son.''

''I'll call.'' Guilt squeezed through Luke's innards as he replaced the phone. He'd have to talk to Katie again and this time he couldn't be distracted as he seemed to forever be whenever she was near. Just the thought of her brought a tightness to his groin and a longing that he didn't want to scrutinize too closely.

''You're a fool, Gates,'' he muttered and grabbed his hat from a hook near the front door. The excavating foreman was scheduled to meet him at the ranch to discuss the addition to the house, and he had just enough time to get there.

He'd deal with Katie, Josh, and Ralph later.

* * *

"Any more information on the Isaac Wells story?" Pat Johnson, Katie's editor, asked as he paused at her cubicle and leaned against the edge of her desk. He was all of five feet six inches, but he carried himself as if he were a foot taller. With a shock of white hair, round eyeglasses and small features drawn close together, he was far from Hollywood handsome, but his sharp mind, bright eyes, and quick wit compensated for his lack of pure physical beauty. Everyone loved him. Including Katie.

"I wish," she said, but shook her head. "I've badgered the police and my brother and a few of Isaac's associates, all to no end. I've even tried contacting whoever sent me the letter through the personal ads in the *Review,* as well as the local paper in California where the last letter was postmarked. So far, nada."

"Too bad." Pat removed his glasses and wiped them clean with a handkerchief from his pocket. "I thought it would be this year's big story."

"Me, too." She offered him a smile. "At least I'd hoped."

"Well, something could still break." He slipped his spectacles back onto his nose and patted the edge of her cubicle's thin walls before moving on.

No one wanted the story more than Katie. Despite the problems and distractions in her life—a new mishmash of a family of half sisters and brothers-in-law, Josh's attitude toward her, Dave's death, and her fascination with Luke Gates—she was still anxious to solve the Isaac Wells mystery and get the byline.

She forced herself to finish an article on the change in the school district's curriculum, then accessed the Internet and, through cyberspace, found the obituary on David Sorenson of Dallas, Texas. So it was true. Her shoulders sagged a bit. She hadn't doubted Luke's word, but seeing Dave's short life in an even shorter article was strangely sad.

"Great," she muttered under her breath. It was bad enough that she'd been forced to tell Josh about his father's death, but now she was trying to get him to call his newfound grandparents and her negotiations with her son on the subject weren't going well. Josh was interested, but wary. Tonight, if he didn't do the deed himself, Katie would call them. She had to. The Sorensons deserved to know their grandson.

She was grateful for the end of the day. At home, she started dinner and turned on the radio. Josh had a ride home from soccer practice, so she threw together potato salad and baked pieces of chicken in herbs. She wasn't used to the thermostat in the new oven, so she was doubly careful, and as she unpacked what seemed to be an endless number of boxes, she kept an eye on her meal.

The phone jangled just as Bliss, with Mason's daughter, Dee Dee, pulled into the drive. "Hello?" Katie answered, waving Bliss and the girl inside. Holding the phone to her ear with one hand, she kicked open the screen door.

"Ms. Kinkaid?" a gravelly voice asked.

"Speaking."

"This is Ralph Sorenson."

Her heart dropped to the floor and she leaned against the cupboards for support. As much as she'd tried to bolster her own confidence and had told herself that she wanted to talk to Dave's parents, now that she was down to it, she was apprehensive. She felt as if all the blood had drained from her body in that one instant.

"Hello," she said, trying to sound calm when she knew that her life was about to shred.

"I don't know how to say this but straight out. So here goes. I know about the boy. That he's David's."

"I see," she replied tonelessly as Bliss and Dee Dee rushed into the room.

"This is very awkward for me."

"Me, too," Katie said and met the worry in Bliss's eyes. "I did try to call you once, but when I didn't get through I'd hoped I could call another time, when Josh was home...."

"Glad to hear it." He sounded appeased and she was relieved. "Difficult as all this is, I have to tell you that I'm pleased to know that I have a grandson, especially now that Dave's gone. It's comforting to know that a piece of him lives on."

"Of course," she replied, her eyes and nose burning.

"But I can't imagine why you chose to hide him from Dave for ten years. It would have done my boy some good to know that he had a son of his own."

"I didn't mean to hide—"

"I guess it don't matter now that Dave's gone—" The old man's voice cracked and Katie crumpled inside.

"I did try to tell him, before he left Oregon," she said, shaking her head at the unspoken, worried questions forming in Bliss's eyes. "He never called or came back to find out."

"So now it's his fault?" The man's voice rose an octave and Katie could almost feel his agitation.

"That's not what I meant."

"I should hope not, missy, because our boy's gone. Gone. It nearly killed Loretta—" His voice cracked again and Katie wanted to drop off the face of the earth.

"Look, I'm sorry about Dave. Really. He was a good person."

"But not good enough for you to contact and tell him about his son."

"That was probably a mistake," she allowed.

"Amen to that one."

"But I was young and scared—"

"Maybe we should be running along," Bliss said as she caught a glimmer of the conversation.

"No, it's fine. Please. Stay," Katie mouthed, placing her hand over the mouthpiece of the receiver.

"Okay. We'll be outside." Without another word, Bliss shepherded Dee Dee outside, found the basketball on the back porch and challenged her stepdaughter to a game of horse.

"I know why you were scared," Ralph Sorenson said. "Can't say as I blame you, but the here and now of it is that Loretta and I have a grandson—the only one we'll ever have—and we want to meet him."

"Of course you do," she said, trying to stay calm. "I think that it would be a good idea." That was stretching the truth a bit, but she couldn't deny Josh the right to see his grandparents, or vice versa.

"Then let's do it. The sooner the better."

She'd forgotten how pushy Ralph Sorenson had been, how Dave had complained of an overbearing father. "Listen, Mr. Sorenson, I said I was sorry and I am. I probably handled this all wrong from the get-go, but the most important person in this situation is Josh. I just want to make sure that he's strong enough to handle this. I think he is. And certainly, very soon, he's gonna want to meet you."

There was another pause, then a sigh. "All right, Ms. Kinkaid. You do what you think is best, but remember, Mrs. Sorenson and I are here waiting, dying to meet Dave's boy."

"I know. I'll let you know when Josh is ready to meet you. Then, of course, I'd love you to visit. You can even stay here at the house, if you want."

"Well...that's very kind." The anger in his voice faded away and she thought she heard him sniff, then blow his nose, as if he were overcome with emotion. Her own throat was thick, her hands sweating over the receiver. But she wouldn't break down, wouldn't allow herself the luxury. It seemed that all she ever did anymore was cry, and she hated it.

"Tell Luke that we spoke and assure him that he'll get paid, just as promised."

"I will," she said, wondering at the turn of the conversation.

"I know he told me not to call, that he'd set it up, but... Oh, hell, the missus and I, we just couldn't wait for him."

"'Wait for him'?" she repeated uneasily.

"You'll let us know when we can visit?"

"Of course." She hung up, mystified. Why was Ralph Sorenson talking about paying Luke for something now? A hint of an idea pricked her mind, but she didn't want to think about it, couldn't let that little niggle of horrid doubt burrow into her brain.

Bliss, as if sensing the conversation was over, lost her game to Dee Dee, then, while Katie was rummaging in the refrigerator for a pitcher of lemonade, returned to the kitchen. Both mother and stepdaughter were sweating, their faces beet-red, their eyes bright.

"I won!" Dee Dee announced.

"Fair and square," Bliss agreed. "But wait until next time. Then we'll see who's the champ of the court."

"I am, I am!" Dee Dee cried excitedly. She turned big eyes toward Katie. "I'm gonna be a big sister!"

"A what?" Katie nearly dropped the pitcher of lemonade. She turned and saw a blush creep up Bliss's neck.

"That's right," Bliss admitted, her eyes shining with her secret. "I'm pregnant!"

Katie left the pitcher on the counter and hugged her half sister fiercely. "I'm so happy for you and Mason! When is the baby due?"

"A long time off," Bliss admitted. "I'm really not sure, but in the spring sometime. I'll find out when I go to the doctor."

"A baby!" Tears threatened Katie's eyes all over again. From the edge of her vision she saw Dee Dee gazing up at them both. "Oh, Dee Dee, how lucky you are," Katie said. "I was never a big sister, always the youngest."

"Not me." Dee Dee's smile was back in place immediately.

"Let's have a toast," Katie insisted. She poured them each a healthy glass, sliced lemons and tossed them into the liquid, added a couple of plump strawberries for good measure, then plopped ice cubes into the drinks. "Here." She handed them each a glass and touched the rim of hers to Bliss's. "To the baby and his big sister."

"No way. It's gonna be a girl," Dee Dee insisted.

"Okay. To the baby and *her* big sister," Katie amended.

"What? Nothing for the mother?" Bliss stuck out her lower lip until she couldn't help giggling.

"You get the best part. You get to be a mother," Katie said, "and change diapers, get no sleep, worry yourself silly and...I'm only kidding. It's the most wonderful feeling in the world."

"I'm already a mother," Bliss said, cocking her head toward Dee Dee. "Well, kind of."

The girl nodded enthusiastically and Katie was amazed at how quickly Mason's daughter had taken to Bliss. But then, who wouldn't? Bliss Lafferty was special. "Well, listen, I'm going to throw you the biggest, most lavish baby shower Bittersweet has ever seen!" She pointed a finger at Dee Dee's small nose. "You can help me give it—you and Aunt Tiffany."

"Can I really?"

"Really and truly." Katie took a long swallow from her glass. "This is the best news I've had in weeks."

"Speaking of which," Bliss asked as Dee Dee discovered Blue, and dog and girl dashed out the back door. "Who was on the telephone?"

"Oh. That." Katie's good mood instantly shattered. "That was Ralph Sorenson."

"Who?" Bliss's features pulled together as she tried to remember the name and came up blank.

"Dave Sorenson's father. You wouldn't know him, they lived here only a little while."

"Sorenson? Isn't that the guy who owned the place Luke Gates bought? I drew those blueprints for him and it seems like I remember the name."

"Small world, isn't it? Anyway, Dave was Josh's father. I just found out a week or so ago that...that Dave's gone.... I mean, he's, uh, dead." Her heart

squeezed again at the horrid thought. "Died in a helicopter crash a few months back."

"*What?*" Bliss eyed Katie as if she'd just sprouted
horns. "Wait a minute. Slow down and start over.
From the beginning."

Fighting a losing battle with tears, Katie obliged and
as she told her story, she felt as if a great weight, a
burden, was slowly being lifted from her shoulders. For
the first time in her life she understood the depth of a
sister's love, the special bond that exists between sisters in times of joy or sorrow. Who else would listen
to her and empathize when she poured out her heart
and unburdened her soul?

Bliss listened and chewed on her lip. "Unbeliev-
able," she said when Katie had finished. "What're you
going to do?"

"Talk to Josh and try to get him to accept Dave's
family. I was afraid that they might want custody or
something, but I don't think so. They just want to know
their grandson."

"Well, if there's anything Mason or I can do, just
call and let us know."

"I will. But I think we're okay, as long as Josh quits
blaming me for not telling him the truth. This is my
problem. I can handle it." The words sounded much
stronger than she felt, but she and Josh had weathered
storms before; they'd get through this. "You know the
old saying—something about that which doesn't kill us
makes us stronger."

"Words to live by," Bliss murmured and Katie
changed the subject.

"Let's get back to the baby," she said, sliding into
a chair at the table. "I think we should have the shower
about a month before the blessed event...." She threw

herself into discussing the joyful topic at hand and turned her thoughts away from Ralph Sorenson and his interest in Josh right now. There was a chance that Josh knowing his paternal grandparents would be a blessing, but there was also the risk that it would turn into a disaster; that the Sorensons would become overbearing and insist upon being an integral part of his life. Katie told herself not to borrow trouble and was already mentally organizing the baby shower when the phone rang.

"I'd better get it," she said to Bliss. "It could be Josh. This is his first day back at soccer practice." She snagged the phone on the third ring and silently prayed that the caller wasn't Ralph Sorenson again. "Hello?"

"I'm calling about the ad you ran in the paper."

Her heart nearly leaped from her chest. For a second she'd wondered if the male voice on the other end of the line belonged to Isaac Wells.

"Yeah, I'm looking for a place to rent, so can you tell me more about the house?"

"Oh." Her excitement dropped. But she couldn't be disappointed, because she needed to rent her cottage. She gave the man a quick description of the house and grounds, quoted him the rent and terms, then asked his name.

"Ben Francis. I'm married, but me and the wife don't have any kids yet. No pets, neither. If it's not too much trouble, I'd like to see the place as soon as possible."

"I could meet you there at—" She checked the clock over the stove, mentally calculated when Josh would be home, and said, "Around seven tonight if that works for you."

There was a pause and for a reason she couldn't

name, Katie felt a moment of doubt, had the odd sensation that something wasn't quite right.

"That would be good," he finally agreed just as the timer on the oven dinged loudly and Bliss, grabbing a pot holder lying on the counter, took over the duty of removing the steaming pan of savory chicken.

"Let me give you the address," Katie offered, ready to rattle it off.

"No need. Got it this afternoon, from the sign on the front lawn."

She hesitated. "But I thought you got the information from the paper." Was it her always-overactive imagination or was something wrong here?

There was a beat of silence. "I did. Once I saw the sign, I checked out the ads in the *Review* to find out how much the rent was. Then I called you."

"Oh." Why the devil was she always so suspicious? "All right, Mr. Francis—"

"Ben."

"Ben. I'll see you there."

She hung up slowly and read the questions in her half sister's eyes. "Someone who wants to rent the old place," she said thoughtfully.

"Someone you know?"

She shook her head.

"Ever heard of him before?"

"No, but before I hand over the keys, I'll check his references."

"Do that," Bliss advised as she drew in a deep breath of fragrant steam escaping from the hot pan. "This—" she pointed at the pieces of chicken "—smells like heaven."

"Does it?" Katie was pleased. "One of Mom's old recipes. I'm really not much of a cook." She winked at Dee Dee, who'd entered the kitchen, followed by Blue. "Don't tell Josh. He hasn't figured it out yet."

Dee Dee giggled and Blue, smelling the food, whined near the counter.

"Ever hopeful," Katie observed.

Bliss drained her glass and scraped her chair back as a station wagon filled with rowdy boys pulled into the driveway. Blue barked excitedly, clamoring to be let outside as Josh climbed out of the fold-down third seat and waved to his teammates. His face was flushed, his hair matted with sweat, but he wasn't limping.

"I think we'd better be taking off," Bliss said. "Mason will be home soon and, unlike you, Ms. Kinkaid, I don't have dinner ready. I think it'll be take-out Chinese."

Dee Dee wrinkled her nose.

"Oh, come on," Bliss said, giving the girl's slim shoulders a hug as Josh shouldered open the door and dropped his soccer bag in the middle of the floor. "I bet you'll like the fried shrimp."

"You could stay," Katie offered.

"I'll take a rain check. We just wanted to stop by and give you the good news."

"Congratulations." They hugged and Katie's heart swelled. When she'd first learned she had two half sisters, she'd been wary, not certain of her feelings, especially since Bliss had been pampered and preened—John Cawthorne's "princess." But, being ever pragmatic, Katie had decided to make the best of the situation and from the minute she'd pushed herself into Bliss's life, insisting that both she and Tiffany be accepted, she hadn't regretted it for a minute. Today was proof positive that a loving family—no matter how tattered and shredded and pulled apart—was the greatest gift in life.

Luke eyed the pile of dry earth that had been scraped away from the building site. Kicking at a dirt clod, he examined the dig and was satisfied with the progress. The excavation would be finished in two days; the setting of forms for the concrete foundation that would link the existing buildings was scheduled thereafter, and by the end of next week the framing crew would be at work. He wanted everything done immediately, of course, but knew better.

As he squared his hat on his head and walked to the stables, he reminded himself that patience was a virtue—one that had eluded him for most of his life. He reached through the slats of the fence and twisted on the faucet for the water trough. Clear water gushed through ancient pipes and spilled into the metal drum, splashing noisily. Several mares lifted their heads at the sound. A light bay with black ears nickered in his direction.

"Hello to you, too, Trudy," he said and felt a sense of belonging, of finally having a place in the world he could call home.

It was just a damned shame that he'd be doing it alone. For the first time since his divorce from Celia, he experienced a need to be connected, to be a part of something bigger than just himself. It was an odd sensation, really—one he'd hoped he would avoid for the rest of his life and that, he suspected, had more than a little to do with Katie Kinkaid. That mite of a woman had bored herself under his skin and he found himself thinking about her far too much.

"So stop it," he ordered. She was just a woman.

Angry with himself, he twisted off the faucet, and saw that the stock seemed settled down. The foals cavorted, running and bucking and nipping at each other while their more sedate dams, ears flicking at each sound, tails forever switching at flies, grazed and generally ignored the antics of their spindly-legged offspring.

It was a peaceful existence right now, though an influx of guests, ranch hands, and house staff would change that sense of tranquillity in the months to come. But then money was money, and somehow this place had to support itself.

"Good night, ladies," he said, but the horses didn't pay any attention. "See y'all tomorrow."

Shoving his rawhide gloves into the back pocket of his jeans, he strode to his pickup and climbed into the cab. Though the windows had been left down, the interior was sweltering. A confused horsefly buzzed angrily between the dash and windshield before finally stumbling upon the open window.

"Good riddance." Luke ground the ignition, jammed the rig into gear and headed for town. Dust and exhaust billowed in his wake and he thought of Katie. Damn, but he'd love to get her into his bed again. He envisioned her dark red hair, spread around a face that was flushed with desire, imagined kissing the freckles on the bridge of her nose, saw vividly in his mind's eye her swift intake of breath and seductively parted lips as he thrust deep inside her and began making slow, sensuous love.

"Cut it out," he growled. At the end of the lane he noticed that his crotch was suddenly uncomfortable, his arousal stiff, and he wondered if he'd spend the rest of his life fantasizing about that sharp-tongued-but-beautiful woman. He looked into the rearview mirror, saw his own eyes and then barked out a humorless laugh. If he didn't know better, he'd think he was in love.

Yeah, and you sold her and her boy out for money. Some lover you turned out to be!

Maybe it was time to tell her the truth. His fingers tightened over the steering wheel. She might hate him for the rest of her natural life, but, be that as it may, it was a risk he had to take.

Yep, he'd face her, tell her the truth and the devil take the consequences.

"I should be back in about an hour," Katie told Josh, who was grumbling about having to do the dishes. "Maybe sooner. I'm going to the old house to try and rent it." He didn't respond and she touched him lightly on the shoulder. "You can come with me if you want."

"Naw." He shook his head.

"Okay. Ellie—Mrs. Ellingsworth—downstairs, is home and she said she'd look in on you if you'd like."

"I'll be okay."

"'Course you will." Katie rumpled his hair, which was still wet from the shower he'd taken before they'd sat down to dinner. For the first time in a week he'd actually talked to her, told her about soccer practice and a new kid he'd met at school, then even brought up Dave, asking a few questions about him. Eventually she'd offered Josh the opportunity of meeting his paternal grandparents. Josh was interested, but wary. They were strangers to him, but he'd agreed to meet them. Soon. *One step at a time,* she reminded herself, since Josh had been forced to face a truckload of issues this past couple of weeks.

Placing a rental agreement and application into a side pocket of her purse, she headed outside just as Blue, who had been lying docilely on the porch, jumped up and made a racket, startling the blue jays that had collected on the eaves. The birds squawked and fluttered off.

Luke's truck rolled into the drive and Katie's heartbeat began to notch up a bit. She set her jaw and marched over to the pickup as he, in worn jeans and a frayed shirt that he hadn't bothered to button, swung out of the cab.

"Ms. Kinkaid," he drawled, his sexy-as-all-get-out crooked grin growing from one side of his square jaw to the other. "You look like you're about to spit nails."

"That would be a good way to describe it," she agreed, throwing out a hip as Blue, finished with his alarm barking, began sniffing the grill and running boards of Luke's truck.

"At me?" He feigned innocence.

"You'd be a primary target, yes."

"Is there a reason?" But his eyes belied him and she saw in their blue depths a hint of worry.

"Ralph Sorenson called today."

His smile fell away from his face.

"He wanted to come out and meet Josh, and during the course of our conversation—which could only be described as tense, at best—he let it be known that he's grateful to you for finding his grandson and that you'll be paid for your trouble."

Every muscle in his body seemed to tighten and his face, so congenial minutes before, took on the expression of a harsh, unbending cowboy. "You want an explanation."

"Not just an explanation, but a damned good one,"

she clarified, her fingers curling around the strap of her purse.

Luke glanced at the house. "Maybe we'd better go inside."

"So Josh can hear this? He doesn't much like you, to begin with. I think this would only make things worse."

"Fair enough." He rested his buttocks against the fender of his pickup, folded his arms over his chest and stared so hard at her she nearly looked away. But she didn't. She was too hurt. Too upset. And too damned mad.

"When Ralph and I made the deal on the ranch, he sweetened the pot a tad."

She was shaking inside. She didn't want to hear his confession, but wouldn't have missed it for the world. This was a man she had trusted, believed in, made love with. She'd given him her heart though she'd die before admitting it. And he'd betrayed her. Used her. Played her for a fool. Well, she wasn't having any more of it. "How did he 'sweeten the pot'?"

"A few more dollars if I found out whether or not his son had fathered a child."

She'd suspected it, of course; been darned-near sure that this was the explanation she would eventually hear after her talk with Ralph Sorenson, but the bald facts, the depth of the deception that went into the lie, hit her hard, like a blow to the stomach. "I hope it was worth it," she said through lips that barely moved. Inside she was shaking, quivering with a rage that burned bright in her soul.

"Katie—" He reached for her, but she ducked away, holding up her hands as she backed up a step and shook her head.

"Enough already."

"Just listen."

"I think I've heard enough to last me a lifetime, Gates." She turned on her heel and marched to her father's Jeep.

"If you would let me explain—"

"What?" Again she turned. "How you lied to me? Deceived me? Seduced me? *Used* me and my son for your personal gain? Is that what you want me to listen to? Well, forget it. It's over, Luke." She felt a tiny shaft of sadness. "It really was over before it began." She yanked open the door of her father's rig. "The only thing you need to remember is that the rent's due on the first." She slid into the hot interior and told herself it was better this way. Pumping the gas and turning on the ignition, she was reminded that she'd done just fine without Luke Gates in her life before; she could darned well do it again. She didn't need anyone but Josh.

She reversed into the street, her eyes trained on the rearview mirror, then she threw the Jeep into first and roared away from Luke Gates. This time it would be forever.

Chapter Eleven

Katie pulled into the drive of her old cottage and felt a tug on her heartstrings. She climbed out of the Jeep and walked the familiar path to the back door, smiling as she saw Josh's old basketball hoop still hanging lopsidedly from the garage. The trail Blue had worn from the front of the house to the back was still visible, a crooked ribbon of dirt in the grass, and the vegetable garden, hardly more than a tangle of weeds, displayed a few pumpkins yet to ripen, a couple of oversize zucchini squash and three vines of tomatoes with fruit threatening to rot.

She'd hired a yard crew to clean up the place and repairmen were scheduled to fix the dripping bathroom faucet, sagging gutters and somehow shore up the garage. Jarrod had promised to mend the screen and the twins had volunteered to patch the nail holes in the walls and help her paint next weekend. By then, she hoped, she'd have a tenant to help pay for the upgrades as well as cover the payments on her mortgage.

She heard the crunch of tires on gravel before she saw the nose of a maroon minivan pull in behind the Jeep. A tall, lean man climbed from behind the wheel and she had the vague sensation she'd seen him somewhere before. His hair was a little long and shot with the same gray that silvered his short-cropped beard and mustache. Dark glasses covered his eyes and the bill of a baseball cap shaded his forehead.

"Are you Katie Kinkaid?"

"Yes."

He grinned and showed off white teeth that seemed in contrast to his disheveled appearance. He wore brown coveralls that had a few oil spills on them and a faded red rag, streaked with grease, poked out of his back pocket.

"Hi." His hand shot out and she noticed his fingernails were dirty as she offered her palm and felt the strength of his clasp. "Benjamin Francis." He nodded toward the house. "This is a nice place, looks like it might work for me and my wife. I work at a gas station in Ashland and she teaches preschool."

That explained his work clothes, though she wondered why there wasn't a logo for the station or his name embroidered on his coveralls. There was something about him that didn't ring true, made her ill at ease, though she couldn't explain why.

"Can you give me a look at the inside?"

"Sure." She told herself her case of nerves was unjustified and unlocked the back door. The heat of the day had settled into the house, leaving it sweltering. As she reached for the latch of the window, she said, "I have a few repairs that will be made before anyone moves in. I plan to paint, clean the carpets, wax the floors and—''

She heard him walk in behind her, close the door and turn the lock. ''Don't bother with the window.'' His voice was low, the command sharp.

She froze. ''But it's beastly in here and there's a good cross breeze—'' Turning, she found him leaning against the door, blocking her way out, and his expression had turned from friendly to hard and calculating.

''I have a confession to make,'' he said.

But she already understood as she mentally scraped off his beard and removed his hat. She swallowed back her fear as she recognized him. Her blood turned to ice.

''I'm not Ben Francis.''

''I know.''

His eyes glinted with a malevolent light. ''I don't believe we've met.''

''We didn't have to,'' she said, fighting a feeling damned close to terror climbing up her spine. ''I know who you are, Ray Dean. I just don't understand what you want from me.''

Luke yanked a clean pair of jeans onto his wet body. His muscles ached and his mind thundered with the accusations that Katie had thrown his way. She was right. Though he hadn't set out to use her, he hadn't been completely honest about his intentions.

''Damn.'' He snapped his jeans closed and silently cursed himself to as many levels of hell as there were, then added a few more for good measure.

If only Ralph had held his patience in check; if only he'd let Luke talk to Katie himself, explain what he'd been doing, try to let her understand his position. "And what good would that have done?" he wondered aloud. Angry at the world in general and specifically at himself, he jerked a towel from the rack and wiped away the condensation that fogged the mirror.

His reflection glowered back at him through the tiny droplets and he felt as if he were about to explode. He didn't bother combing his hair, just raked his fingers through the wet strands. Muttering under his breath about hardheaded women and the stupid men involved with them, he threw on a pair of old sneakers and a T-shirt that had seen better days, then buckled the worn leather strap of his watch.

He was outside and down the stairs before the door slammed shut behind him. Crossing the yard in swift, ground-eating strides that led him straight to the back door, he ignored the low rumble of a growl old Blue gave him.

Banging loudly with his fist, he waited until Katie's kid, eyeing him with unmasked suspicion, stood on the other side of the screen.

"Yeah?"

"Your mom here?" He knew better. The Jeep was still missing in action, but he thought he'd start at the beginning with Josh.

"Naw."

A wealth of information, this kid. "Do you know when she'll be back?"

Josh's eyes narrowed a fraction. "Yeah."

Luke's patience was wearing thin. "And when is that?"

"Later." He gave a lift of one shoulder. "She said about an hour."

Luke calculated that she'd already been gone twenty

minutes or so. He was going to ask Josh where she'd gone even if it wasn't any of his business, but at that moment Tiffany's car pulled into the drive. She was out of the car in a second. Her son, Stephen, who'd been in the passenger seat, was right behind her.

"Is Katie here?" Tiffany asked, climbing the steps.

"At the other house."

Bingo.

Josh opened the door for his aunt and cousin. "Someone's looking at it."

"Good. I need to talk to her, so Stephen and I'll wait if that's okay."

"Great. Where's Christina?"

"She wouldn't get up from her nap, so J.D. stayed with her." Tiffany rolled her palms to the air and winked at her nephew, as if they shared some private joke. "So, I guess it's just you and Stephen."

"Too bad," Stephen said sarcastically. He didn't seem inclined to hide the fact that he was sick to his back teeth of a sister who was little more than a toddler. "She's a pain."

"She is not. You're lucky to have her."

"Yeah, right."

"Stephen," Tiffany warned, about to say more when her eyes met Luke's. "You'd think that with all the years that separate them, they'd get along."

Josh grinned from ear to ear, eager, Luke supposed, to hang out with his older cousin. He opened the door and Stephen bolted through, followed by his mother, who took over the duties of keeping the screen door from shutting by using her body as a wedge. The boys were already up the stairs. Tiffany smiled at Luke. "Why don't you come in and keep me company while I wait? I'm sure Katie won't mind. That way you can tell me what's happening with the ranch you're fixing up.''

"You know about that?"

"Katie happened to mention that you were going to open it up to the public and take in guests sometime next spring.''

"That's the plan," Luke allowed as the boys, eating red licorice, ran through the kitchen again, grabbed a couple of skateboards that had been propped on the porch and took off toward the front of the house.

"Hey, wait. Where're you going?" Tiffany asked.

"Just to the store." Josh was already around the corner.

"Be careful and come right back!" Tiffany yelled, then, when Stephen threw her a look that silently told her he wasn't a baby anymore, she turned back to Luke. "Moms are really just pains in the neck for teenage boys.''

"Is that right?" He wouldn't know, of course, since he hadn't been raised by his own mother, but there was no reason to confide in her. "He'll grow out of it."

"I hope." She sighed and he saw a glimmer of the worry she'd carried with her as a single mother, a grieving widow. He decided it was a good thing that she'd linked up with J.D. She glanced around the kitchen. "It's starting to come together, isn't it?" Shaking her head, she admitted, "I never thought I'd move out of here. Never planned to remarry." A tiny smile played at the corners of her mouth. "I guess that just goes to show you that you never know what's around the next corner.''

"Nope."

"So—" she motioned to a chair "—just for the record, I think a working dude ranch is a great idea. Why don't you tell me all the details?''

"You sound like your sister."

"I'm not a reporter, but I'm interested. Besides, it looks like we both have a little time to kill before Katie gets back.'' She offered him a brilliant smile. "I feel kind of strange about sitting in *her* house waiting for her, but knowing Katie, she wouldn't want it any other way.''

She heated coffee on the stove as Luke explained his plans. He was hesitant at first, didn't know if he wanted his entire life exposed to a woman he barely knew, but Tiffany, like her dynamo of a half sister, was easy to talk to. The difference was that this woman was calm and chuckled softly as she cradled her cup in her hands. Katie, on the other hand, was a bundle of energy and would have dominated the conversation while doing a dozen other things.

Tiffany asked questions, made a few jokes, and generally kept the conversation rolling as the minutes ticked by. The boys returned, the wheels of their skateboards grinding on the concrete. Hastily they constructed a jump out of some two-by-fours and plywood, and immediately took to their boards to practice becoming airborne.

"I hope they don't break their necks," Tiffany said looking worried.

"They'll be fine."

"But Josh is still recovering from spraining his ankle.'' She started to yell something out the window, thought better of it and held her tongue. "Once a mother, always a mother.''

"I hear it's a hard habit to break."

"The hardest." They laughed and watched the boys

through the window and Luke checked his watch for the dozenth time. He was starting to feel antsy, though he had no reason. His talk with Katie could wait.

"So, I wonder what's keeping her?" Tiffany finally asked as Luke finished his second cup of coffee. He'd been in the house nearly an hour. "It's odd that she'd leave Josh alone so long." She sighed and lifted a shoulder. "Maybe she had to go to the store." She scraped back her chair, walked to the sink and placed her cup under the faucet. "If Katie doesn't show up soon, I'll have to leave her a note."

"I could take a message," Luke said automatically, but he was starting to get that same damned feeling of anxiety he'd had before when she lived in the other place and she'd been receiving the crank phone calls. *Don't overreact,* he told himself, but found it impossible whenever Katie was concerned. He couldn't do anything but wait.

The phone jangled and they both jumped. "It could be Katie," Tiffany said, glancing to the backyard. "She might be calling Josh to explain why she's late."

For some reason he couldn't explain, the muscles in Luke's back tightened and he snagged the receiver before it had time to ring again. "Kinkaid residence."

"Who's this?" a male voice demanded. Luke's fingers tightened over the mouthpiece in a death grip.

"Luke Gates. I'm a neighbor. Ms. Kinkaid isn't in right now."

"Where is she?"

Luke's eyes narrowed and he thought of all the hang-ups Katie had received. "Who're you?"

"This is Jarrod Smith, Gates," the voice said with more than a trace of irritation. "I'm looking for my sister."

He relaxed a bit. The voice fit. He'd only talked to Jarrod a couple of times, but he was convinced that Katie Kinkaid's oldest half brother was on the other end of the line. "She's not here right now."

"So where is she?"

Leaning a shoulder against the door and meeting the questions in Tiffany's eyes, he said, "According to Josh, Katie went over to her old place to meet a potential renter."

"When?"

"Over an hour ago."

"Damn!" Jarrod let fly a blue streak and Luke's momentary feeling of calm vanished into thin air. "Let's hope it's legit."

"What do you mean?" Luke demanded.

"It's probably just a coincidence, but Isaac Wells, with his lawyer, walked into the police station not two hours ago. He seems to think he's in some kind of danger from Ray Dean, an ex-con. He also thought maybe because Katie's shown so much interest in the story that Ray might want to talk to her."

Luke didn't like what he was hearing and he'd never put much stock in coincidence; the fact that Katie was late at the same time Isaac Wells had suddenly turned up made him anxious. Still...no reason to panic. Not yet. "How do you know all this?"

"I have connections with a friend on the force. We used to be partners. He keeps me informed because I've been working on this from the outside. I'd been checking with lawyers in Eureka, where that letter Katie received was postmarked, widened the circle to include Oregon as I figured Wells would want an in-state attorney. I was on the right track, only hadn't located the guy. Anyway, he and Isaac strolled into the police station this afternoon." Frustration edged Jarrod's voice and Luke decided Katie's oldest half brother wasn't used to having his quarry elude him. "Katie wanted to know the minute he came into town, so I thought I'd pass on the information."

"I'll let her know," Luke promised.

Jarrod hesitated, as if weighing whether he should confide in Luke, as if there was something more.

"Anything else?" Luke prodded.

"I don't know."

Luke could almost hear the wheels of suspicion turning in Jarrod's mind. Tiffany was standing by this time, her eyes fixed on Luke's face, her expression growing more concerned by the second.

"Maybe I'm just borrowing trouble," Jarrod allowed, "but Wells is starting to claim that Ray Dean has been involved in a lot of crimes the police couldn't pin on him."

"How does Wells know?"

"Wells?" Tiffany repeated, her eyebrows shooting up. "Isaac Wells?"

"Because Wells is claiming that he was his silent partner," Jarrod said. "Says he helped mastermind the crimes and case the places Ray would rob. He left town because Ray was getting out of prison and he was afraid for his life, or something. Anyway, now he's willing to turn state's evidence against Ray Dean in return for immunity from prosecution."

Luke's mind was racing ahead. He didn't give a hoot about Isaac Wells or Ray Dean or how they were involved in crime together. But he sure as hell was concerned about Katie and it looked as if, because of her articles, and the letter Isaac sent her that she published, she might be a link between the two thieves. "Did Isaac Wells write the letter to Katie?"

"That, I don't know. But if he did, he didn't contact her again because his attorney wanted him to deal directly with the police."

Luke's throat felt like sandpaper. He thought about the crank calls she'd received, about the feeling he'd had that someone had been watching her, waiting in the shadows at the hotel and at her home. Even after she'd moved this close to him, he'd spent more hours than he'd like to admit, sitting in the dark, staring out his window, watching the main house, scouring the darkness for any hint of a prowler. But he wasn't convinced. "Do you think Katie's in any danger?"

"I don't know. Hell, I hope not." But there was a note of apprehension in Jarrod's voice that Luke couldn't ignore. "Just let her know what's going on. When she gets in, have her give me a call."

"I will," Luke promised and promptly hung up.

Tiffany motioned toward the phone. "What was that all about?" she demanded. "You said something about danger."

"Isaac Wells is back in town." He gave her a quick rundown as he reached for the handle of the door. "If you want more details, call Jarrod back. There's probably nothing wrong," he said, disturbed and telling himself that he was being a dozen kinds of fool. "I'm going to check on Katie."

"I'll stay here with the kids," Tiffany said, her usually dark skin turning an ashen shade.

"Do that." He ran to his pickup and climbed inside as the two boys stopped their jumps for a second. The way Luke figured it, he could be at the cottage in less than ten minutes. He reminded himself this was probably just a wild-goose chase. Katie was probably safe. She might not even be at the cottage, but he wasn't going to rest until he found her. He backed his truck into the street, flung it into first gear and roared down the street.

He didn't give a damn if he looked like a fool; he wasn't about to take a chance with the life of the woman he loved.

"I think you and I should go for a ride," Ray said and Katie, rooted to the floor of the cottage, tried to maintain her rapidly escaping wits.

She shook her head.

"Whatever it is you have to tell me, you can say it right here." It would certainly be more dangerous to leave with him. At least she was in an environment she knew, with neighbors just across the fence.

"We could be interrupted."

"So what?" She was thinking fast, trying to get her bearings. If she could get over her fear and if Ray meant her no harm, she might have stumbled on the answer to the Isaac Wells mystery. But what if he did intend to hurt her? What then? Her legs threatened to give out on her and for the first time since her interest in the Isaac Wells disappearance began, she questioned whether or not she wanted to be involved. "You're not in trouble with the police, are you?"

"Always." He lifted a shoulder and she tried to determine if he was carrying a weapon. There were no bulges in the pockets of his coveralls, but a knife would be easy to conceal. Even a small handgun could be hidden somewhere on his body. Not that it made a huge difference—not when there was the size of him to consider. At over six feet and two hundred pounds, he was way too strong for her to try to overpower him. No, she'd have to use her brains.

"Do you know where Isaac Wells is?" she asked Ray.

"No."

"Is he alive?"

"I think so."

"Why?"

He studied her carefully, as if, now that he had her full attention, he wasn't sure how much of his story to divulge. "I have connections."

"Connections? Who? What?"

"Someone trustworthy."

Her mind was racing, her skin prickling with dread. "A snitch? A *trustworthy* snitch?" She tried to keep the disbelief out of her voice.

Ray's lips flattened at the insult. "Has he contacted you since you got the last letter?"

"No." She shook her head. "I thought he would, but I haven't heard a word. No letters or phone calls...well, except for some hang-ups."

"That was me."

"You?" She was sweating now, adrenaline rushing through her system.

"But they started coming before the letter was published...." Her voice faded away and she wondered how long this man had been watching her, following her. Her skin crawled at the thought of what he might have seen. "You...were watching me?" She thought she might be sick.

"I had to know what was going on."

So Luke had been right. She'd dismissed his concerns as some kind of overprotective paranoia, but his sense of dread had been justified. "Look, if you want me to help you..." She let her voice drop off. "Is that it? You want me to do something?"

"I want you to level with me. I think you know where Isaac Wells is."

"I don't." She shook her head. "I swear. The only contact I've had with him is the one letter."

"My source said he was returning to town. Was gonna turn himself in, but first he would contact you."

"Why?"

"Good question. I thought it was so that he could give you some more B.S. and lies that you'd publish in the paper."

"No," Katie insisted and heard the familiar sound of a pickup turning in at the drive.

Ray's nostrils flared, as if he'd encountered a bad smell. "Who's here?" he demanded.

"I don't know."

"Liar."

"Really. No one knows I'm here."

Ray's face clouded. He reached into his pocket and Katie couldn't help but back up a step. There was a horrid click; the sound of metal snapping. A switchblade flashed. "Oh, God," she whispered.

At that moment, the sound of Luke's boots hit the back porch. She looked through the window and shook her head as she spied his rugged face, twisted with concern. "Katie?" He knocked loudly as Ray stepped away from the door. "You in there?"

"Go away!" she yelled.

"Shh." Ray reached forward, grabbing her arm, but she resisted, pulling away, kicking at him with her feet, hearing the sound of Luke swearing and banging on the door.

"Let go of me!" She yanked away, but he grabbed

her again, forcing her close, the smell of grease from his uniform filling her nostrils. Hard muscles restrained her and the knife was ever-present in his left hand.

"Katie!" Luke's voice thundered through the house.

"Who's that?" Ray snarled.

"A friend."

"Tell him to get the hell out."

"Luke, go away!" she cried, as worried for him as she was for herself.

There was a split second of silence.

Crash! Glass splintered and sprayed. A body, huddled against the impact, burst into the room and rolled over the broken glass.

"Damn." Ray twirled, lifting Katie off her feet as Luke, recovering, found his footing and, all muscles flexed, eyes glimmering with fire, advanced.

"Stop!" Ray commanded.

"Let her go," Luke ordered through lips that barely moved.

Ray's grip tightened. Katie could scarcely breathe. "Get out!" he shouted at Luke.

"Are you okay?" Luke's gaze touched Katie's for an instant.

"Get out or I'll cut her," Ray threatened. The knife was poised high, glinting in the fading sunlight. "I swear it, man."

"Leave her be." Luke didn't move, just crouched, his gaze trained on the knife.

Fear congealed in Katie's blood. "Let me go," she demanded. "There's no reason for this."

Tense, appearing as if he'd lunge at any second, Luke took a step toward Ray. "Who are you?"

"Stop right there."

The arm around Katie's waist jerked hard and she

gasped. Luke froze. Ray pulled her backward, toward the living room, his boots crunching on the bits of glass scattered on the old linoleum.

Katie's heart thudded wildly. There was nothing she could do. "You—you haven't been in this kind of trouble before, Ray," she said.

"Ray?" Luke repeated, his expression wary. "Ray Dean?"

Sweat streamed from Ray's face.

"Just let her go and we'll talk this out," Luke insisted.

"Nothin' to talk about."

"Sure, there is. You told me about Isaac Wells," Katie said. "That you think he's going to frame you or something. Why don't you let me write *your* side of the story?"

She felt him hesitate.

"If you do anything now you'd be thrown back in prison for a long, long time. And Isaac would get away scot-free. Think about your kids," she said, sensing him listening, hearing his breathing slow a bit. "Laddy and Miles need a dad who isn't in prison."

"They're used to it." He glanced at Katie. Luke sprang forward. Startled, Ray stumbled a bit. His hold on Katie loosened a little. She threw herself away from him. "Don't move!" Ray's knife arced downward. Katie screamed and looked for something—anything—to use as a weapon. Luke caught Ray's wrist, and the knife trembled as the men struggled.

Grunting, swearing, muscles straining, they wrestled each other to the floor. Glass crunched. Katie ran for the door, her feet slipping on the shards. She threw the bolt, shouldered open the door and, screaming for help, grabbed the only thing she could find—Josh's old base-ball bat that had been left in the corner.

Sirens wailed in the distance, and a truck roared to a stop behind Ray's van. From the corner of her eye, Katie spied Jarrod bolting out of his pickup. "Get away!" he yelled, running up the steps, two at a time.

But it was already over. Luke, straddling Ray's chest, had him pinned to the floor.

"Hell, Katie what were you thinking?" Jarrod de-manded as she followed him into the house. Outside, a police cruiser slammed to a stop.

"I thought I was renting my house."

"What happened here?" a female cop demanded. She and her partner, weapons drawn, ran through the back door. She stopped when she recognized the man sprawled on the floor, pinned by a strong-willed cow-boy. "Well, well, well. Ray Dean. Why aren't I sur-prised that you'd be in the middle of this?"

"Butt out."

"Don't think so." She motioned for Luke to get up. "We'll take over from here, but all of you—" her gaze swept the group and brooked no arguments "—will have to come down to the station to give your state-ments."

Luke didn't look at the cops, but walked straight to Katie and folded her tightly into his arms. "Thank God you're okay," he said, his breath hot as it ruffled her hair. She felt him tremble, heard his heart pounding and wanted to cling to him forever. Tears blocked her throat and her eyes burned. "I was so worried." He kissed her crown and something inside her broke. She let the tears rain from her eyes and drooped against him, all of the fight and fire of her spirit finally col-lapsing. "Shh. You're okay. I'm here." She felt like a fool, an idiot of a woman, but was grateful that he was here, holding her, coming to her damned rescue.

"It's all a mix-up," Ray insisted as he climbed to his feet and the second cop, Officer Barnes, a thin man of thirty or so with an expression of someone who had already seen far too much, yanked Ray's arms behind his back and snapped handcuffs on his wrists.

"Take it easy! I haven't done anything wrong."

"Right," the policewoman mocked. "Not a damned thing."

"Ray Dean, you have the right to remain silent—" Barnes began reading Ray his rights, but the prisoner would have none of it. He looked at Katie and beneath the anger in his eyes, was a silent plea. "Look, I messed up."

"Big time," Katie said as Luke's arms tightened around her.

"Shut up. You have the right to remain silent..." the officer began again.

Ray ignored him. "I want you to write my story. In your paper."

She hesitated.

"Forget it, Dean," Jarrod said. "Just get him out of here," he ordered.

Luke wouldn't let Katie go.

"You said you'd write it!" Dean argued.

"For God's sake, man, you had a knife to her throat!" Luke's face was red, his eyes narrowed in fury.

"I'll think about it," Katie said.

Luke tensed.

"Are you nuts?" Jarrod was in her face now, his finger jabbing at her nose. "Do you know what he almost did to you? Katie, use your damned head!"

"This is my life, Jarrod," she replied.

"And you nearly lost it! Get a clue, would you?"

With a prod from Officer Barnes, Ray was led away and slowly Luke released Katie. Jarrod, still fuming, kicked at the broken glass and muttered under his breath about women who didn't have the common sense of fleas.

With Dean in the back seat, the police cruiser pulled away and a few neighbors who had gathered in the yard peeked inside. One, Leona Cartwright, an elderly woman with keen eyes and a hearing aid that helped her miss nothing that was going on in the neighborhood, admitted calling the police when she heard the commotion. "I just thank the Lord that you weren't hurt," she said, basking in the bit of glory that came with being the person to inform the authorities. "I just knew something wasn't right."

"Thanks."

"You'll write about this in the paper, no doubt."

"No doubt," Katie confirmed and Leona, like a preening peacock, beamed, looking from one of her neighbors to the next.

Luke didn't leave Katie's side and by the time the mess was cleaned up, they'd given statements at the police station and had returned home, it was nearly ten o'clock.

Katie, exhausted, was greeted by her entire family. Her father and mother, half brothers and half sisters were all milling and pacing around her kitchen, their faces drawn, lines of worry etching their features. At the sight of her sliding out of the Jeep, the family poured onto the back porch.

"Katie, oh, thank God!" Brynnie, smelling of cigarette smoke and perfume, dashed through the door and down the porch steps to fold her only daughter into her arms. "I was so worried."

"We all were," John said as Luke, who had parked behind the Jeep Katie had been driving, walked slowly across the lawn. He hung back, letting the family surround her while Jarrod's truck screeched to a stop. Rushing over to join the rest of the family, he was still wearing the role of protective older brother.

"I'm okay, Mom," Katie assured Brynnie.

"Thank God." Again, Brynnie's arms tightened around her, then she let them drop. "You're still my baby, you know."

"Yeah, I know."

"Lord, what I wouldn't do for a cigarette."

"Mom!" The screen door opened and banged shut. Josh flew down the steps to hurtle himself into Katie's arms.

Her throat was suddenly swollen, at the gesture of her son. She blinked hard and silently thanked God for her boy. "Hi, bud."

"Are you okay?"

"Fine, fine." She kissed Josh's crown and for once he didn't seem embarrassed that his mother was displaying her heartfelt affection for him.

"What happened? I thought you were just going to try and rent the house." His eyes were wide and now that the worry of her safety was over, he was keyed in on the fact that his mother was some kind of heroine.

"I did. I guess I was duped," she admitted, ruffling his hair. So much for heroics.

"So the guy was a phony."

"Big time."

John Cawthorne stepped forward. "You'd better

come into the house and slow down a mite. You look all done in."

"I'm fine," Katie lied.

"Dad's right." Bliss, ever the worrier, held the door open. "Maybe you should rest."

"That's a good idea." Jarrod glared at his half sister. "And give up the ridiculous notion that you're going to interview Ray Dean for your story."

"Ray Dean? Laddy's dad? He was the guy?" Josh asked, his eyes round as saucers as his estimation of his mother and her bravery soared into the stratosphere.

"Stay away from the likes of him," John growled.

Tiffany squeezed her hand. "Oh, Katie. Jarrod and...and John are right. Ray Dean's a criminal and you're a mother, you can't be taking any chances." For once, Tiffany sided with her estranged father, and Katie saw that this family—ragtag and filled with more than its share of bitter memories, distrust, and skeletons tucked away in every available closet—had come together during this crisis. Unintentionally, she'd drawn them to one another.

"Maybe everyone should hear what Katie has to say." Luke, the outsider, finally put in his two cents worth. He was standing beneath a madrona tree, one shoulder propped against the trunk, his hands shoved into the back pockets of his jeans. "Seems to me that it's her life."

Jarrod was about to argue. He opened his mouth, snapped it shut and then lifted a hand as if in surrender. "He's right."

"Tell us what happened," Bliss insisted.

"Everything," Tiffany added. "Come on, I think we can all fit into the parlor." She held the door open and John urged everyone inside. There wasn't enough of

Katie's odds and ends of eclectic furniture to hold everyone, but Stephen and Josh sat on the hearth, Christina was huddled in her mother's arms while Bliss and Mason stood at the windows, Brynnie sagged onto the couch, and the rest were scattered throughout the room, either seated in kitchen chairs they'd dragged into the parlor, or on the floor.

At John's insistence Katie took her place in an over-stuffed wing chair and Blue, toenails clicking, entered the room to curl into a ball at her feet. His ears twitched and his eyes moved from one member of the family to the next while Katie launched into her story. Everyone, even her ever-restless twin brothers, listened raptly. Few questions were asked and when she described Luke's dramatic rescue, all eyes turned his way. He stood in the archway between parlor and foyer, his face without much expression. Aloof. And still as sexy as any man she'd ever seen. Her throat caught for a minute as his eyes held hers. In that heartbeat she forgot that he'd betrayed her; remembered only that he'd put his life on the line for her. Before anyone had noticed, she looked away.

"I guess we owe you a debt of gratitude," John commented, eyeing Luke and sizing him up.

"No trouble."

"Nonetheless, you should be rewarded—"

"I don't think so." Luke's back stiffened in stubborn pride, and then Katie remembered that he'd probably already been paid for locating Ralph Sorenson's grandson. Her teeth clamped together; now wasn't the time to bring that up.

"You saved Katie's life," John said adamantly.

"She was doin' okay before I got there."

"Like hell she was," Jarrod retorted, his lips compressed over his teeth, his eyes flashing with frustration at his half sister's bullheaded streak. "I don't call it 'okay' when you're locked away with a known criminal who has a weapon at your throat!"

"It wasn't like that," Katie protested.

"Damned close."

There was no arguing with him. She glared at Jarrod for a second, then smiled. After all, he was only angry because he cared. "So what happened on this end?" Katie asked, hoping to defuse some of the tension that lingered in the air.

"After Luke left, Tiffany called me. Explained what was goin' on," John clarified.

Tiffany, smoothing Christina's curls, nodded. "I was worried. Luke had already left and I just had this feeling that there might be trouble, so I decided your folks should know what was going on." Her eyes met Katie's and a moment of understanding passed between them, a connection only true sisters share. "So, I phoned the ranch and talked to John."

Katie couldn't believe her ears. For Tiffany to have reached out to her estranged father was a major step. Major. Maybe there was hope for this ragtag family yet.

"Since I was there when John got the call," Jarrod added, "I decided to find out what was going on for myself. Bliss and Mason gathered everyone together here."

"I talked to the police," John said. He stood behind the couch where his wife was ensconced and patted her shoulder. Brynnie reached up and grabbed his fingers in hers. "But they'd already been tipped off. Some neighbor, I think."

"Leona."

"Helluva way to get us all together," Nathan joked.

Katie managed a laugh. "I promise I won't do it again."

"Good." Brynnie pushed herself upright. "I don't think I could live through it again."

"The next time you meet someone interested in looking at that place, give me a call," Jarrod said.

"I don't need—" Katie stopped short. How could she complain about his overbearing, big-brother tactics when he'd risked his life for hers? "Okay, I'll be more careful and take someone with me."

"I'm gonna hold you to it," Jarrod warned, leveling a finger in her direction. But he couldn't hang on to his glower and the smile that twitched at the corners of his mouth let her know that all was forgiven.

The conversation grew lighter and the kids strayed upstairs. Luke, seeing that all was well, tried to leave, but Jarrod stopped him in the foyer near the staircase. "Seems to me you might just be the reason my sister's alive."

Luke's gaze touched Katie, still seated in the chair near the fire. She felt her heartbeat elevate from just that one glance. What was it about him that made her so crazy? It seemed that she was either ready to murder him because he was so bullheaded, or she was melting at his touch, dreaming of making love to him forever. The man was just plain confusing. There were no two ways about it. She climbed out of her chair and went swiftly to the entry hall. A slow smile stretched across Luke's mouth. "My guess is that your sister here would have done just fine on her own," he said to Jarrod. Again Luke's blue eyes found hers. "I just didn't want to take any chances."

"I'm glad you didn't. Stick around," Jarrod invited.

"Please. Stay. I'm sure this clan is going to be clamoring for food at any second," Katie agreed.

"I'm already taking care of it." John joined them in the foyer. "Everyone's invited out to the ranch. I know it's late, but we need to celebrate. Brynnie and I'll pick up ribs and chicken down at Mel's Barbecue. Meet us at the ranch in an hour."

Luke started to protest, but John put on his I-won't-take-no-for-an-answer smile. "It isn't every day someone saves my daughter's life, though it has happened in the past." His gaze slid to Mason for a second, before returning to Luke. "Please, son. It's the least we all can do." He stuck out his hand and Luke clasped it firmly. "All right. I'll be there."

"Good." John turned toward the parlor and announced that the entire family was invited.

"It's so late," Tiffany said, blushing as Christina yawned and rubbed her eyes. "We need to get her home."

"She can bunk down on one of the beds in the guest rooms," Brynnie offered.

"I don't know...." Tiffany looked at Katie, then, moistening her lips, glanced in Bliss's direction. "Okay," she finally said, her shoulders straightening a bit as she seemed, for the first time, to accept her position in John Cawthorne's family. "We'll be there."

Katie could have dropped through the floor. Never would she have believed Tiffany could capitulate.

"Good! Good!" John said, practically beaming. "Come on, Brynnie, we'd better get a move on. We'll see you all in an hour."

Katie was stunned. Every member of the family had agreed to show up at Cawthorne Acres. In a flurry of activity, they left, climbing into individual cars and trucks that roared away from the apartment house, leaving Josh, Katie and Luke standing in the moon-washed backyard.

"Who would've thought?" she said, tousling Josh's hair.

"What d'ya mean?"

"I never thought this family would get together. Never. This is a red-letter day," she said to Luke as everyone dispersed.

"I'm just glad you're okay, Mom," Josh admitted.

"Me, too."

"Why don't you go check on Blue and we'll get ready to go?"

Josh hesitated, as if he were about to argue, then lifted a shoulder. "Sure."

"Good." She turned back to face Luke. "Now," she said as a cloud shifted over the moon, "you and I need to talk."

"Do we?" In the half-light his teeth flashed white and she reminded herself that despite everything she was still angry with him. That he'd deceived her.

"Yep. Just because you probably saved my life today," she continued, "doesn't mean you're off the hook, Gates." She angled her face up to his and said, "There's still that little matter of your deal with Ralph Sorenson. No matter what happened with Ray Dean, I think you used me and my son. For your own purposes."

He stared down at her so intensely she had trouble meeting his gaze. For a brief second she thought he might kiss her, but then she changed her mind when he looked away. His eyes narrowed as he stared into the distance, but, she suspected, he saw only what was deep in his own mind.

"I guess you have the right to think anything you damned well please," he finally muttered. "Can't say as I blame you." He turned on his heel and started toward the carriage house. "Give my regrets to your father and Brynnie."

"But— No. Wait." She caught up with him, touched his arm and he spun again, facing her with an expression of exhaustion and pain.

"Just for the record, Katie," he said slowly, his gaze drilling into hers as if he could somehow find her soul, "I never intended to hurt you." With that, he turned and walked out of her life.

Chapter Twelve

"I don't want the money."

Luke had never thought he'd say those particular words. Since he'd grown up poor, he'd thought, for as long as he could remember, that money could buy him happiness. Not that he needed a lot. Just enough to get by and give himself a little nest egg so he wouldn't have to work until he was ninety. But he'd changed his mind. Katie Kinkaid had seen to that.

Ralph Sorenson, on the other end of the line, and woken from what must have been a deep sleep, wasn't in the mood for Luke's change of heart. "You earned it, boy. It's yours."

"No."

"What the devil happened to you?"

I fell in love. "I just had a change of heart." That wasn't a lie.

"You're just mad 'cause I called my grandson's

mother before squarin' it with you," Ralph said. "Well, I admit I was a little impatient, but then you've got to understand there's no reason to wait. That boy is Dave's son. Our grandson. It's time we met."

"I don't think that'll be a problem."

"So you'll get paid."

"Give it to Josh," Luke said. "I'm out of this. Good night Ralph."

"Well, ain't that a fine howdy-do?" The old man hung up and Luke felt only slightly better than he had a while before. He strode to the window and stared into the night. He'd never gotten used to living in town and the blue glare of the streetlights seemed harsh and unforgiving.

Just the way he felt. Staring at the huge apartment house as if it were an enemy, he tilted back his bottle of beer and took a long swallow. He thought of Katie, and deep inside there was an ache—something primal and painful and, in his estimation, way out of line. So she was a beautiful woman. So she had an outlook on life he found fascinating. So what? Disgusted with himself, he drained his long-neck, considered another, then tossed the idea aside.

Alcohol wouldn't help. Not that it ever had.

His conscience was eating him alive. What he'd done to her was unforgivable, and calling and telling Ralph that he was out of the deal was hardly compensation enough. Nope, his refusal of Ralph's bribe was just another incidence of too little, too late.

Which seemed to be the story of his life.

"Where's Luke?" Bliss had asked.

Tiffany, too, hadn't let Luke's absence go unnoticed. "I thought he was coming."

"I specifically invited him," John Cawthorne had grumbled. "Helluva way to act, if ya ask me."

Of course no one had asked John's opinion; John was just forever willing to offer it. While the rest of her family had laughed and talked, eating ribs, chicken, bread and coleslaw, Katie had scarcely been able to take a bite. Everyone had assumed it was from the trauma she'd suffered earlier in the day, but the truth of the matter was that no matter what she did, her thoughts turned back to the rangy cowboy with the Texas drawl and easy smile. Dammit, she'd missed him.

As soon as it was polite, she'd located Josh and said her goodbyes. All of her brothers had warned her to be more careful, whether while renting the house or chasing down stories. Her sisters had told her how great they thought Luke was.

As if they were a couple. What a laugh—a miserable, heart-wrenching laugh. Driving through the darkened streets of Bittersweet, she told herself that she couldn't love a man like Luke Gates. She wouldn't. It was just too painful.

He used you, she reminded herself as she shifted down and turned into the drive of the apartment house. The beams of her headlights washed up against the tailgate of Luke's truck. He was home. Only a few yards away. She told herself it didn't matter if he was living next door or in the middle of the North Pole.

But of course that was a lie. "Lord help me," she whispered under her breath.

"Huh?" Josh, eyes closed, stirred in the passenger seat.

She parked and set the emergency brake. "Come on, bud," she said. "Time for bed."

"I can't make it." He yawned and let his head loll back against the seat again.

"Sure you can. Just try." She managed to help him out of the Jeep, then guided him toward the house and upstairs to his room. He managed to make it as far as his bed, then flopped, facedown, onto the mattress.

She brushed a kiss across the top of his head. "I'll see you in the morning."

As she snapped off the light and closed the door, Josh lifted his head and tried to stifle a yawn. "I'm really glad you're okay, Mom."

"Thanks, kid." Her heart swelled. "I love you."

"Me, too. And Mom? You know what I said about Luke before, that I didn't like him?"

She nodded, vaguely recalling a conversation when Josh had sprained his ankle. "Yeah."

"I changed my mind. He's okay."

"Good." Why it mattered she didn't know, because Luke had used her. And Josh. "See ya in the morning." She closed the door and went down the hallway to her room. It seemed empty and dark. Even after she turned on the bedside lamp and pulled down the quilt, it felt cold somehow, vacuous and barren.

What had Jarrod said—that she needed a man? She'd never believed him. Until now. Because of Luke Gates. "Oh, Katie, you've got it bad," she said, realizing the aching truth that she loved Luke Gates.

"I never intended to hurt you." His final words had rattled through her brain all night long. But it didn't matter what his intentions had been. He had hurt her. And loving him only made it worse.

"Okay, Katie, I should be shot for this, but I think I made the rash promise to let you know anything I found out about the Isaac Wells case," Jarrod said when she answered the phone the next morning.

"Sounds like you've had a change of heart." She poured herself a cup of coffee and looked through the back window only to discover that Luke's pickup was missing.

"No way. You be careful. But I figure someone down at that rag you work for is going to write the story, so it may as well be you."

"Can't argue with that." Holding the receiver between her shoulder and ear, she scrounged in a top drawer for a pen and a notepad. "Okay, brother. Shoot." She sat at the table and listened.

"Okay, the deal is this. It seems that Isaac isn't quite the loner everyone thought. In fact, he was a crook, or the guy behind the scenes with all the brains. The police don't know for sure, but they suspect Isaac was involved in a string of burglaries that happened around Medford and Ashland a few years back. Ray Dean was his accomplice, the actual thief. Ray took all the risks and got most of the money. Except for one job—the big one."

"Which one was that?"

"When Octavia Nesbitt was robbed."

Katie stopped writing. Her hand froze over the paper. "Wells and Dean were involved in that one?"

"It looks that way. They got away with it and were about to split the loot when Dean was caught for his part in an earlier break-in. He was convicted and, as they say, sent up the river. All that time in prison he kept his mouth shut about the Nesbitt job because it was the biggest one he'd ever pulled off. He had some phony alibi, so the police were thrown off. No one suspected that Isaac Wells might be involved and eventually Dean ended up paroled. The problem was that Isaac had used all the money—either gambled it away, paid off back taxes, used it to keep up that car collection of his, whatever."

"He told them this."

"Not everything, of course, but it's what the police have pieced together. So when Ray was about to be released, Isaac decided to disappear rather than face him. Ray has a track record of being thrown back in jail within months of being paroled, but this time it didn't happen. Isaac began to get worried that Ray would talk, so he turned himself in yesterday and is cooperating with the authorities."

Dumbstruck, Katie leaned back in her chair. "So what about Octavia's jewels?"

"Pawned."

"And her cat?"

"I don't think anyone asked him about her cat. He's probably long gone by now."

"Wow." Katie scribbled as fast as she could. "Why was Stephen a suspect?" she asked, remembering that her nephew had been questioned.

"Never a suspect, but he did have a set of keys that belonged to Isaac Wells—keys that Ray Dean hoped would lead him to the loot. The police didn't know the connection, of course. Not until now."

"So what happens now?"

"Your guess is as good as mine. I think Ray will be sent back to prison and Isaac will get a lesser sentence for turning himself in. I think Octavia's insurance company will probably sue and Isaac will have to give up whatever he has left to pay off the claim. But I'm not sure. That's just conjecture."

Katie chewed on the end of her pencil. "So how did they break into Octavia's home?"

"Isaac knew someone who had once cleaned Octavia's house and knew where she kept the extra keys. The old lady was foolish, I think."

Katie stared out the window toward Luke's apartment. A squirrel was racing along the gutter, then scrambled into the overhanging bows of a pine tree. Blue was barking, running along the edge of the carriage house, his nose tilted into the air, his eyes trained on his quarry. But Katie didn't pay any attention to the squirrel's antics or Blue's frustrated cries. In her mind's eye she saw her story forming, but some of the joy she'd expected to feel—the satisfaction of getting her big scoop—was missing. "I owe you, Jarrod."

"Just take care of yourself."

"I will. Thanks."

"No problem."

"You know I'll have to talk to Ray Dean," she ventured, ready for her brother's temper to explode.

"Go ahead. As long as he's behind bars."

The next couple of days were busy. Too busy. Somehow Katie avoided Luke, though she suspected he was the one doing the avoiding. By the time she got up each morning and peeked out the window, his pickup was gone; she didn't hear it return until after midnight. She'd talked to Ralph Sorenson a couple of times and Josh had tentatively gotten on the phone and spoken to his grandfather. Things were still tense, but working out. Eventually they would all meet.

So close and yet so far away, she thought on the second day after Josh had flown out the door, his backpack draped over one shoulder, his hair flopping as he raced up the street to meet the school bus.

She finished cleaning the kitchen, then, against the wishes of everyone in the family, drove to the jail where she planned to interview Ray Dean. She'd already written the story about his arrest and how she was involved. Her editor was impressed, but he wanted more.

Ray, seated on his cot, looked at her through the bars. She sat in a folding chair and listened as he smoked and told his side of the story in painstaking detail. In the end, it seemed, his version only backed up Isaac's rendition. They were both crooks. But Ray, she assumed, because of his record and the fact that he'd actually done the deed, would draw a much longer sentence.

Nonetheless, she got her story.

So where was that overwhelming sense of satisfaction she'd been certain she would feel? Where was her emotional payoff? Instead of a feeling of elation, she experienced a sense of loss. The mystery was over and, though she would probably get to work on more interesting stories in the months to come, she was still the same woman she'd always been—just with a different set of problems.

She drove home and found a bouquet of flowers on the front step. She bit her lip as she carried the roses, chrysanthemums, and baby's breath inside. Her fingers trembled and she mentally crossed her fingers that the bouquet was from Luke.

The card was simple: "We're proud of you. Congratulations. Mom and Dad."

"How nice," she said, but couldn't ignore the overwhelming sense of disappointment that dwelled deep in her heart. Though she'd pushed Luke away, now she missed him. "Yeah, well, you're an idiot," she said as she mounted the stairs, started removing her earrings and, once in her bedroom, checked the clock. Josh wouldn't be home for another couple of hours, so she just had time to—

The phone rang shrilly. She snatched up the receiver before it had a chance to ring again. "Hello?"

"Katie Kinkaid?"

The voice was familiar. "Yes?"

"It's Ralph Sorenson again. I've been doing a lot of thinking and even though we've talked a few times, I didn't really tell you what I'm thinking. Mainly that I guess I owe you an apology for the first time I called and I don't want there to be any bad blood between us."

"There isn't—"

"Just hear me out," he insisted, on a roll he didn't want to stop. "When I first called you I was just so damned anxious to get to know Josh, you know, because of Dave's death and all. Anyway, I made that deal with Luke, offered him money to find the boy, because I was so damned lonely."

Her throat ached all over again, as he explained how empty his life was without Dave but that he'd decided that Katie, as Josh's mother, knew what was best when it came to his grandson. He and his estranged wife only wanted what was best for Josh, and to that end they planned to set up a trust fund for him with the money he'd set aside for Luke.

Katie was thunderstruck. Her fingers clamped over the receiver. "But I thought Luke already got the money."

"No way." The old man chuckled sadly. "That boy

taught me a little bit about what being a family and putting other people's needs before your own is all about. It's funny, really. Luke never really had a family, didn't know much about his folks, and then his own marriage was a mistake from the get-go, what with his wife running around on him and all.''

Katie felt a tear slide down her cheek. What a fool she'd been.

"Listen, Mr. Sorenson—"

"Call me Ralph. We are like family whether we want to be or not."

"I want you to come and visit Josh. I've talked with him and we need to all get together."

There was a moment's hesitation. "You're certain about this?"

"Positive."

"Well...sure. I'll let you know. Thank you, Katie."

"And thank you." She hung up, wrote Josh a quick note in case he got home before she returned, then flew out to the car. She needed to talk to Luke and tell him how she felt. She had to swallow her pride and, no matter what happened, admit that she loved him.

Once behind the wheel, she took a deep breath, then jabbed her key into the ignition and prayed that she hadn't let the one man in the world she needed slip through her fingers.

Luke, pounding nails that had worked their way out of the stable's old siding, raised his hammer again and heard the Jeep before it rounded the corner of the lane. He half hoped it would be Katie driving out to see him, but told himself he was being a fool. Whatever they'd shared was over. Somehow he'd have to get used to living in the same town with her and knowing they'd never be together.

"Tough," he muttered to himself and slammed the hammerhead into the siding so hard as to leave a dent. A whirlpool kicked up dust in the corral, spinning a few dried leaves and blades of grass in a crazy dance. Overhead a hawk circled lazily.

Katie's Jeep appeared and for a moment Luke thought he was seeing things. What could she possibly want? Probably another story—now that the Isaac Wells mystery was cleared up she'd need another topic. Maybe she wanted to do a piece on this place. The concrete foundation had been poured; in less than six months he hoped to be open for operation.

He slid his hammer into a loop on his jeans and walked across the gravel lot to the spot where she'd ground to a stop. She hopped out of the cab and marched up to him.

"Do you have anything to say to me?" she demanded.

"Such as?"

"I just got a call from Ralph Sorenson."

"And—?"

"He seems to think he's going to send Josh some money for a trust fund." She threw up one hand and he couldn't tell if she was furious or pleased. "I think this has something to do with you."

"I told Ralph I was out of it."

"Well, you're wrong, Gates," she argued, her eyes crackling like green lightning. "You're in it big time."

"How's that?"

She drew in a long breath and he braced himself. Her cheeks were rosy, the pulse at the base of her throat beating erratically. The fingers of one hand opened and closed as if she was so nervous as to be tongue-tied and the scent of her perfume tickled his nostrils. Damn, but she was beautiful. And she didn't seem to know it. "Because I want you to be," she said, her voice a little softer.

"You do?"

"Yes." She licked her lips and he found the movement ridiculously provocative. "I—I want you in my life, Luke." She seemed embarrassed, but held his gaze. "I love you."

He didn't move, didn't feel the wind play with the tails of his shirt or ruffle his hair. "What?"

"I said, 'I love you.'"

He couldn't believe it and before he could respond, she started to turn. "Wait."

"Why?" She was halfway to the Jeep, when it finally hit him. He caught up with her before she reached for the door handle.

"Katie—"

She shook her head and disappointment darkened her eyes. "Look, just let me go, okay? I've embarrassed myself enough as it is, and—"

"I love you."

"You don't have to say anything. Really."

His fingers tightened over her arms. "I love you, Katie Kinkaid, and I've known it for weeks." All the words that he'd bottled up started tumbling out of his mouth as he tried to convince her of the truth. "It's just that I felt like such a heel because of the Ralph Sorenson thing."

"No—"

"Believe me."

"No, I—"

"Katie, will you marry me?"

The world seemed to stop. The breeze died and the hawk disappeared. It was as if they were entirely alone in the universe with that one simple question hanging precariously between them. "Wh-what?"

"Katie Kinkaid, I want you to be my wife." He reached for her then, and drew her close. "You're not going to make me get down on my knees and beg you, are you?"

She laughed. "No...but...it would be a nice vision." Swallowing hard, she stared up at him and in her eyes he saw his future. "Of course I will," she said with a grin, "but just tell me one thing."

"What's that?"

"What took you so long to ask?"

Epilogue

The preacher smiled as he looked at Luke and Katie. "You may kiss the bride," he said, then turned to J.D. and Tiffany, "And you, too, may kiss the bride."

The guests filling the hundred-year-old church whispered and chuckled and Katie leaned forward as Luke lifted her veil and kissed her as if she were the only woman on earth.

This double ceremony had been Katie's idea and now, as she felt her heart flutter and broke off the embrace, she grinned broadly.

"Ladies and gentlemen," the preacher announced, "I give to you Mr. and Mrs. Luke Gates and Mr. and Mrs. J. D. Santini."

Katie slid a glance in Tiffany's direction and was rewarded with a smile. *This is the way it should always be,* she thought, with Bliss as their maid of honor,

Christina as their flower girl, and their sons as well as John Cawthorne giving them away.

She'd thought Luke would balk at the idea when she'd first suggested it, but he'd agreed, happy to finally be part of a family. Even Tiffany, at first resistant, had gotten caught up in the extravaganza. As the organist began to play, Katie, holding Luke's arm, walked down the aisle. Between the sprays of flowers and the candles, she saw the faces of the townspeople she'd known all her life. Her mother was crying, of course, and John Cawthorne was sniffing loudly. Octavia, Tiffany's grandmother, beamed. She'd been reunited with her cat—the result of a woman who'd bought the Persian years ago—reading Katie's article on the Nesbitt burglary, which was picked up by a paper in Portland. Brynnie and John were considering moving into the apartment house, while Katie, Luke and Josh would take up residence at Luke's ranch.

It seemed fitting, somehow, that Josh would live in the very spot where his father had lived.

Outside, the late-October sun was gilding trees already starting to turn with the coming winter. Katie imagined being snowbound with Luke at the ranch, sleeping in the room with the river-rock fireplace, watching as his dream unfolded and the ranch was up and running. She would still write, of course, but she thrilled at the thought of spending her days and nights with the man she loved.

The two brides and grooms formed a reception line and Katie accepted kisses, hugs and handshakes from friends, neighbors and relatives. Ralph and Loretta Sorenson had met Josh and had stayed for the nuptials. Even Rose Nesbitt had stood proudly and watched Tiffany marry, though, Katie decided, it would be a cold day in Hades before Rose would ever say a kind word to John Cawthorne.

But time could take care of a lot of the pain.

"It was a great wedding," Bliss said as the line dwindled and she stood between her two half sisters.

"The best," Dee Dee said.

"Oh, I can think of a better one." Mason winked at his wife.

J.D. laughed and kissed Tiffany again. Luke's arm surrounded Katie's waist. "I wouldn't trade this one for the world," he whispered into her ear. "Now, can we go somewhere private."

"Soon," Katie whispered back.

"Not good enough, wife." Not waiting for another second, Luke pulled her behind a thick laurel hedge and, holding her face between his two callused hands, he looked deep into her eyes, then kissed her as if he never intended to stop. Because he didn't.

* * * * *

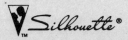

If you enjoyed what you just read,
then we've got an offer you can't resist!

Take 2 bestselling love stories FREE!

Plus get a FREE surprise gift!

Clip this page and mail it to Silhouette Reader Service™

IN U.S.A.	IN CANADA
3010 Walden Ave.	P.O. Box 609
P.O. Box 1867	Fort Erie, Ontario
Buffalo, N.Y. 14240-1867	L2A 5X3

YES! Please send me 2 free Silhouette Special Edition® novels and my free surprise gift. Then send me 6 brand-new novels every month, which I will receive months before they're available in stores. In the U.S.A., bill me at the bargain price of $3.57 plus 25¢ delivery per book and applicable sales tax, if any*. In Canada, bill me at the bargain price of $3.96 plus 25¢ delivery per book and applicable taxes**. That's the complete price and a savings of over 10% off the cover prices—what a great deal! I understand that accepting the 2 free books and gift places me under no obligation ever to buy any books. I can always return a shipment and cancel at any time. Even if I never buy another book from Silhouette, the 2 free books and gift are mine to keep forever. So why not take us up on our invitation. You'll be glad you did!

235 SEN CNFD
335 SEN CNFE

Name	(PLEASE PRINT)	
Address		Apt.#
City	State/Prov.	Zip/Postal Code

* Terms and prices subject to change without notice. Sales tax applicable in N.Y.
** Canadian residents will be charged applicable provincial taxes and GST.
   All orders subject to approval. Offer limited to one per household.
   ® are registered trademarks of Harlequin Enterprises Limited.

SPED99   ©1998 Harlequin Enterprises Limited

FOLLOW THAT BABY...

the fabulous cross-line series featuring the infamously wealthy Wentworth family...continues with:

THE MERCENARY AND THE NEW MOM

by **Merline Lovelace**

(Intimate Moments, 2/99)

No sooner does Sabrina Jensen's water break than she's finally found by the presumed-dead father of her baby: Jack Wentworth. But their family reunion is put on hold when Jack's past catches up with them....

Available at your favorite retail outlet, only from

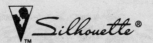

Silhouette®

Look us up on-line at: http://www.romance.net

SSEFTB5

Bestselling author

LINDSAY McKENNA

continues the drama and adventure of her
popular series with an all-new, longer-length
single-title romance:

MORGAN'S MERCENARIES

HEART OF THE JAGUAR

Major Mike Houston and Dr. Ann Parsons were in the heat
of the jungle, deep in enemy territory. She knew Mike's
warrior blood kept him from the life—and the love—he
silently craved. And now she had so much more at stake.
For the beautiful doctor carried a child. His child…

Available in January 1999, at your favorite retail outlet!

Look for more **MORGAN'S MERCENARIES** in 1999,
as the excitement continues in the Special Edition line!

Silhouette®

PSMORGMERC

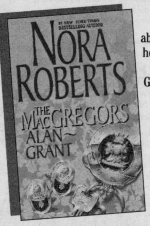
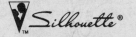

COMING NEXT MONTH

#1225 BABY, OUR BABY!—Patricia Thayer
That's My Baby!
When Jake Hawkins returned to town, he discovered that one unforgettable night of passion with Ali Pierce had made him a daddy. He'd never forgotten about shy, sweetly insecure Ali—or how she touched his heart. Now that they shared a child, he vowed to be there for his family—forever!

#1226 THE PRESIDENT'S DAUGHTER—Annette Broadrick
Formidable Special Agent Nick Logan was bound to protect the president's daughter, but he was on the verge of losing his steely self-control when Ashley Sullivan drove him to distraction with her feisty spirit and beguiling innocence. Dare he risk getting close to the one woman he couldn't have?

#1227 ANYTHING, ANY TIME, ANY PLACE—Lucy Gordon
Just as Kaye Devenham was about to wed another, Jack Masefield whisked her off to marry him instead, insisting he had a prior claim on her! A love-smitten Kaye dreamt that one day this mesmerizing man would ask her to be more than his strictly *convenient* bride....

#1228 THE MAJOR AND THE LIBRARIAN—Nikki Benjamin
When dashing pilot Sam Griffin came face-to-face with Emma Dalton again, he realized his aching, impossible desire for the lovely librarian was more powerful than ever. He couldn't resist her before—and he certainly couldn't deny her now. Were they destined to be together after all this time?

#1229 HOMETOWN GIRL—Robin Lee Hatcher
Way back when, Monica Fletcher thought it was right to let her baby's father go. But now she knew better. Her daughter deserved to know her daddy—and Monica longed for a second chance with her true love. Finally the time had come for this man, woman and child to build a home together!

#1230 UNEXPECTED FAMILY—Laurie Campbell
Meg McConnell's world changed forever when her husband, Joe, introduced her...to his nine-year-old son! Meg never imagined she'd be asked to mother another woman's child. But she loved Joe, and his little boy was slowly capturing her heart. Could this unexpected family live happily ever after?